Crystal Lake
Cerrig Forest
Bromton
Jay Woods
Pinestock Forest
Valley of Desire
Oliverwood
Bengorn
Gardon Forest
Northstead Highlands
Toaren Mountains
Atlios
Felmid
Excalibur
N
E
S
W

Ocean of Manar

Isles of Avalon

KING CROW

Copyright © 2024 Miriam Yvette

ISBN: 979-8-3304-9407-1
Publisher's note.

Excalibur's
King

CONTENTS

Three Kingdoms

Excalibur
Felmid
Atlios

Gods

Orendor – The Blacksmith God
Mother Nature – Mother of life and magic
Varil – Iron Spear God

Coin system

King's Coin: Highest value
Gold: 50 gold coins and more
Silver: 25 silver coins = 1 gold
Copper: 100 copper coins = 1 silver

Hear my story.

THE AFFLICTION WAR

For two centuries, Man has endured the oppressive dominance of the supernatural. Living under the iron heel of charlatans of magic that roam these sacred lands, their insatiable hunger favored their flesh to near extinction. Through my guidance, three kingdoms banded together to even the odds. Atlios, the kingdom of the wise, Felmid, the kingdom of the spear, and Excalibur, the kingdom of the mountains.

The pursuit for monsters began without adjournment, but such a campaign was met with fierce pushback from the fiends who rejected Mother Nature's call to the Isles of Avalon. Among them were dragons and underneath their wings were Dranyths, servants with incredible strength who sided with the monsters and launched a direct attack upon Excalibur, wounding Orendor the blacksmith god, creator of the rarest metal on Earth, tanium.

The war endured for decades, plaguing the lands with unending cries from both monster and man alike. Proud towns and villages crumbled to dust, and the stench of death lingered in the air. When the war was near its end, Ecarus Sol, the firstborn son of my friend, King Murenten was killed in battle. The king, vowing for revenge, pushed a tired war through its limits, wiping Drantyhs, but the cost seemed too great. King Murenten, the great king of Excalibur perished after a long-term illness. Without a ruler, Queen Lailon appointed her second son, Tungsten, the stronghold of the kingdom and keeper of Excalibur's borders, to reign as king. Though faced with opposition from within, the laughing giant took the mantle and served for a decade.

Forgive me, for I have been deceiving you. I, Merlin the Old have also perished. I hope the one who comes after me will heed my call. Beware of the shadow that lurks beneath your feet.

I

YOU DARE LEAVE YOUR BROTHER IN ARMS WAITING?

Fall
October 28ᵗ
Valley of Desree
40 miles left for Crystal Lake.

I t was past midday, but no light from the sun could shed the gray mists and crawling fogs. On King's Road, Tungsten felt like an arrow, following the course of its trajectory for days. The north was preparing for winter, an inconvenience to the grim farmers they saw a day ago. But alas, desire and reality were never on the same side of the coin. In the South, the soil was still warm. Lush green trees still filled the forests where their cascading mountains lived richly with life and sport; their peaks were the only indicator of winter during the night.

Tungsten looked back with a lingering grudge that lodged in

his throat. His memory of home carried the aroma of honey and citrus trees, not this enduring odor of damp grass, and the constant, crisp breeze tethering burnt-looking leaves wherever it went.

"You've been looking back every time we cover a mile." His companion, Lancelot, wore plated armor with a purple pauldron on the right. "Moreso, you've grown awfully quiet since we left."

"Hm." Tungsten laid his hand on the head of his feline ride. His thick coat was a yellow to light orange, with stripes ranging from dark brown to black. The stripes extended from his back to his belly, continuing onto the interior, while his tail was adorned with black rings.

Lancelot raised his map to the sky. "We have less than forty miles to cover, but the sun appears to be descending behind the mountains."

"Hm."

"Your Majesty," Lancelot stressed.

"Oh, what now, friend?"

"It appears we have visitors."

Looking far ahead, a wagon was coming up the hill with speed. The driver was a man with dark hair, back hunched, and a long coat with a wrinkled hat. On his left was a young woman, covered from head to toe with a wool blanket.

The wagon slowed before the startled horses came to an untimely stop. Seeing the growling cat pulled the color from the driver's face, and he jerked on the reins to steady his alarmed team. His wife could only hold her breath, gripping the side of her seat.

"L-Lord of the South." The driver inhaled, eyeing Tungsten's gauntlets where the feather-like metal quivered past his knuckles. "What can we do you for?"

Lancelot encouraged his horse to move forward and circled the wagon. Behind, barrels of wine were stacked, one had toppled over, and the rest were poorly covered by a ragged cloth. "Quite a fine load you have there." His voice gave a metallic echo as he spoke behind the small opening of his helmet. "Are you aware that you're on King's Road?"

"Why—yes, I know." The man answered sharply, though his chattering teeth couldn't be veiled behind his wiry beard. "We just finished our delivery and are heading back home."

Suddenly, the young woman rose from her seat, but the driver grabbed her arm and forced her to sit down. "W-Winter is coming soon and our home is two moons away." His hold remained steady on the young woman, who in response squinted her eyes. "Pardon us for taking this road. We are eager to return to our family."

Once again, Tungsten stroked his hands against the coat of his tiger. His eyes fell upon the young woman, who was nibbling on her lower lip. When her gaze flicked to him, she quickly looked away. She wouldn't look up, in fact, she appeared afraid of him.

"Is she alright?" Lancelot asked. "The girl looks distressed."

Tungsten chuckled. With equal judgments like that, he and his friend might run the same beating heart.

The man caught Tungsten's amusement and gave his unruly wife one look. Droplets of spit hung on the jumbling movements of his lips. "Nuthin' to worry about, my daughter is homesick." In response, the young woman inhaled and nodded. "I beg of you to forgive us this one time Giant Lords, we'll never cross these roads again. That's a promise."

"Is that so?" Lancelot turned to him, seeking permission. The man, in return, looked both at his friend and him.

The silent stare endured before Tungsten unleashed a hearty laugh. The driver jumped, pulling the reins to calm his startled horses. "Well, that covers it!" he said. "Fare thee well." His mount started to leave.

Lancelot stayed behind to speak to the startled couple some more. "The king has long permitted humans to use this private road. You should've known that."

The man said nothing, but his wagon soon went into motion.

A few moments later, Lancelot caught up with him, but not before he gave a deep sigh. He was a habitual worrier. Even on this long trip, he was back to looking at his map.

"And you said I was homesick," Tungsten probed.

4

"You are," his friend answered. "And from your fidgeting, you're ailing like you've gotten the plague."

"There's no ailing in my mind, nor any eagerness to see my sister."

"Aye? And a good brother would want to see her well."

"Calibor is a woman in love, not the Captain of the Royal Army. A visit from her brother too early during her honeymoon would be repugnant."

"Aye, and *we* have no choice in our coming this soon; the Queen Mother requested for the Sun Princess to make her return." Lancelot grabbed the goat's foot lever from his belt. His crossbow was already in the other hand. "Gods know how I prayed you were more honest with yourself."

Tungsten squeezed the reins, and his ride stopped. "Indra, think they went far enough?" The large feline lowered his head, and his claws extended, digging into the soil.

Lancelot's horse, Marigold, nickered from the quick turnaround. Before taking off, he hooked the goat's foot lever on and locked it on the trigger. "I'm nearly ready, Your Majesty, just need to lay the bolt."

Indra leaped to the trunk of the nearest tree and turned around.

They moved at a slow trot before picking up speed. Lancelot caught up to them in no time, and surged ahead, leaving Indra to snarl and quicken his pace.

The driver and his daughter were going up the hill now, about to descend before the man turned around and saw them. Without hesitation, he slapped the reins upon his horses' back and took off.

"And there they go!" Tungsten laughed. His tiger let out a mean roar, forcing his friend's horse to whinny.

"Oi!" Lancelot cursed. "We're not in a race!"

"Indra is certainly in one!" Tungsten laughed again.

The daughter, seeing them, climbed over her seat, screaming. Her hands reached out to them as she attempted to climb off the seat. The man grabbed her arm, keeping her in place. Amidst the struggle, she slipped through the blanket and jumped off the wagon.

"See to it that she's alright." Tungsten pushed his war tiger to carry forward. At this pace, it was just the wagon and him. "Where are you going?" he blared.

The man unleashed a shrill wail. "Your Majesty, you have it all wrong!"

"A true local would know these roads are public to them and you did not, correct my friend?"

"You fooled me!"

"The one who's fooling is you. What monster *are* you?" He eyed the fleeing man. "By your poor form, you're no shapeshifter."

"It's nun' of your business!"

6

"Or perhaps you're a drape, a hideous green beast who wears the skin of their victim?" The man arched his back, his guilt leading Tungsten to release a good one. "Hah, ha-ha-ha!"

The road was reaching a hairpin where, at the current speed, would smash the wagon into the sizeable chestnut tree and shake its few remaining golden leaves. With little time to react, the man pulled the reins with one hand and shoved the brake lever with the other. The wagon bounced before the wheels slammed to the ground and the team neighed.

In one cry, the man jumped and landed on his hands and knees. He studied Tungsten with a low hiss, layers of his face starting to wrinkle over his eyes. He barked and crawled into the woods.

Tungsten stopped at the border. "Stay here, old friend." He dismounted Indra and entered the woods, his steps pounding on the layers of crunchy leaves.

By the silence, the pursuit was fruitless. Tungsten stopped when a low fog rolled between his feet. A sense of emptiness started to fill the space, lacking any sign of life or the wind's songs.

"You are unhappy," Tungsten told the woods. "Is that what you wish to tell me?"

The woods did not answer. Perhaps it was upset with him since long ago Excalibarians cut through their trees to make a pathway, clearing the place of monsters and stopping them from

7

migrating near King's Road and its entire four-hundred-mile stretch. As a result, disarrayed people from The Affliction War, abandoned their homes and migrated to King's Road to build their villages and farmlands from the chaos, but still, these monsters hadn't learned their lesson.

A foul-smelling fog blanketed the forest and rose to his knees. *"Blood"* the woods answered. *"I want blood."*

Tungsten stopped and listened. Since all signs of life had been sucked out of the place, the slightest sound led him to his target. "This was an unnecessary chase," he sang as if he was about to break to a song. Red slime had been dripping onto the soil. "But if it makes you feel safer, I came alone."

On a high branch, the man sat slouched with his hands and feet balancing on the branch like a dog. The pale skin he wore tightly over his body loosened, revealing his green wrinkled skin. His eyes were turning yellow, glowing as he snarled at him.

Amused, Tungsten placed his hands on his hips. "Can you come down so we can have a little heart-to-heart?"

"Giant King," he hissed, his shaky voice turning dark. "Ill-bred, saboteur of homes and giver of wars."

"Well then, I suppose you expect me to climb up there?"

The monster hissed. Yellow claws ripped through the skin of his victim's fingers, and bits of flesh and fingernails fell onto the ground. "When I kill you, the horse of death will drag you into his master's undying inferno."

Tungsten crossed his arms and studied him. "And you tally me with threats."

A shadow hovered over him, and he made out daggers in mid-air. Dozens of glowing eyes grew closer as he spun, their scream and weight fell upon him, covering him from head to toe, striking their blades upon his armor, scratching, and biting. Tungsten walked along intent on his target then the dozens of drapes who pounced on his back. Their blows did nothing to his armor, their claws couldn't penetrate the slightest surface.

When a blade poorly squeezed through his visor. Tungsten turned his head and swiped the dagger off the grip and onto the damp grass. As he reached for the hilt of his sword, the drapes scattered, their feet scrambling away.

Tungsten took one step toward the man's tree, and he hissed. "Say your piece, for my journey shall not be delayed."

The drape spun back until he was hanging upside down; a pair of red eyes were now peering at him. "Tell me, for how long can that armor sustain you without your God's protection?"

"Perhaps you can ask himself when you return to the Isles of Avalon."

The drape spat a blotch of dark mucus before his feet. "Not I! May Orendor, God of the hammer and anvil, rot in those cursed Isles!"

Tungsten tilted his head, giving no riposte to the drape's lofty comment.

9

The monster, seeing his unmoved demeanor, released a horrid call and leaped from the branch. Tungsten unsheathed Excalibur, a two-handed blade he named after his kingdom. In the time it took the drape to fall, the marking on his blade began to glow.

In one strike, the man was cut in half, revealing a drape, with long bony fingers slowly curling in.

With a flick of his wrist, the blade glowed with fire, turning the blood into steam. "Sorry." He squatted before the man who lay still, his eyes never leaving him. "It was not my wish to feed this malevolent forest any blood, but I also don't pardon any vile remarks about Orendor."

• • •

Back on King's Road, Indra followed faithfully at his side, his long tail swaying side to side. The startled team of horses had calmed and were perhaps still capable of turning back to the road.

Lancelot was halfway to meeting him, holding the distressed young woman in his arms. She gasped, still uneasy at the sight of him. Was it because of their unnatural height? Giants they were, and Tungsten knew he was the biggest of them all.

"Did he escape?" Lancelot asked.

Tungsten turned toward the forest that witnessed the drape's last moments. He then looked at the young woman, her breath still shaken. "Are you alright my dear?"

Her shoulders pinched in, but she nodded. "T-That creature tore my father's flesh. It fused into his skin, taking his likeness, but it wasn't him!"

"What you encountered was a drape," Tungsten said. "But it's over now, dear."

"No—it is not—I can't rid his face from my mind!"

"Horrific acts aren't that easy to shake off, Miss…?"

"Igraine."

Tungsten went to his tiger and took a dagger from his holder. He gave it to Igraine, who seemed surprised to be offered a weapon. It was made of their best steel and decorated with gold dust. "Take this and be swift on your way home."

"She sprained her ankle badly," Lancelot said. "Will you be able to take the road on your own?"

Igraine nodded, squeezing the blade and shaking it as a result. "If you hadn't returned… that drape would have led his group to my village." She took Tungsten's arm in a desperate plea. "He demanded my mother and my son! I have no one else but them!"

Tungsten gently patted her shoulder. "At ease, dear, the others will meet the same fate should they overstay their unwelcomed lingering upon King's Road."

Lancelot turned to the woods and gripped his sword. The eyes that had been watching them from the shadows crawled back, their hissing lingering in the shrubs.

Igraine, seeing they had been around them all this time, froze.

"Ignore them, you must be on your way." Tungsten offered his hand, but she stared at his gauntlet with some unwillingness to touch it. The metal glistened like sheer plated armor and in poor light it darkened. It was impenetrable to anything manmade or magic, but perhaps there was something more, something the war was responsible for. By tightening his hand and opening his palm, layers of his tanium armor receded from his fingertips to his knuckles until they split over the back of his hand and stopped at his wrist.

Surprised, Igraine blinked at the leather glove he wore underneath.

"Is this better?" he asked, moving his fingers to show he was flesh and bone underneath. It was as far as he was willing to go anyway. His skin had never touched a woman that wasn't his kin. Igraine took his hand, and he noticed her trembling when he boosted her to her seat. "A word of caution, my dear. If you fail to reach your destination before nightfall, do not heed the cries at night. No matter how infantile they sound or how unwell they appear. Do that and you'll find your way back to your family."

The reins quivered in her hold. "And if those drapes take

me again?"

Chuckling, Tungsten tapped her chin lightly and guided her to the road ahead. "Think only of home and you will find yourself at her doorstep."

She gave them one last look and smiled weakly, tired from what she had gone through.

Tungsten watched her go, just in case the drapes wished to follow her. She had his mother's eyes, a soft brown but too young to bear her gentle crow's feet. Mother wanted to join their travel to Crystal Lake, but the kingdom was about to confront a change, and there was no one more suited to prepare his people than her.

"Your Majesty." Lancelot made his way back to their intended path. "I'm afraid we lost some light."

"Hmm." Tungsten brushed his fingers through his tiger's fur. "Then let's continue."

Cerrig Forest was further north. A dirt road parted from King's Road and led the way to Bromton, a small uncontrolled town of a young lord. At the crossroads, a wooden sign brought them to a stop.

"What will His Majesty choose?" Lancelot asked.

"You know that answer, friend, but first, we have yet to celebrate our recent rescue."

"Celebrate?"

Tungsten raised his elbow and extended it toward his friend.

Lancelot scowled. "You know I don't participate in elbow

bumps or any of those celebratory gestures."

"You do when Calibor requests it, but you dare leave your brother in arms waiting?"

Lancelot whipped around, hand squeezing his dagger. "*Who told you that? Present to me the name and I will smite that blabbermouth!*"

Tungsten laughed. "Siblings bury each other's secrets. You would know that if you had any."

Lancelot muttered something under his breath. With a reluctant groan, he raised his arm and met him halfway. Their elbows hammered against one another with a *clang!*

II

AN OATH GIVEN SHANT' BE LOST

The rustling of Cerrig Forest persisted well into the night; weak branches had fallen on the road from the strong pulls of the wind. Lancelot and his horse had to snake through the forest and with little light, there was much more reason to be vigilant. Tungsten remained on the wide road that led them to the lake.

"Your Majesty?" Lancelot called from a fair distance.

"I'm nearby," said Tungsten. "The road appears to be clear from here on."

"Easy for you to say when you have a cat that can leap higher than Marigold and climb trees with ease."

"That's not his fault!" Tungsten trailed his fingers down his coat and Indra growled.

"That cat never likes any affection you provide, does he?" Lancelot brushed a twig off his pauldron and cleared the leaves off his horse. "We both know he could easily kill you in your sleep."

Tungsten chuckled, for the cat was never meant to be his. It was during his fight with the Giantess Florenda that he acquired Indra. He was a cub then and her pet. Indra attacked him after he defeated the giantess, but a wounded cub against a man like him was no match. He spared the young tiger and tended him in his palace, ignoring his retaliation, clawed walls and gnawed furniture. It was well within a month that Indra had grown and recovered, but when he set him free, the tiger didn't leave.

A crack disturbed the woodland, and Lancelot cursed. "These weak northern forests are beginning to irritate me."

"You can complain freely, my friend, but we shan't be delayed with more detours and breaks."

Lancelot tapped his horse to a trot until he rejoined him. "So, His Majesty *does* miss his little sister?"

Though he couldn't see his face, Tungsten gave him a hard look.

Lancelot clicked his tongue. "And it is here in October that my friend counts his silence as his confession."

Tungsten petted Indra's shoulder. He listened to his quiet growling; as his cat's tail snapped back and forth at the touch.

Sure, he didn't like to see Calibor outside of Excalibur, nor out of his sight, but he couldn't give Lancelot the pleasure of knowing he was right.

His petting stopped after Lancelot gave a partly suppressed laugh. Worriers and sometimes short-tempered men like him rarely joked around, so Tungsten had some joy in hearing him.

"You know, you could remedy your problem by sending a letter to Calibor, stating you had finally decided to marry Princess Casana."

Tungsten stopped Indra as he could not lead him further. "Marry?" He patted the hilt of his sword as if the mere word could summon a monster. "It was only at Calibor's wedding that I picked up courting her to please my mother, you know better than to think I would break my long-standing oath."

"Princess Casana has been patient for you all these years."

"Calibor campaigning the outer borders of the country is enough womanly troubles to worry about, don't you agree?"

"And are our king, not the stronghold prince of our borders."

"I've done both quite well."

"Is it because Lady Casana was Ecarus' betrothed?" His friend dared to ask. "She's favored you since we were children. Surely you saw that, everyone to this day knows it."

"She's a good friend, and it's not because she was my brother's promised woman."

"Then perhaps you could do with the softer women of the neighboring kingdoms?"

"Like Felmid?" Tungsten exclaimed. The name itself made Indra glare at Lancelot. "Their God has left them, leaving scrawny, pampered women who could not bear the weight of Excalibur's crown nor her armor."

Lancelot pounded his chest. "Bengom's noble women then. I saw one was quite affectionate to you at the wedding."

"And I tossed that hen across the room for attempting to swim her little hands between my faults."

Lancelot laughed, only this time, Tungsten didn't share the same sentiment. "Are you done?"

"Pardon my amusement at your discomfort with the fairest maidens, but you must take advantage of what youth you have left. You're thirty-five and speak like a man of retiring age, calling women older than you, 'dear.' Anyone who wishes to marry you must rely on the benefits of the union than worry if you're ugly behind that armor."

Tungsten held his breath but continued down the road, barely able to grasp the imposing interrogation. "My mother made you talk to me, didn't she?"

Lancelot fell silent.

Tungsten harrumphed. "You know no one from my family line has ever shown his face to anyone but his kin and you dare use my missing sister as a reason to sweet talk me into this subject?"

A drawn-out lungful escaped Lancelot's visor. "Then will you continue a life of celibacy and give Excalibur no heir? Now when we need it the most?"

Tungsten encouraged Indra to pick up his pace. "We will leave your inquiries to dry. I hope next time you consider my choices."

• • •

Past the dense forest, a clearer path opened to their destination, lighted by the flaming torches the guards oversaw.

Tungsten wondered what his sister would say when she heard of his arrival. She'd been looking forward to their reunion at Crystal Lake, but the death of his father had robbed him of his love for their family retreat. But to Calibor, such a place could not be tarnished.

As children, they often looked forward to family retreats, breaks from the war or talk of it, seeing their parents together, and their older brother Ecarus reading rather than leading another campaign. Their then-king father, Master of the spearhead, would go fishing with them. He and Calibor would dig for worms and bask in the sun all day. Tungsten could remember the scars on his father's back and his gray beard that danced on his chest as he laughed heartedly.

It wasn't until The Affliction War ended that Merlin the Old sent his father to the lake for his last days, and overnight, the fond memories became cold.

"Your Majesty." Lancelot's voice pulled his thoughts back. "May I have a word?"

"Speak friend."

"I request your pardon for my poor choice of words. You made an oath to Orendor, and you're not one to break promises."

Tungsten turned to his friend. "Your pecking is because of your recent engagement, isn't it? You have gone beyond the marrying age and now want to settle with that big-breasted tavern woman?"

"Well, as you know, Excalibarian men have a weakness for strong women and Lucia displayed them exceptionally well on the night I saw her wrestle two hammered men out of her business."

"Then allow me to fund your wedding. It's the least I can do for you after joining me in the single life."

"Then I graciously accept! My mother says I'll never provide her a grandchild; she thinks I'm trying to pull white hairs out of her scalp."

"So, it seems!" Tungsten laughed, aware that his friend had

grown silent, peering at the road ahead.

The iron gates were empty of their knights.

"What the blazes?" Lancelot dismounted his horse. "Excalibarian knights, make your presence known!"

After a moment of silence, Tungsten pushed the gates, and they creaked open. He pushed them again, leaving them wide open, and rushed up the hill.

A two-story cottage with a tower in the back waited in the dark. The torches on the stands remained unlit. The only thing that provided any light was the sparkling lake. Diamond-like shards floated from the surface until they faded where an old, crooked willow tree grew in the center; its crawling branches sinking into the water.

"Your Majesty?" Lancelot said.

Tungsten dismounted Indra, blade held tightly in his grasp. It was awfully quiet, but that didn't stop him from breaking through the double doors.

III

WHAT MUST I FEEL?

Tungsten stood in the foyer. There was only the sound of his labored breathing breaking the stillness of the place. How could such a silence hold the night like this? Twenty of Excalibur's best knights joined Calibor and Prince Valte in Cerrig Forest. Five archers, five-foot soldiers, and ten of her best spear women.

"Here." Lancelot lit a torch and passed it to him.

Tungsten gripped it and raced through room after room. In one, he expected to see Calibor, humming as she painted another portrait of the lake, or reading books on smithing in the library. But there were no recent paintings, no books left open, no Calibor.

"Calibor!" Tungsten shouted, this time desperate. "Sister, heed my call!"

Room after room lay in darkness until the first floor was deemed empty. He marched up the stairs expecting a different outcome, his armor clanking as his flared nostrils blew through the openings of his helmet. He paused briefly when he noticed flickering lights from a door toward the end of the hallway. The door belonged to a bedchamber—Calibor's room.

"Your Majesty," panted Lancelot after catching up with him. "The windows are open, but why on such a cold night?"

Though determined to move forward, Tungsten's pace slowed, he couldn't evade the feeling of a sinister presence lingering in the room. The wooden door creaked as he opened it just enough to allow him to see and enter the room. The fire inside the fireplace was flickering weakly.

Whatever unknown he was going to unveil stirred fear in him. He felt like a child again, caught in the middle of a battlefield, watching death's horses roam over the bodies of his people, leaving him with a sinking weight in his chest, one that no armor could block.

He only made it a few steps before he discovered a slumped figure. She wore a white gown and lay over the table facing the fireplace. A blot of darkness soaked the wood where her arm was tucked under it. Black blood oozed from her side, slowly dripping into the pool it made.

"Calibor?" A cold moisture invaded his hand, and the pulse in his chest throbbed in his temple.

Tungsten breathed deeply. His lungs had not drawn any air until he forced himself.

Lancelot, hearing his surprise, tried to go in, but Tungsten held out his hand, commanding him to stop. "Not a step closer." His mouth had gone dry. "You will not enter, nor will you look inside this room."

Lancelot gripped the torch. "But—"

"I will not have you gaze upon my sister without her armor! If you dare yourself to try, I'll kill you myself!"

Lancelot stepped back, his breathing growing heavy. "Where's her armor?"

Tungsten ignored him, looking at him one more time. Lancelot had pulled back his visor; his eyes filled with fear. Trusting his friend would not barge in if he left the door open, he approached the maiden on the table.

"Your Majesty!" Lancelot implored. "Tell me where her armor is. I will fetch it! Just tell me she's alright!"

"Quiet." Tungsten kneeled next to the table. His breathing was fast as he inspected her closely.

Calibor's head dangled at the edge, face turned slightly sideways as if she was watching the fireplace.

His boot bumped into something, and he looked down, finding a gold armet helmet with eagle wings that protruded from the ends of the visor. Observing his sister once again, he grasped her intentions before she lost consciousness. Her cheeks remained a pale soft pink and sweat appeared to be glistening on her forehead.

A ragged breath left her and her fingers curled and uncurled, still reaching for her helmet that had fallen on the floor, still out of her reach.

Tungsten took off his helmet and dropped it on the floor, leaving a loud clank that could cut flesh. He scooped Calibor off the table and carried her over to the bed. She let out a sharp cry before he steadied her. Black bruises darkened her right eye, and blood had trailed over the bridge of her freckled nose. He cupped her cheek where a blade had carved through, and she winced.

"Calibor." Her golden hair, touched by the Sun Goddess herself, had been reduced to red.

Calibor's eyebrows scrunched together, and her eyes suddenly locked on him. She let out a shaky sigh and smiled. "Dearest brother. You're here."

Tungsten enticed her with a hug. She winced, and he pulled back. "Who did this to you? Tell me and I will wipe them from existence."

The shadow overhead hadn't stopped moving, and it was unlike the chandelier to shift with little wind. Hanging from one post was a man, looking down at them with a swollen face, lips pushed out, with his eyeballs left to hang from his sockets. He was unrecognizable, but his attire and body were alike — Prince Valte.

25

"Shadow," she uttered. "A shadow came into our room."

"Your Majesty?" Lancelot's voice startled him. "May I enter?"

"No," Tungsten said, clinging to what life his sister had left. "Leave us!"

"Brother," she whispered. Tears started to well up in her eyes as a gentle smile formed on her face. "It matters not, let me see Lancelot one more time."

Tungsten buried his face in her chest. Words should have jumbled together; his throat should have felt like a lump. Even now, he felt as if his heart had been plucked from his chest, but he couldn't shed a single tear. He should be in shambles, but it's happened again, just like when Ecarus died—Father took his last breath.

He jumped, noticing Calibor's fingertips dancing on his cheekbone before going down to his chin. "Do not weep for me, for I fear you will break."

"You are worthy of breaking for," he pleaded.

"Our people still need you," she replied with a weak whisper. "My brother is strong and favored by Orendor. You will laugh as you always have and paint this world with the love and hope you always poured unto me." Calibor's eyes softened and despite the pain, she smiled. "Will you miss me?"

"More than I can say with words."

She mustered her strength to lean on him as if reaching to

embrace him. "If only I could go where you go. Wouldn't that be nice?" Her breath stopped, and she fell back, her head hung back before Tungsten caught her.

• • •

Tungsten dried his clean hands before dipping them in mint oil. He cleaned Calibor's face until there was no blood to tarnish her skin. He studied her arms for any marking he may have overlooked. Without a doubt, a blade had gone through her back. The blade that caused it was likely the one hanging above them, still deep in her husband's chest.

With Calibor neatly laid on the bed under a silk sheet and pillow, he prepared her for the journey home.

Tungsten went to pick up her gold helmet. Blood had streamed from the top and down the side. He found a cloth in a drawer and wiped it until the stain was gone. Calibor must have used all the strength she could muster to reach for her helmet to go to battle with her assailants, but it was all for naught.

After tying her hair neatly up, he placed the helmet back on her head. Seeing it back on, it was as if she was alive again, her high-pitched laugh muffled within the tanium metal. He didn't have to observe her to realize she was at peace, but while he didn't feel sadness, a darkness grew inside.

"Well now," Tungsten said, the muscles in his throat still tight. "You look better this way, but perhaps never as good as you did on your wedding day. The halls sang when you arrived. Mother glowed with pride as you and Prince Valte were joined as man and wife." He chuckled, recalling giving her a tight embrace, and swinging her into the hall of the palace before she left for Crystal Lake.

Tungsten grabbed his helmet and placed it back on his head. The room was now small from what his visor could offer. He carried Calibor and looked to the exit. He sat back down on the bed and held her a bit longer.

The owls hooted in the night, the same distasteful wind carried on, and the branches rustled in the distance. So many broken promises resided in this place, dreams he and Calibor shared that The Affliction War stole from them. The war had been over for a decade yet this was how her sister would die?

Lancelot leaned on the wall with arms crossed, staring out the window. Surprise revived his rigid posture, but seeing Calibor in his arms froze any word he wanted to throw at him.

He looked at him, almost frozen. "Is she?"

"Move aside, friend. For we shall bury her in the lake."

Lancelot looked outside the window. His shoulders were shaking and yet he promised himself to the view of the night. "She deserves a royal burial, to rest amongst tombs of her kin!"

"I've made my decision," Tungsten made his way down the hall his voice still echoing. "Prince Valte is hanging in the chamber. Free him so he can be reunited with his family."

"No, I'll join you and the Sun Princess," he said, in mid-pant, urgently at his heels.

IV

BECAUSE OF ME

The night never felt like a stranger like it did tonight. The stars turned their back on him, and the moon lay hidden behind a cloud. Even now, he hadn't slept, not since they left Excalibur.

Crystal Lake was downhill. A stream of floating crystals hovered over the chilly waters. It was as if the night had dropped the stars themselves. Whenever one of the crystals hit one another, they would chime into the night.

As he made his way down, Tungsten looked at his sister. "When you left Excalibur, I asked myself, who am I going to drink with without my armor? Who can look at my face and remind me to shave?" he told her. "The answer now carries a frigid answer that I am reluctant to voice."

It was no secret he didn't know how to mourn like others mourned. Growing up The Affliction War forced his sole focus onto the well-being of Excalibur's walls. While he couldn't convince others he could feel the sense of loss, the countless deaths from the war desensitized him from showing it.

Tungsten stopped, realizing he reached the lake's shore. The sound of the crystals gently clashing with each other grew noticeably louder and crisper than they gracefully rose in the air.

Before taking a step, he watched the water ebb and flow. Admittedly, he hadn't been this close to the lake since his father passed away. Countless promises to Calibor and their mother were made to visit for the winter, but he'd never go.

Perhaps that's why Calibor wouldn't leave until he came, denying herself an early return home.

Is this my fault?

"Well then!" To shatter the thought from his mind, he spoke with the same vibrancy and timbre to echo across the waters. "Let's not wait any longer."

One step and his foot clanked on a firm surface, not its icy waters. It crystallized, creating a path to the center of the lake.

"It's bewitched," Lancelot warned unsheathing his sword. "Step back, Your Majesty."

Instead of heeding his friend's worry Tungsten looked at his sister. She appeared like a child, shoulders tucked in his arms. "No, I shall not."

"But Your Majesty!"

Tungsten took another step, and he could hear the chiming

of crystals, bits floated like glimmering stars that drifted into the sky. Finding the surface secure enough to carry his and Calibor's weight he continued, each time the crystals rang before breaking off. He looked down, and stared at Calibor's helmet, the feathers on the end of her visor were painted in gold. "Strange," he told her. "I'm suddenly beginning to remember all those fits you threw as a child because Father couldn't bring us for the winter." As he got to the center he brushed through the floating crystals. "When Father broke, you wanted us to spend his last moments here, at our favorite place. But he passed while you were on a campaign, far from Excalibur's soil. I don't think I can forget how disappointed you looked when I told you he passed. Surely you know it was because of Father that I never wanted to come here, and yet you made no complaints. Because of me, you didn't return and stayed with me."

"Your Majesty!" Lancelot cried.

Before he took another step, Tungsten haled. A woman was in the water, staring back at him.

The water rippled as she came out. A silver gown adorned her figure the gold trumpet sleeves flowed with the wind as if she had not been wet at all. Instead of webbed hands like the sirens he encountered, her fingers were bejeweled with silver rings.

Lancelot sheathed his sword and now had his crossbow aiming at the woman. Seeing the threat, she turned to him and gave him a sharp look. Crystals from the lake were embedded in her temple and her eyes. It was as if they were in her iris too.

"I wouldn't try, Sir Lancelot."

Lancelot gritted his teeth, half blinking. "How do you know me?"

"She's not a siren," Tungsten announced. "This woman is fairy-kind."

V

WALKING TO AN UNKNOWN FOG

The woman's gaze shifted back to him. Her pale skin radiated enough to illuminate against the dark. The uncomfortable sensation he felt told him she could influence him if she wanted to, and if she not had already tried it was because his tanium protected him.

"Few can tell apart a siren from fairy kind." Her ethereal voice caused ripples to dance around her.

Tungsten seeing he was not in current danger responded. "It is no foresight. I've met every kind of siren to know you're not one."

She blinked and a sly smile cornered her lips. "Well then, why does one such as yourself cross into our realm carrying death upon thy arms? These waters are not a place for the dead."

"Before I answer, who am I speaking to?"

"Morgên is my name, and you are trespassing upon our home."

"Our?" he repeated.

She turned slightly behind, where another fairy rose to the surface, followed by another. "We are the maidens of the lake." Her silver eyes focused on his dear sister. "Bury your kin on your land."

"And if I refuse?"

More fairy maidens surfaced from the deep, eyes faintly glowing, their stare widening with curiosity. Morgên glided closer as if to show she was their voice. "We revealed ourselves to tell you should you leave her here, we will expel her body for the wolves to eat."

Tungsten pressed his sister to his chest. "Calibor deserves a just burial and you will provide it."

"You do not have command over us," a maiden said, she looked like she was in her mid-twenties, her hair was dark blue, eyes radiated gold. "Your sister indeed had the foresight to know we existed, but she'd never mark her grave upon our home."

Lancelot was heard from the back, telling him to abandon the idea and return to Excalibur. Back home, his sister would be mourned by her people, but this was her favorite place—this is where she would want to be buried.

"Perhaps I can work out a deal," Morgên said. "Are you

interested?"

Tungsten observed the shore as more fairy maidens peeked from the waters to listen. "What kind?"

Using the rolling waters under her feet, Morgên circled him. She had no weapon on her person and no staff to put a spell on him, but he followed her, unwilling to let her see his back. "Even as a child, Calibor would not give us the sword of the old king."

The same blue-haired maiden pointed at the weapon on his hip. "We are bounded and connected by many running rivers and lakes, oceans you dare not cross. Ever since Orendor's waters stopped flowing out of his mountains, we have grown weak. The fire from his anvil, the minerals from the tanium you possess on your body, it once nurtured us, but most importantly served as a failsafe for our realm."

"Give it to us," a fairy said, her slender finger emerging from the waters as she reached for him. "Lay Excalibur upon our hands."

Tungsten stepped back from her reach. He turned to see the commotion erupting behind him. His loyal friend stood a few feet behind outnumbered by the fairies. The maidens grew closer, bringing him to swing his sword to steer them back. "Stay back wenches," he cursed. "How dare you ask the king for a sword deemed sacred to him!"

Morgên's leaned towards him, her fingertips gently grazing Calibor's helmet. "Younger brothers always want to imitate their older brother, don't they? As you looked up to the late Prince Ecarus. Calibor looked up to you. Is that not why she had her helmet made to look like yours? Did she not consider a life of celibacy to imitate her brother."

Tungsten exhaled. With such intimate knowledge upon her lips, she might as well take off his helmet. He pivoted from her reach, keeping Morgên from laying another finger on his sister. "Orendor made this sword to serve Excalibur, not to be used as some exchange or currency."

Morgên's movements stopped, and she retreated, eyes narrowing. The sun started to rise, and the fairies turned to see it. They didn't fear the light like most monstrous beasts but appeared drawn to it like a moth. Seeing closely with such light, they were beautiful women, skin bearing the mix of every tone that dazzled like the crystal lake.

"The night is over," Morgên said. "Should you deny my request, then leave my lake before I sink you and your friend to the bottom."

"Lay one finger on my king and I'll have your head floating for the crows to pick," Lancelot warned.

A small smile cornered Morgên's lips. "I won't deny that you might try."

The wind picked up, moving the crystals to dance his way. Instead of marveling at the beauty it held, Tungsten could only stare at Calibor's helmet, where it remained faithfully shut, where nobody ever saw the beautiful girl he knew. Warm freckles, a small gap tooth, and a smile that could repel the storm.

"Lancelot," Tungsten said. "Unsheathe my blade and place it in Calibor's hands."

"Your Majesty!"

"Do it!"

Although his friend showed clear opposition, progress was made when he eventually moved to his right. The fairies had grown quiet, observing his friend. He unsheathed Excalibur, grunting from its weight before he laid it over Calibor, delicately placing her hands on the hilt like a king's burial.

"Take Excalibur, in exchange for my sister's resting place."

Morgên rose from the water, still powered by the current that rolled under her feet. Translucent wings opened from behind, and her gown glistened a brighter white. Her arms parted, once more leaning towards Tungsten. He raised his sister's body and laid her in the fairy's cold and wet arms.

Morgên shifted back, her gown swaying as she created distance between them. "Fare thee well, recluse king."

Lancelot stormed back to land, shouting curses, boots pounding hard on the solid water.

As the fairy descended into the water, Tungsten didn't take his eyes off his sister until Morgên faded.

Tungsten took a sluggish pace. The fairies, unaffected by the solid surface he walked on, swam at his side, following him. They would reach out and brush their hands against his feet and legs.

"Your strength is alluring," one said.

Another reached his arm and swam her fingers down to his hip. "Your armor has endured much death, and yet it radiates with so much power."

"Do you know what happened to Calibor?" he asked. "What became of her soldiers?"

The fairies stopped, forcing Tungsten to turn back.

One sprang from the waters and leaned into Tungsten, her hair flowing as her pale hands cupped his helmet. "We saw shadows," she answered. "Screams that never infiltrated this peaceful lake." The waters of her feet ran up as they carried her to him; her pale lips pursed as she leaned over and kissed the side of his helmet. In a flash, Tungsten saw a moment of last night, the torches in both the gate and in the property extinguished at the same time, followed by the clashing of steel and sudden screams.

"These shadows took down the unwary guards." Another fairy had risen and wrapped her arms around his waist. "Sensing the disturbance, we came to the surface. Your subjects living in this place and your knights were hauled off into the forest."

"Were they man or monster?"

The red-haired fairy who embraced him trailed her finger down to the middle of his chest. "Neither, Your Majesty, just shadows."

Shadows.

Tungsten pressed forward, dragging the maidens until they released him. This time his fists clenched, feet hitting the surface as if wanting to sink.

The fairies swam by his feet, hands brushing his calves while they asked him to not be so sad.

"If you need company, we offer it gladly." The fairy pulled at her sleeves, exposing one of her breasts. "In return, you will give us your seed."

"And we will keep the child," another answered.

Tungsten went on until he made it to the shore. He turned to see if they would follow him out of the water, but the fairies moved back as if repulsed by the dry land.

"You are as they say." Without sharing their disappointment, the maidens bowed their heads to him and sank into the water.

Tungsten smudged where the fairy had kissed his helmet. They weren't sirens, but they behaved just like them with their seductive comments and desiring his seed.

Lancelot was uphill, prepping his horse. Indra was resting under a tree, staring at them.

Mauled down.

Gutted.

Whatever happened, it happened swiftly. "Go to the tower," he told Lancelot. "See if any pigeons remain and send word to my mother what has happened."

"Your Majesty," Lancelot said, his urgency seeming less than his. "Pardon my choice of words, but you were most unwise to give away your sword, you might as well offer them Excalibur while you're at it."

"I know you're upset."

"Orendor made it for you! Just as he had made the other twelve that now rest on the Round Table."

"I'm aware."

"No, you do not!" His voice echoed out. "Your blade, humbled and crafted to serve became the sword of the king! Now it's gone because you bent to the will of those harlots. We could have taken Calibor home, to her rightful place in the royal tomb."

Tungsten stared at the lake. The fleeting emotions still pressing in his chest. "I wanted her to go down like the queen she was."

"Queen?" Lancelot delayed saying. "You mean to say…?"

"Upon her return, Calibor was supposed to assume the role of Excalibur's queen. She accepted, and old Grand Advisor Edmun was overjoyed by my stepping down. Upon our departure, Mother was to announce it so I could avoid explaining my choice to others."

Lancelot muttered something under his breath, and joined him, where they both stared at the lake. "That's why the Queen

Mother didn't come with us, no matter how much she desired to see Calibor."

"The ceremony was to take place upon her arrival. It was to be a grand welcoming to the new queen."

"You... never told me any of this."

It was why Tungsten agreed to take the mantle as king, but such a position was for the first born to lay claim—to Ecarus to take. "You should have at least suspected it would come to this. Grand Advisor Edmun and General Armin still oppose my rule, and I cannot go against my father's loyal subjects for the law forbids me from touching the wind sword, my father's ceremonial blade."

"Calibor a queen."

"Merlin the Old always called her a shieldmaiden, but she was much too young to lead after Ecarus fell. In the last decade, she proved herself. But if what occurred here was deliberate then returning with Calibor's body would warn the enemy and I will not use my sister as a smoking signal."

Indra who listened stared at them, aware of the growing tension between them. Lancelot's silence reeked with disappointment. He clenched his fists and returned to the back of the estate.

Tungsten looked at the betraying stir of the wind, shifting in the leaves. Calibor becoming queen would not change what was already in motion. Like many gods before him, Orendor had long left for the Isles of Avalon, leaving Excalibur vulnerable to the changes of the winding world.

• • •

By the afternoon, dense and heavy clouds covered Crystal Lake like a gravesite. Tungsten scouted the property with no rest. No rock was unturned, no footprint was unmarked, and no spill was undetected. There was, however, some hope. The soil in the back of the property revealed indentations of hooves before cutting into the forest. There appeared to be only one rider, but one was enough.

Swift like a shadow.

The halls of his estate gave a colder grim welcome; each room had droplets of the would-be guards.

What kind of shadows discard any trace of my people and flee?

In the principal home, the grand frame of his parents hung over the fireplace. His father stood in full armor behind the lake, with his mother, also in full armor, standing beside him. The painting was old, completed at Crystal Lake before Ecarus was born.

The door opened, and a pair of steps sought him. Lancelot found him but didn't greet him. "I came across one pigeon hiding in its coop; the others were killed."

"What message did you convey?"

Lancelot took a deep breath. "Princess Calibor has passed along with Prince Valte and her knights. We will make the journey back with haste."

"I see." Tungsten crossed his arms. "Strange. I did not say I would return with such haste."

"What else is to do but to return?"

"Really? You sound too calm and that is unlike you."

Lancelot would typically voice his inquires, but maybe he was still disappointed in the secret he kept from him.

"Enough, you don't need to hide it."

Lancelot cursed. "Your Majesty, we both know I'm upset about what you've done—it's a betrayal of our people—of Orendor!"

"No, you are masking it once again." Tungsten placed his hand on his pauldron. "What does your heart want?"

Lancelot shook himself free and marched toward the exit. "We must depart of course; Excalibur awaits."

"You loved Calibor!" His friend took a shaky breath, but he proved him right by saying nothing. "Now tell me, as a man who admired and fought alongside my sister, what do you feel?"

Without warning, Lancelot kicked the table to his right, sending it crashing into the wall. "I never liked that buffoon prince! Ever since the God of Fortune left them, that foreign-born became weak! Never did I have any confidence he could protect her, and he proved me right—Gods, I wish he didn't prove me right!" He slammed his fists on the stone wall, cracking it. "We need to get the bastards who did this."

Tungsten released a hearty laugh and patted his friend's shoulder once more. "That's the Lancelot I know!" He marched to another room, eyes nearly souring at the many trips. "Well then, where do we begin? This was no work of vagabonds or mercenaries. Someone wanted to kill my sister and Prince Valte. They nabbed plenty of valuable items, but they didn't ransack the place. Every chair and table are precisely where it belongs."

"Where are you getting at?" Lancelot said, breath still short. "This place was attacked last night."

"I discovered fuzzy bacteria coated several unwashed bowls from the kitchen."

"You mean…are you saying Calibor laid on that table for days without anyone to aid her?"

Tungsten gave the furnished room another look. He kneeled on the carpet and found no mud stains the weather would carry, no footprints of smell. "A thief or murderer can leave disorder behind, especially in a resort that was guarded by Excalibarians, but a careful planner would never clumsily knock over a chair like you did."

Lancelot spun around, surveying the windows and how neat the drapes still decorated the place. "They attacked in the night when she would be less likely to wear her armor. Otherwise, she would have crushed them."

"Precisely." Tungsten got back to his feet. "I know you didn't want to enter the room Calibor died in, but her nails were awfully dark."

"Poison," said Lancelot. "But of what kind?"

"I'm unsure but it did not kill her; being Excalibarian, she can endure a dose that would kill a normal human. Perhaps she was slowly poisoned until our arrival. There was no meal in her chamber, so it must have been taken as a drink before bed, possibly served by someone she trusted." Tungsten exhaled. "Alas from my inspection, Valte had barely put one boot on before someone dragged him across the room and beat him with a candleholder that was tossed on the ground. The attackers took her jewels, her feathery crowns, and most importantly, Calibor and Valte's wedding rings."

Lancelot lowered his head, slowly balling his hands into fists. "Such a death is unbefitting, but as grand as we're perceived, reality would have us fall for the same trap." He let out a curse, his anger uncontained. "If the killer knew we were coming, then they're far gone."

"Aye, and that makes the seek is impossible," Tungsten said. "But we have one track to follow. For now, we shall invite ourselves into the unknown fog."

VI

YOUR SILENCE

Bromton

The Sour Ol' Inn

Lancelot rushed into the Cream Tavern, but Tungsten trailed behind. Rain was the prime enemy against armor. Even iron gradually corrodes when it encounters it, while steel loses its protective coating and rusts. Tungsten's armor was made of pure tanium, a rare living metal that is both flexible and impeccably strong against blows and magical properties. While water stood no chance against it, it was also like all other armor, heavy, hard to see out of, and uncomfortable in both the winter and summer.

When Tungsten entered the lobby, he breathed the woodsy smell of the place. The porter had a scared look focused on Lancelot and now, seeing him enter, he winced. Who knew what he did to scare that poor worker but it was likely that his friend must've threatened him, as his short-temperedness had not diffused.

A dry cough ceased all movement when a short, stocky man came from the back of the room, dragging his feet and releasing a long yawn. He patted the porter's shoulder and dismissed him with a curse. By the gold rings on his fingers, he was likely the owner of the inn. "Careful, Giant." One eye squinted while the other soured at him. "Ye'r cut through my ceiling if ye don't slouch."

"Are you going to give me a room or not?" Lancelot demanded. "Or are you going to stutter like the other?"

The owner grumbled, and a pinky went to one of his nostrils. "Wha'tta a night to be woken by two overgrown Excalibarians."

Lancelot leaned on the counter. "And I will not repeat myself."

"A bit late to be traveling, ain't it? Gates close for the night and you..." He looked Lancelot up and down. "Well, 'suppose you two must've hopped over my gates. But it matters not. I can refuse who I wish, especially by ye unnatural bastards for barging in here and making a spill on me good floors!"

"I won't deny the hour is late." Tungsten ducked under the chandelier so he could join the conversation. "And as you can see, we were poorly prepared for the rain."

The owner sneered, outwardly unconvinced by his explanation.

Tungsten laid a coin on the counter. "Perhaps this will serve the late inconvenience and buy your total silence?"

Under the dying candlelight, what he offered improved the owner's glowering eyes. His chair creaked as he leaned down, his nostrils blew on the wooden surface. It was a silver coin with a gold edge; the rim encased with tiny diamonds, crammed together but still capable of gleaming under such a poor light.

"A King's Coin?" He wheezed as he looked up at them. "Why I've nev'ah dreamed, me eyes, poor as they may be, wud' behold such a sight."

"We can start our exchange with a room," Tungsten said. "Two beds, a warm bath, some oil and buffer to polish my friend's armor, and some meat, beef, and pork will do just fine."

"Why yes, of course, mighty sirs!" The owner's attitude flipped, he took the coin and pressed it to his chest. "Anything else? Got some good-looking whores who come now and then."

"Your silence," Tungsten cut in, leaning in to examine the man closely. "You failed to mention that."

"Aye, as far as I'm concerned, yer not here." He tossed his record book on the ground and spilled his bottle of ink in the process. "Such a coin would not leave yer mighty hands if ye weren't someone important."

"You're quick to lick our boots," Lancelot asked.

"Oi, if I was upset it was yer fault!" He turned to Tungsten. "Why, by yur' height, it's as if I'm staring at King Tungsten

49

himself."

Tungsten roared a sharp laugh and rested his hand on Lancelot's shoulder. "Did you hear that? He thinks I'm the king of Excalibur."

"How he's gravely mistaken." His friend answered, shaking his shoulder free, his mood still as damp as his armor. "And if you let that tongue slip." Lancelot took out his dagger.

"May I suffer a gruesome death, giant lords!"

Tungsten leaned his hand on the counter, his weight and armor creaking the wood. "Well then! We're ready to be shown to our rooms."

"Aye, eff'course." The owner fumbled under his desk and brought out a key.

Upstairs, the dim hallway had an odor, like a wet dog had run through. It lacked the presence of a welcoming inn, but in Bromton there was no other choice to make.

The few rooms they walked by were very active, beds rattling the walls, and moans seeping through the cracks.

"Nott'a worry, I got the biggest room in mind," the owner said, "no old fool here can afford it anyway."

Tungsten followed behind. The inn was decorated like a war room, as if the owner had an affinity for swordsmanship. Old rusty blades hung on the wall as they passed, dull and covered in dust.

"Before ya' say anything I ain't got no time to polish the

place up." The owner's voice led him to a room in the far back. "I'll prepare the hot baths in the other room."

Lancelot rolled his arm and reached to undo his gauntlet. "This blasted rain is the last thing I needed."

"Here," Tungsten said, offering to help him. Without a squire, there were areas only he could reach.

"I can do it myself," Lancelot snapped. "Just give me time."

Tungsten dropped his hands and gave him space.

"Fall is dyin' and winter is 'wakening," the owner said, returning with wood to prepare the fire. "If I could, I'd run from it, perhaps see Excalibur me'self, heard of her tropical plants plenty, and the hot air."

"You wouldn't be able to stand the elevation," Lancelot bickered. "*Or* our people."

"Let the man dream," Tungsten said, surveying the spacious room. It was much better than watching his friend untie his greave. The room was spacious, with high arched windows and vaulted ceilings. "Besides, a King's Coin is too dangerous to spend here."

The owner turned to him, his face turning pale. "My... that's true, ain't it? Ye fooled me and gave me a death sentence!"

"I'm afraid that was your greed," he corrected.

"It's trickery, that's wah' it is. How will I spend this coin without getting' me throat sliced?"

Lancelot groaned, plopping on his bed and nearly breaking

it by the crack. "The big cities, you fool, allies of Excalibur will accept the currency, His Ma—my friend here was trying to warn you."

The owner nodded. Color returned to his face as his smile widened with greed. "You won't be getting cleaned, Mi'lord?" he asked as if his prior worries had become thin air.

"Hmm." Tungsten noticed a knight's helmet displayed on the wall. Intrigued by the workmanship, he whistled to get the owner's attention.

The man barely glimpsed at it. "That there is junk from the ol' war. Widows and old retired men sold 'em to me."

"Dead or alive, a knight's armor is a channel to their soul. I trust you gave them a fair price?"

The owner laughed. "Business is business." His work froze when he noticed Tungsten and Lancelot staring at him with a penetrating silence. He coughed in his own spit, for even his lie cowered in his throat. "B-But of course, if you need it—it's yours." He paced out of the room and shut the door.

Tungsten locked the door and went to the wall table. He laid Calibor's sword and went to fetch a cloth to clean the blade. Lancelot gave a long sigh. The man had not returned to the present, the maze he put himself in his thoughts left him awfully pensive. While he agreed to find Calibor's killers, the tracks they followed were lost to the rain and his map went to mulch.

"Let's see where we go from here." Tungsten took the old,

wrinkled map that was pinned above the fireplace and spread it on the table. "The tracks Indra has been following continue to the south miles before the rain came and washed away the blood trails. I'm certain the rider we're trailing has been venturing further and further from King's Road. After this, we shall venture deep into Pinestock Forest."

Lancelot nodded and plopped his boots on the ground.

"What could those shadows be?" he continued. "Many monsters take a similar shape. Shapeshifters, drapes, werewolves even." Lancelot didn't respond. A cautious, worrying fellow like him would at least share his thoughts as he did so often. Tungsten rolled the map, deciding not to pry. "We'll leave as soon as the rain passes, so get some sleep."

"And you?" Lancelot had taken his helmet off and looked at him. A scar ran up his neck and touched his right ear, a wound he received after battling Giantess Florenda and her pet cat, Indra's mother. His eyes were heavy from their travel, but in them, he noticed his eyes were still pink. Had he been weeping in silence?

"I shall keep watch should that owner decide to pull a sly one on us."

Lancelot grabbed his covers and yanked them up, but the blanket wasn't enough to cover his feet. "You know, just because you're the stronghold that kept the kingdom safe, it doesn't mean you have to do it here."

"Sleep, friend. I can go for a few more days without."

It was only mere minutes before Lancelot started to snore. Tungsten quickly retrieved his blanket and gently draped it over the bare half of Lancelot, ensuring he was shielded from the cold. His mood and temper were normal signs, mourning Calibor in the way she deserved.

"Lancelot," Tungsten said.

His friend grumbled. "What?"

"Nothing."

Lancelot turned sideways and tucked his pillow under his arms. He curled like a child to fit onto the mattress, but even that wasn't enough to comfort him.

Tungsten sat by the fireplace. Lancelot was angry about what happened to Calibor, and that gave him comfort. Excalibarians were mighty, but could fall ill from stress in the soul and, if neglected, they could slowly die from heartbreak.

When Ecarus died, Father went to his brother's room and refused to leave for two weeks. He wouldn't talk to anyone, not even to Calibor who brought him food when her own eyes were fresh from crying.

In the end, Ecarus's death affected Father greatly, and he worsened after news came that Merlin the Old had perished. He stopped eating and would stare off into nothing, ignoring all the comfort and support they offered.

Tungsten leaned back and looked at the ceiling. How could

he have gone through the same losses and more and still not break? If only he was like Lancelot, if only he could shed some tears for his dear sister.

His gaze fell back to the swaying flames. "Calibor, when did I become the stronghold itself?"

• • •

The rain picked up again, pouring without rest. Tungsten raised the map under the protection of a tree. He ran his index finger from Bromton and glided over to Pinestock Forest and circled where Cardon Forest should be. "Lancelot, I do believe we're lost."

Lancelot yawned but said nothing.

Tungsten tucked the map in his satchel. "Does our navigator have anything to say?"

"My map turned into mulch from the rain, and I'm not in the mood to learn those barbarian scribbles."

"Barbarian?" Tungsten tsked. "You've been mute since we left Bromton, and I'm growing tired of it."

"Fine, you want me to navigate, then I shall navigate, your heaviness!"

"Heaviness?"

Lancelot encouraged Marigold to a trot, and with a nudge of his heel, they sped off. Ingra growled, shifting from side to side.

"Lancelot come back!" Tungsten shouted. "With a pace like that, you'll alert a monster!"

"Well, I guess that means we'll both be meals, now won't we?"

Tungsten patted Indra. His feline growled once more. "Come now, Indra, you don't have to ask. I expect you to outrun him."

His cat charged, and Tungsten wobbled back, nearly losing his hold on the reins.

The forest blurred as he gave chase with Lancelot ahead. The terrain rose and fell, fresh orange leaves swirled by their passing, and the wet ones on the floor clumped the mud.

The shrill neigh from Marigold made Tungsten pull on the reins, and Indra dug his claws into the ground until they stopped. The forest they thought they would never escape opened to a dirt road.

"Oi!" A girl with a felt hat was crouching behind a bush. She sprang back to her feet, tying a string around her baggy brown trousers. "You blubbering fools got no meaning of privacy?"

Tungsten reached into his satchel and reopened his map. The road was a proper one; it lacked the wild grass from the depressions of wheels passing by, but there was no mark of a cut-off through the forest.

"Well, you got tongues, don't you?" The girl appeared no older than thirteen. She wore a tunic with missing buttons on the collar, and her leather gloves were tied at the wrist as they appeared to be made for an adult man. Her boots looked soggy, missing the laces that held the top flap together. When she moved to the side, dead squirrels were neatly tied to her belt.

Tungsten raised his hand midway to prove otherwise. "Greetings, child."

The girl crossed her arms, her cheeks coated with soot. "I'm sixteen, *not* a child."

"Child, do you know where this road leads to or its nearest junction?"

She scrunched her face, spat at Indra's feet, and turned back. Her dirty blond hair was in a high ponytail and tied into one braid. She went to untie the horse that had been waiting for her return, but she stopped and glanced at him once more. "Give me your map."

Indra growled, but Tungsten patted his head. "At ease boy." He was reaching to give her his map before she swiped it from his hands.

"You got some manners?" Lancelot pried.

She stuck her tongue out at him and stared at the map, squinting. "You old fool, this map is outdated. This road has been standing for three years."

"Oh." Tungsten took it back and stared at his map. "I suppose it was another item sold from the old war."

The girl laughed and mounted her horse. On the satchel, she

had some traps for small animals. She turned east and pointed. "This path shall lead you to Olivewood, a small wheat town made up of all things sin. Beyond yer yonder will lead you to King's Road."

"And if I continue to cut through here?" Tungsten asked.

The girl shrugged. "Then you'll be encountering your grave. I'd advise against it, as the recent killings disturbing the town are coming from that ol' region."

"Killings?" Tungsten glanced at Lancelot, who appeared more alert by his straightened back. He then turned to the girl. "If it's so dangerous, what are you doing here alone?"

"Wadd'aya think?" She raised the squirrels for them to see. "Da and I still gotta eat, even if these forests are the home of kidnappers and monsters."

"Finally, some good news," Lancelot muttered.

"Good?" the girl asked with an arched eyebrow.

"Ah, he means about there being a town, not the killings."

"Olivewood is the only town in this blasted forest." She flipped her ponytail to her back.

Lancelot turned to his friend. "We might find some news."

Tungsten nodded; aware this was the most his friend had spoken since they left.

The girl wasted no time and marched onward. Indra followed closely, but Lancelot stayed a bit back, looking at their surroundings.

At least he's still cautious.

"Quite a little tiger you got there," the girl said. "Too bad his kind don't venture here, would make a fine meal." Indra growled, and she chuckled. "What are Excalibarians doing here anyway?"

Tungsten patted Indra's back shoulders to calm him. "We've decided to take a detour from King's Road in hopes of finding something... exciting."

She turned to sour at him. "What a doltish thing to do!"

"And you, child? Hunting this far from town?"

"I told you I'm not a child—I'm sixteen, almost a woman." She shrugged. "Anyway, I'd have better results hunting after the rain, but this is all I could catch, which means little food or money to make."

"Might you have some place for me and my friend to stay?"

"Oh? Living like vagrants now?" She raised her arm for him to see the hole in her sleeve. "You think I have something to offer?"

"We don't want to impose but if you have the room, we'll take it."

"I gott'a barn, but I'd have to talk it over with my da first."

• • •

From a distance, a gray establishment expanded before them with smoke swirling from the crooked-looking chimneys. The road leading to it was all muck, and horse manure in the country meant there would be more in town.

"Quite the place," Tungsten said.

"Aye, quite the worst place in the world," the girl said, turning to the other road that led to the farmlands. There wasn't much to look at even then.

"Pardon, but may I have your name?" Tungsten asked.

"Pardon but mind your own business."

"Mind your manners," Lancelot intruded.

The girl rolled her eyes. "The name is Lily."

"I'm Rode." Tungsten fibbed. "This over here is—"

"Lancelot." His friend promptly answered, choosing not to hide his real name.

"*The* Lancelot?" Lily asked before blowing raspberries. "No, you can't be him."

A small house lay ahead, facing the untouched farmland. A barn stood on the left, with a charred side that gave off a smoky odor as if it had survived a recent fire and the rest was deep-rooted from decades of standing.

A man in his fifties sat on a rocking chair outside an old cottage with a warped roof. Seeing them, he got up, arms shaking as he could not lift his own weight. He was tall, with a muscular build, but there was a look of weariness in his eyes, something Tungsten knew too well.

"Da," Lily said, dismounting her horse and bringing her squirrels with her. "Got us some food."

"Lily," the man said. "I told you not to venture far."

Lily opened her mouth, but she clamped it shut, noticing the bruise on his right eye. "Aben was here, wasn't he? What did he want now?"

"Don't worry your pretty mind about that fool." His one working, cataract-clouded eye looked up at them. "Who are these people? I trust you're not in trouble?"

"I'm renting them the barn for the night. We'll finally have some coins."

"No... not happening." The man soured at them. "These folks are strangers, they don't smell right."

"We mean no harm." Tungsten dismounted Indra and Lancelot followed. At their approach, the man grew stiff. His poor eyes widened, and the color of his face that wasn't sunburned paled. He grabbed his daughter's wrist and yanked her behind him. "Lily, flee!" He limped for his scythe and swung it toward them. "Get back! Get back!"

"Da!"

"You'll not get near, ya hear!"

For the man's sake, Tungsten and Lancelot backed away, even so, Lily got between them. "The war is over, Da. It's been

61

over for ten years! When are you going to let it go?"

The man heaved, sweat beading on his face as he covered his eyes. "No, the war prevails. It lives in my mind, circling, torturing me with memories of my wife, my friends, my comrades... everyone I loved."

Tungsten approached the man, who seemed to shrink, gripping his scythe.

"What are you doing?" Lily asked.

Tungsten moved the girl aside. "You're a soldier of The Affliction War?"

The man parted his legs and gripped the scythe with both hands now. The scythe swiftly lifted and then descended upon Tungsten who didn't move. Upon impact with his armor, the metal shattered the handle and resulted in the metal swinging aimlessly in the air.

"He didn't mean to," Lily yelped. "Just leave, go!"

"It doesn't get better, does it?" Tungsten asked. "The cold sweats, the dead who visit your dreams."

The man looked up. "As expected, you were in the war, you murderer—murderer!"

"Aye," Tungsten answered. "But I did not fight beyond my homeland. My job was to serve Excalibur by clearing the threat of monsters who dared come for our dying god. Soldiers do what is necessary and mine was to serve the then Prince Tungsten."

The color in the man's face came back. "Tungsten?" His

stiff shoulders soften. "You were in his ranks?"

"Both me and Sir Lancelot over here."

"You really *are* Sir Lancelot!" Lily exclaimed.

Lancelot crossed his arms, unimpressed. "And what of it?"

She ran to his side and peered at him. "Heard you got skill with that bow, say, how about teaching me?"

"No."

The man scowled. "Doesn't matter. I don't like your giants, prideful, ever looking down on us men." He rubbed his back as he tried to straighten himself. "But I have heard of the giant king, of his mercy for the weak, and his swift decision to help the people of Birch during the collapse of the last Dwelling Devil."

"Such news has reached you?" Tungsten was but a boy then. No older than Lily when he went beyond the borders to take down the Dwelling Devil who held a village hostage.

"Were you there?" the old man asked.

"He was the biggest Dwelling Devil I had ever seen," he answered instead. "His dark tendrils rolled the terrains like it was cotton."

"Excuse me," Lancelot said. "But we must be getting back on the road if we don't intend to stay."

The man grumbled and looked at his daughter. "Go prepare their room in the barn, but don't let 'em wander." His eyes drifted to him before his legs wobbled back to his chair.

Grinning, Lily skipped away from them before running to

the barn. "Well, come on!"

Lancelot took his horse by the reins and followed her. Tungsten stopped. He looked at the man once more, rocking in his chair and frowning at his abandoned field. "What was your occupation?"

"I was a commander, Olivewood's champion but such a title died with everything I held dear."

"You must've been a volunteer, which kingdom did you serve?"

"Bengom. We were supposed to push a migration of drapes before we were hit by Dranythian bombs." His right hand went over the shoulder of his cloak, showing his arm was missing. "It happened in the Valley of Desree. They came like a bat in the dark, unseen, and lit their explosives. When I awoke, I was the only one breathing the stench of burnt flesh. All my men were dead."

"Dranyth bombs," said Tungsten. "Those things have claimed the lives of many Excalibarians." He remembered that fire envelope in Orendor's temple. The bridge leading to him was destroyed, his wails echoed, and he was powerless to reach him. His duty was to stay at the borders while Father and Ecarus went to his temple. He remembered the waves of Dranyths that flooded the front, their supernatural speed, and the damage they did to their walls in a short time. "Excalibur met such a fate many years ago but things have changed, the war is over."

64

"You'd think after the war, my life would get better." The man groaned back to his rocking chair, not caring to cover his left shoulder. "I was discharged from my position. Lily was only six months old. I suffered many fevers, carried my shame, and watched this once vibrant village rot. If I'm alive, it's because of my dear Lily."

"Big guy!" Lily called, waving at him. "Hurry up—I don't got all day!"

"Excalibarian, before you leave."

Tungsten stopped.

"I appreciate you not harming her. She's young and the world is cruel."

Tungsten nodded and went toward the barn.

Lily who waited for him stood cross-armed, tapping one foot. "How'd did he take it?"

"Better than our first encounter."

Before he passed her, she uncrossed her arms and joined him. "You know, Da doesn't like to talk about the war."

"Few like to talk about such things." Tungsten looked for the road, the one leading back into town. "Child."

"Child again?" she pouted. "I'm sixteen!"

Tungsten placed his hand on her blond hair. "Might you provide me an extra cloak for my friend and me? We wish to visit the tavern, one that sees all and knows all if you understand."

She groaned and took his hand, barely capable of lifting it

on her own. "The Cream of the Crop is where anybody who's a somebody goes. It is sinful, awful men and whores rot the place."

After Lancelot left his horse in the stall, he brushed his shoulder, softly muttering something to him before going to sit on the hay bales. He was ignoring him again, taking his crossbow so he could busy himself with an already clean weapon. The barn reeked with the scent of manure, but it was bearable with the open window. The loft above could offer him privacy.

Lily returned with two cloaks and laid them across the stall. She set out a lantern for them and grabbed two blankets for them to sleep. "We can share some of our squirrels if you're hungry."

Tungsten reached into his pocket and gave her five handsome gold coins.

Lily's eyes widened. "What are you doing with those?"

"These are for you, child."

"What for? My da was the richest farmer in Olivewood, and even that didn't save him."

"This isn't to make your life comfortable," he said. "You need help to run this farm again and with these coins, you can do it."

Lily said nothing. She cupped her hands together, allowing his coins to fall on her palm. "Well, good night," she said by the barn's exit.

For privacy's sake, Tungsten went outside to see her go. She was halfway down the road with hands in the air, twirling her fingers to the stars.

In the loft, he undid his real armor with ease. Squires weren't needed when every piece could detach at will, from his helmet to pauldron to down his sabatons. The chilly air brought goosebumps to run up his arms and back as his skin could finally breathe. His cuisses and gambeson were left on the hay bale to dry. He sat on the floor in his braise and enjoyed his comfort in silence. There, he tied his armor, one over the other until they were evenly on Indra's back.

He patted his growling cat, who saw his face and knew every feature. "Stay out of trouble."

"Must we go to that tavern?" Lancelot interjected from below. "I'm exhausted."

"Lily said the folks of weary here, we must find out why."

Lancelot said nothing after.

After squeezing into the helmet he took from Bromton, he detected an odor of rust somewhere. If only he thought to clean it before putting it on, but it was too late.

VII

FAR BE IT FROM ME TO BACK DOWN FROM A CHALLENGE!

A drizzle followed them onto Olivewood's wide cobblestone roads. Barrels crowded the sidewalks between their buildings built with timber and thatched roofs. People who skulked in the nighttime were cautious, halting their walk to observe them as they went by.

A shop owner, who was closing his store, gasped at the mere sight of them. He raised his hand to his heart and appeared relieved as if he confused them for a monster.

"Excuse me, sir," Tungsten said. "Do you know where I might find The Cream of the Crop?"

"Ehm, follow the noise over yonder." He stepped around him and went in the opposite direction before crossing the street.

Lancelot lagged, his steps heavy from being forced to join Tungsten while suffering the ache in his heart. He also left his armor in the barn and complained when he said the cloak Lily gave him smelled like a skunk. Without his helmet on, Tungsten could read him better, lips drawn in tightly, eyebrows squeezed together. The light rain dampened his hair, and he didn't care to use the hood to cover himself.

Contrasting the dark and dank weather was a round building, offering the most light in town. Despite the promise of rain, beating drums and laughter stemmed from the open windows. The smell of ale reached the steps of the door, where a group of working women chattered. And the men poured outside because of their presence.

Before they entered, a scream stalled them. A young woman with a red shawl was being cornered by a man, and she told him she didn't work for free. He was pulling her away while the other women followed them, daggers out, telling him to release her.

"This is the last call, Aben. Leave her alone!" When one reached for his arm, he kicked her stomach, sending her crashing into a puddle.

"Go back to whoring," he roared. "This one owes me money and if she won't pay me one way, she'll pay me in another!"

Tungsten was about to mediate before Lancelot broke through the crowd of women, surprising them at the same time.

The man saw him and stopped. "And wad'aya want?"

"This is the second time I've heard your name, and I don't like what I'm seeing."

"Yeh? Well, go suck a thumb."

Lancelot picked the man up by the neck, lifting him four feet off the ground. As always, his friend's methods were nothing short of mediation. He threw him the same way he had done to the woman, except with his strength, Lancelot tossed him a few feet before he rolled to a stop.

Grunting, Aben climbed to his feet and unsheathed his sword. He ran at Lancelot, roaring. Tungsten patted his hip, realizing he left Calibor's sword in the barn. He flinched as Aben's blade went into Lancelot's side.

"Lancelot!"

His friend gripped the blade and plucked it out. "If I see you terrorize that old farmer and his daughter, I'll make sure you no longer have feet to stand on. You will then know what it's like to feel helpless." He punched the man in the face, and Tungsten winced.

Aben flew over the woman, twirling before he crashed into the water trough.

Among the gasping women, one started to clap, quickly approaching them. "Why I haven't seen Excalibarian men in ages!" Even with the light rain, she wore only a shawl, but she didn't use it to cover or hide her bulging cleavage. "Now Sir

Lancelot, friend of the King is here!"

Lancelot squeezed his side and marched inside the tavern.

"Heavens, you look like the giants," a younger one said as the others surrounded Tungsten. He'd been cornered by such women, human and beast too many times to be surprised.

When he tried to enter the tavern, the older one blocked him. Her smoldering gaze danced around his armor. "I serviced a few in my younger days, knights who came to my hometown for rest. I would certainly love to mount a mountain again."

"Leave the man alone." The woman with the red shawl said, arms crossed and shoulders shivering from the cold. The hit she suffered darkened her left eye. "If we draw out any customers because of your babbling, we'll be given the boot."

Tungsten nodded at the woman. "Thank you, dear. I much appreciate the aid!"

"You're welcome," she said, smiling and turning to the tavern. "Is… your friend going to be alright?"

"I would hope so."

Tungsten went inside, ignoring the next prostitute who brushed her feathered fan against his arm.

In contrast to the poorly lit town, the tavern greeted him with the odor of tobacco and belched ale.

Lancelot claimed a table at the very end of the room as if to keep away from prying eyes, but it was impossible for men like them.

Tungsten joined him; the wooden floor creaked under his weight as he became aware the music and voices had stopped. Lancelot, who likely started the silence with his mood, didn't look up or care that the others were bothered.

The quiet patrons watched to see what Tungsten would do. A group with daggers in hand seemed to be waiting for some blade to come out of his cloak. It was for that reason he didn't take Calibor's sword with him; why he told Lancelot to leave him, and he got injured for it.

When he sat, the patrons relaxed and their voices blended once more. A fiddle joined the din as the player returned to his old tunes.

"Quite a noisy place," Lancelot muttered.

"You should smile," Tungsten said, noticing blood drip off Lancelot's seat. Excalibarians bled slower than humans, but that wouldn't stop him from checking on his friend now and then. "There could be spies about, and your grieving will make us stand out."

"Look at us, we already stand out." Lancelot didn't look up. "Besides, that's one command I can't fake, Your Majesty."

"My name is Rode until we're home, remember?"

"Yeah, yeah."

"I know you're in distress, old friend, but you have a wound to look into." He said nothing when a round man with a balding head approached them.

"So it's no spell, Excalibarians in my tavern." The tavern owner's mustache was long and neatly curled at the ends. "How can the Cream of the Crop service you?"

Lancelot left a coin on the table, bloody from having touched his injury. "Give us your best ale and keep it coming."

The owner picked it up and looked at it. It was no King's Coin but their silver coins were Excalibarian. "Very well," he said, turning to Tungsten. "And for you, big man?"

"Give me your best meat, ham, beef, venison; I'll take them all," he said, charming the owner to smile.

"I wouldn't take a bite," Lancelot said, wincing as he readjusted himself in his seat. "The food here will probably make you sick."

"Hold your horses, we serve our guests well!" The owner said. He patted away, calling for the women to get to the kitchen and start cooking.

Across the tavern, a group of unruly-looking men have been watching them. By how long Lancelot kept his coins out, spinning them like a game, they likely assumed they had enormous bags.

Tungsten took off his cloak, though he wore only the knight's helmet he took from Bromton, he wanted to show the simple trousers and tunic to prove he wasn't here to fool around. The men, seeing this, turned away.

"Cowards," Lancelot said, appearing to notice the change in

the room. "Don't think they've seen muscles like yours but green hasn't ever stopped anyone from being reckless."

"Is that a compliment?"

Lancelot huffed and looked away.

"Here we are," the tavern owner sang, setting down their ale.

Lancelot muttered to himself, bothered by the presence of the townsfolk. He drank his tankard with little care for drawing air. "Keep 'em coming," he cautioned the owner.

Workers from the kitchen brought a cured leg of ham and cut slices off the bone. Another set out plates of roasted venison smothered in butter and chopped mushrooms. The last one was a bowl of beef stew bubbling in dark gravy sauce.

"This looks exquisite!" Tungsten grabbed a roasted cow leg from the plate and barely opened his visor. Lancelot who was always curious of his identity, peeked when he shouldn't have. After years of never knowing his face, his greed to know his face made him reckless.

Tungsten turned the other way and took a hearty bite. Lancelot blew air through his nostrils and went back to drinking.

"If there is anything else, we can accommodate," the tavern owner said, hands clasped together.

"I would like to indulge in delightful melodies of this hospitable place," Tungsten said amid his second bite of juicy meat.

74

The owner, surprised by his request, looked at the servers. "Well, you heard him." He clapped his hands. "Start dancing and bring those whores inside."

With a flick of their aprons, the women wiped their hands and gracefully twirled around the table, swaying their hands in the air like Lily had. As the music grew strong, the fiddler player went to them, eager for coins and perhaps the food they were enjoying.

The women from outside flooded their space, and the scent of their wet clothes permeated the room. They danced around Tungsten, leaping and twirling as they hummed. Be it the alcohol or the entertainment, the patrons started to laugh, and the walls of unfamiliarity crumbled.

Amidst the dance, Tungsten noticed the woman with the red shawl talking to Lancelot, but he seemed to ignore her. She carried torn pieces of cloth and asked something, which his friend ignored. Without his response, she raised his cloak and lifted his shirt for him. He meant to stop her until she placed the cloth on his open wound.

"Giant." Two women took his arms. "Dance with us."

"Oh, I mustn't," he said, watching their futile attempts to move him.

"Please?" They grabbed his arms and turned him around, chuckling.

"Do it," the tavern owner said. "Surely Excalibarians can

dance?"

"Can we dance?" Tungsten asked. "Why I believe I'm offended!"

"Then dance," someone shouted from the crowd. "Or do you giants only know how to fight?"

Tungsten laughed. He finished his beef stew and set the bowl down. "Far be it from me to back down from a challenge!"

Taking hold of his hands, the women directed him toward the center of the room. The fiddler and his band were in tow as he moved along, while the curious crowd observed from all sides. The ones with a rougher appearance kept their distance, but now that he was towering over them, they appeared more troubled.

"Show us your strength!" A woman said. "Carry me!"

"No carry me!" Another cried, trying to climb his arm.

Tungsten balanced two women over his shoulders. They laughed as he spun, and the clapping drunks became a blur.

At that moment he saw Calibor with the crowd, spinning in her dress away from the eyes of others. Her hands swayed to the tune of her hums; her laughter high-pitched as she gazed at him.

"Brother, do I look like a fairy?"

Tungsten laughed harder this time. His throat was pinching, but he laughed and laughed. For now, what else could he do? His mother would soon know of the fate that befell his sister. She would not take another lost child well and would need him standing.

Strong.

Unbreakable.

The night carried on until the juices from the stack of plates were cleaned up from the table. The dancing women went back to work, and tired drunkards left, rubbing their eyes like the sandman sprinkled dust into their eyes.

In his gloomy state of mind, Lancelot resumed seeing the joy in the tavern through a veil of sadness. Excalibarian men only have flushed cheeks as children, so seeing Lancelot's flushed from alcohol swaying side by side was unlike him.

"How?" Lancelot asked, tipping his tankard side to side. "Where do you draw the strength to behave like nothing has happened? You were the same when Ecarus died, and the old king, did you even weep?"

"You think I'm heartless?"

"I think you're a little too accepting of death."

"I mourned the loss of my brother in my way."

Lancelot raised his eyebrow. "Did you?"

"A man can shed as many tears as he may in the privacy of his own home. Others weep in silence. As for my father, I don't go to the lake because it reminds me of him, of the moments we cherished. There was no talk of war there. Calibor would ride her horse and do laps around the lake, the kitchen always carried the aroma of Mother's pastries, and Ecarus would tell us stories by the campfire. I cannot deny that his death spoiled those

77

memories."

"You never told me that."

The rain started to come back, pulling him out of his memory. He looked out the window. "I miss Calibor dearly, but we agreed we would find answers and you pouring a cloud on us isn't helping."

Lancelot sighed and brushed his hair back. "You're the stronghold of Excalibur, perhaps you weren't taught to show it."

"No, my mother and father never made me feel like the stronghold everyone calls me. Both my laughter and sadness are behind this wall of metal, and though you do not see it, it's lonesome here."

"Lonesome." Lancelot rubbed his thumb against the edges of the wooden table. "But you're never alone."

"It's easy to exist when people can recognize you. Even if my voice is muffled by metal and recognizable to many, you have never seen my face. In a way, I don't exist, except to the ones who have seen me, and losing another, my sister opens her absence more."

Lancelot stared back at him. "I suppose I never saw it this way. That it would burden you."

"Everyone carries a burden, but this is not a burden, it's just something I feel, something I can't explain."

Lancelot wrinkled his narrow nose. "I've been meaning to ask..."

"Hmm?"

Lancelot looked up, eyes sunken but glossy. "How did you know I longed for Princess Calibor?"

"Is that why you've been in a blasé mood?" His friend lowered his gaze. Tungsten drummed his fingers against the table to the tune of raindrops. "It's remarkable to think back to our childhood when we were boys and how people would frequently comment on the striking differences between us. You were silent, and I was dubbed the laughing prince."

"Yeah?"

"You may not read me easily, but I can read you. Why else were you so interested in that tavern woman shortly after Calibor announced her engagement?"

Lancelot scratched the back of his neck. "Well…"

Tungsten leaned against his chair and looked at a couple embracing one another, his hand over her leg as he kissed her. "Calibor could have married you. A princess she may be, but she could marry any man regardless of their birth, but she saw more of a brother in you than a man."

"As she should," he said. "I'm ten years her senior, of course, she must see me that way."

"If you assumed correctly, why did you fall for my sister?"

Lancelot stopped moving. "It wasn't a matter of why but how."

"How?"

Lancelot shrugged, half smiling. "You know Calibor is a tomboy and swagger. I never found such women appealing."

Tungsten leaned on the table. "It appears you have a tale to share. Go on."

Lancelot tapped his thumb on the tankard. "Don't think you'll approve."

"Then I demand it."

His friend scowled and wiped his hand over his face. He appeared embarrassed or mortified. "It was a year after The Affliction War ended. Back when the frontal attacks of the monsters never sought rest. Calibor was more of a risk taker then, no thanks to you.

"My unit had pushed back those flying sirens, the masses that were flying to the Isles of Avalon. Calibor's group had arrived to support but amidst the battle she had taken a blow to the head by Mother Siren. Using her talons, she raised her to the skies, but Calibor killed her. She fell beyond our reach, I thought she had died and my heart broke at the thought of telling you the news. But then, I saw Calibor standing over the Mother Siren's corpse as the victor. She turned toward me and called me by my name. Her blond hair had broken free by the crack of her helmet and flowed against the wind."

Tungsten drummed his fingers hard on the table with a hard *thump-thump-thump*. "You saw *my* sister's hair?"

Lancelot raised his hands in panic. "Just her hair. She was

80

humiliated that I had seen it, but I turned my back. I gave her my helmet and held her cracked one during our walk back to the others." He snorted and smiled. "It was the first time we could talk with it just being us. I thought she was going to talk about her usual foolery, but our conversation turned serious. She asked if there was anything interesting besides being the renowned Sir Lancelot who served her brother." The smile shifted as if bearing the weight of sadness. "So I served her the same plate and asked if there was anything more to her than being that boastful Sun Princess who chased after her brother. We were laughing by the time we reached the border. But when we met the others, she took the role of the Sun Princess again and thanked me cordially. I hoped to see that side of her again, but as the years passed, it never happened." Lancelot inhaled and looked at him. A look of shame overcame him, and he covered his face again. "Forgive me, Tungsten. It was wrong of me to bear any feelings for your sister."

"It couldn't be evaded. You were a lost cause when you witnessed her strength." Tungsten looked at his drink, seeing his reflection. It was every story he had ever heard. Excalibarian men only fell for strong women. His father's story of how he fell for his mother was no different, watching her in combat and seeing her talent and strength shine beyond what beauty could give. For beauty cannot disarm a soldier and defend a man. But a woman capable of being his equal can save his life.

• • •

Tungsten carried Lancelot over his shoulder. The tavern owner opened the door for them, begging them to come back again. Tungsten gave no promise and thanked the working women, who were disappointed to see them go.

When he made it to the second block, the woman with the red shawl followed them a bit down the road, her eyes dedicated solely to Lancelot. Her stare lingered until she realized he'd been watching her. "Is something the matter?" Tungsten asked.

She blinked and looked away. "No, nothing at all."

Calibor used to look at his friend with those same eyes. In the privacy of their rooms, she would parade the halls in her royal dress. Her long locks hair bounced as she strode the floors with her mighty steps.

When Lancelot was in the courts, she would watch him from the upper floors. Without her helmet, he could read all her thoughts, interest, and attraction for his friend. Everything she could never quite admit to anyone, not to Mother, and back then, not to him.

When morning came, Tungsten leaned by the stables, watching Lancelot grimace as he stirred and scowled at the light in the room. "My head," he moaned. "I feel as if I've been stabbed."

"Just your side," Tungsten said.

"Did you sleep?"

"How could I after knowing you had seen Calibor's hair?"

Lancelot frowned and rolled out of bed, holding his head. "Dammit all so it wasn't a dream. Damn those tavern's drinks!"

"Ah, but it was just what we needed," Tungsten answered. "Your moping bought us an admirer, and she gave us a hint."

"Admirer?"

"The lovely night woman you helped paid us a visit." He picked up a piece of paper from the side table and handed it to him.

Lancelot peered at it before covering his face. "I can't. Please, my head is spinning."

"Then I'll read it to you." He cleared his throat and held the note to the light so he read it better. "Raiders clad in dark clothing were here not two hours ago, asking if two Excalibarian men were about. The women said nothing, and the tavern owner chose silence—not to protect you but to protect themselves. They meant trouble, even as they dined. The one I entertained for the night said he would go south. Please take care of yourself and inform your friend I have settled my debt. If he wishes to see me again, he knows where to find me."

Lancelot rubbed his face, his eyes growing sober by the news. "Well, I'll be, and here I thought she was a spy drowning me with her questions about my personal life."

"I shall inform Lily of our departure; perhaps you can thank the woman in the meantime?"

"No," said Lancelot, touching his side. "We leave now."

VIII

I MISTAKENLY BELIEVED
I KILLED THE LAST ONE

Summer in Excalibur was unbearable in full armor, but there was no better way to cool oneself than taking a dip in the many lakes and rivers. Because Tungsten could not bathe in any public spaces, the palace had many private pools for him to immerse in, and Indra took much advantage of this.

Unlike most cats who detested water, Indra cared about his guard hair and underfur, and for good reason; tigers were a symbol of beauty and power, but such a time was far away.

Indra's paws were now caked with mud and a thunderstorm had followed them deep into Cardon Forest. Broken trunks, scratches, and corpses that remained uneaten by the elements forewarned anyone daring to meet them.

Forests have always been a monster's nesting grounds. And

two Excalibarians impeding what little claim they have is sure to disturb them. The Affliction War was a rude awakening for them, but what else can man do when facing extinction?

Humans could now populate the area, they could live their lives without becoming someone's meal and it took brave souls like Lily's father to make it happen. His sacrifice and the sacrifice of his father, and Merlin the Old brought upon a world where crooked men like Aben could exist, and equally so for girls and boys in Excalibur to be born after the war and breathe a peace he didn't know the scent of.

"This downpour is growing heavier, and the ground is sinking Marigold's hooves," Lancelot said while assuring his ride.

Tungsten looked up, the branches creaked in ways that they should now but he couldn't justify an uneasy feeling growing in his stomach.

Indra sniffed the ground, the hairs on the back of his neck lifting. "You notice it too?"

Lancelot readied his crossbow. "Shadows, at long last."

Indra made a sudden leap. A stoney hand crashed into the ground, nearly taking Lancelot and his horse.

A humanoid creature with stone skin, unborrowed from the ground, shaking the foundations of their feet. With limbs and arms intact, his face exhibited a lack of symmetry that rendered it challenging to determine the exact arrangement of his eyes.

Tungsten led Indra around the creature. He expected to run

into someone but not a creature as big as a rock troll who used the thunder to conceal his presence. The outer layer of their bodies could material any shape and color of any rock. Even the shape of bricks and cobblestones.

The rock troll turned, sensing Tungsten had moved. They had no eyes but their noses and affinity with the ground was more than enough. Slowly the outer layer turned silver, taking the shape of ores.

"Curses," Tungsten uttered. Ordinary trolls were reliably slow and killable. The ones that could mimic metal could only be taken down by magic. Without Excalibur buried at Crystal Lake, this fight was lost.

"Behind you!" Lancelot cried.

Tungsten squeezed the reins as his tiger dodged the troll's grasp. He ducked under the branches as they fled into the denser pine trees. Upon their return, Lancelot and Marigold wrestled with the mud and its grip on them.

"Get me closer," Tungsten commanded.

Indra surged forward and slipped between two trees before leaping onto the back of a troll. Tungsten leaped off his Indra when the troll tried to grab him, but the tiger dove back into the forest.

"Don't you know it's rude to go for someone's ride?" Tungsten said. "Their task is noble."

The troll, let out an ear-splitting roar. His hand crashed over his back as he tried to grab him, but Tungsten leaped from one shoulder to the other. He'd never tease an opponent, much less a rock troll.

The unspeakable things; only magic could penetrate their hardy exterior, his father's wind sword, and Excalibur.

If only...

Lancelot clicked his tongue to move Marigold, but his ride could barely lift one hoof from the thickening mud. This was unnatural and after seeing his friend try again unwilling to leave his ride, Tungsten grew worried about what they could be facing.

The troll reached Lancelot in which Tungsten ran his shoulder against the head of the troll, forcing him to stumble sideways and crash on his elbows. He snapped his ragged teeth at him. Their mouths served only for chewing, as they were always hungry.

"Friend," Tungsten called. "Hurry and free Marigold!"

"I'm trying!"

"And if you can't?"

"Don't say that!"

The troll rolled on his back, forcing Tungsten to leap off. The mud sloshed up to his, but his movement was free. The troll had crawled to his friend forcing Tungsten to call his name.

The troll reached for the hind legs of Marigold, leaving Lancelot dangling, still caught by his foot.

As Tungsten climbed the troll's back, he could hear the low

rumble of its growls reverberating through the air. He grabbed the mouth of the troll and pulled. The troll swung his arms until he slapped him off. He somersaulted but managed to land on his feet.

Lancelot freed his boot and crashed to the ground. The troll, who still had his horse, brought him to his mouth. Lancelot scrambled, searching his surroundings until he found where his crossbow fell. He dropped to his left knee and fired; the arrow split through Marigold's head, killing his companion instantly before any pain fell on him.

In that split moment, the troll squeezed his horse, ripping the flesh before taking a bite of the cavity of his stomach.

"Hurry!" Tungsten shouted as the cracked trees swayed. It was a disadvantage to think they could fight them when the mudslide was bewitched, something Trolls had no influence over. This was the work of someone else.

Lancelot fled as the troll chased after him. Water continued to rise quickly from the ground, carrying with it a surge of waterlogged rocks, branches, and debris.

Indra swiftly made it back, allowing Tungsten to climb on. They rode around the chase until they were able to get close to Lancelot. "Take my arm!" he commanded.

His friend reached toward him, his fingers inches from him, but the mud was trying to sweep them apart.

"My crossbow!" Lancelot yelled before the mud buried him.

Tungsten grasped the limb, pulling his friend out. He barely laid him on Indra's back as the cat started to slide from the mud.

"Brace yourself!" Tungsten warned.

Indra didn't give in. He struggled through the pull until he leaped through the forest, and away from the pool of mud.

As if aware of their escape, the ground started to sink, prompting Indra to climb one of the trees. They held on, watching the troll follow them.

The mudslide worsened, growing larger and ripping pine and oak from the ground. A further delay on their part would result in a premature burial.

Tungsten eased off his seat before Lancelot stopped him. "Don't."

"We're here to find Calibor's killers, not to fight monsters." He patted Indra's shoulder. "Take Lancelot and flee. Meet me outside of the forest."

Lancelot inhaled. "Alright, but don't stay to fight."

Tungsten leaped off his tiger and landed in the mud flowing through. The mudslide grew like a rolling wave until it stopped.

"Who dares bother my pets?" A groan came as bony arms crawled out of the mud with spurting flames. Stepping closer was a creature in dark robes, bearing the skull of an ox. Behind him were wiry crawling branches that controlled the terrain.

"My... my, my." The charred humanoid tree spouted more flames. Branches grew from his back, raising him above

Tungsten and out of his sword's reach. "The recluse king has paid us a little visit."

"Dwelling Devil!" Tungsten let out a hearty. "And here I thought I killed the last one."

The trolls growled, but the demon stopped them. "Not now, my pups. I. am. Speaking." Instead of feet, clouds rolled under towering over him. His eyes were piercingly narrow, blood never stopped leaking from them as his breath discharged black smoke. "Mountain King, these are unsought lands you claim no ownership of. Your mere presence violates it."

"It was not my intention," Tungsten answered, knowing Indra and Lancelot were far away.

"I'll forgive you this once, for I always wanted to meet the man who killed the second last of my kind."

"Here I am."

The Dwelling Devil laid his hand on the troll's head, calming his anger. "In the old days, we ate what we wanted, slurped as many little children as we desired, and you took that from us."

"You made humans your primary source of nutrition. It was time we fought back and sent you back to the Isles of Avalon."

"And who are you to pour judgment upon me!"

"The reign of monsters has been declining by Mother Nature's will and with that, your dominion over man." Tungsten unsheathed his blade, and a silence fell. The thunderstorm had passed, and the rain was thinning.

The demon moved back, shifting the ground as he slid toward him. "Hmm. That is not the blade of the king, nor is it the one that smote our friends."

"No, it is not," Tungsten answered, retreating.

"Oh, stop that now. I know you want to flee." The Dwelling Devil smiled. His bony fingers with black stings went towards the air. The trees moved as if drawn by some possession. Indra's roar was cut short and the smell of the place changed to a colder atmosphere.

Within a few seconds, the landscape changed from mudslides to a stunning mountain encircled by pines and fir trees.

"Where did you transfer me?" Tungsten asked.

"Where you will never be found, recluse king," the Dwelling Devil said with a taunting chuckle. "You will remain in my forest until the end of your meaningless existence."

Tungsten fled in one direction, but before he got far, a shadow fell from the high branches and blocked him. It was a drape. He was in his true form and not the skin of their human victims. More came down and surrounded him.

By the look in their eyes, they recognized him, and by their smiles, they had waited for this.

Tungsten readied his blade.

The drape stared at it and snickered. "Where is Excalibur?"

"Did you lose him?" Another said.

"This time you won't cut us down like you did to our leader," an ugly one murmured, his long black tongue hanging from the side of his teeth.

A drape leaped on his back. The other held onto his arm as if to restrain him. Tungsten grabbed the one on his back by his folding skin and tossed him into the others. He drove his sword into the chest of the one who dove in his direction and whirled his blade cutting the others.

The survivors backed away but showed no intention to retreat.

"Hmm." Tungsten parted his legs. "It's time you start fearing a new weapon."

• • •

Two days passed, and the clouds remained a dull gray, greedily retaining water, and keeping any light to shine through. For shelter, Tungsten found a bear's cave and started to clean his armor. The recent blood he had to wash belonged to that bear. He felt sorry to disturb the beast but appreciated they were both willing to fight for the den and become each other's meal.

He looked at the meat roasting by the fire, its fat juices sizzling. He had to eat something if he planned to escape. The constant whispers of the Dwelling Devil warned him that escaping would only bring him back here, and that's exactly what happened so far.

Tungsten poured some water on Calibor's sword and wiped the blade from hilt to tip. Up close the blade looked like it was made of marble lacking the even blade and sheer Excalibur had. It's not that Orendor didn't reserve tanium ore for her, but that there was little left. Much like this blade she was without but Calibor never complained.

Father offered his spear and out of rage, he melted his cherished weapon for Calibor to have. Though nobody said it, he knew he hadn't mourned the fate of their mountains.

After putting Calibor's blade back in her hilt, Tungsten set it aside. There was one more piece of armor to clean. He looked around first to see if any more drapes were looking.

Tonight, the forest was as quiet as it had been the past day. Convinced he was alone, he placed his hand under the backplate of his armor, just a bit way down the right side where it protected his lower spine. He grazed his thumb against it, finding the metal particularly different from tanium. He never asked Orendor to mend it, sharing the same fear as Father that it would take away what little tanium was reserved for Calibor. Even so, he never regretted the gamble he took. That backside was his one weakness but his enemies were oblivious, not that he'd gamble exposing his back to them.

"Do you miss the Sun Princess?" a whisper stirred among the trees.

Tungsten turned his armor and set it aside. The Dwelling Devil was back, intruding as always. "Tremendously."

The Dwelling Devil's figure began to manifest, his steps stirring around Tungsten leaving behind a trail of black smoke. "Then you know what loss is like."

"I lived through loss," he answered.

The Dwelling Devil liked to have these conversations but despised his desire to get away. "And what will you do now that you are all that remains?"

"I still have my mother."

"And is she capable of handling a kingdom lacking their God?"

Tungsten didn't answer.

"I didn't think so," the devil chuckled as his voice faded.

• • •

Bear meat had a particular taste of pork and venison. Some salt would improve the flavor but the juices from the fat atoned for it. Midway through eating, Tungsten opened his eyes, realizing he had closed them.

How long has it been since he fell asleep? A week? Two? The soft padding of feet brought him to put down his meal. He grabbed Calibor's blade and swung it in the direction of the sound, stopping at the neck.

An alarmed girl stared back. Her skin was fresh green, with specks of dots on her shoulder blades and pink cheeks. Her eyes were entirely blue, hands raised from shock. She touched her neck, relieved to find it in place. Her blond hair was still in a ponytail with the same braids.

"Lily." Tungsten lowered his sword.

A small gasp left her, eyes widening. "How'd you know it was me?"

"A shapeshifter can take any form and fool the most wise but their eyes are never the same. When we first met, I saw you for what you were, a twelve-year-old girl in the body of one who is sixteen." Tungsten raised the lower half of his visor and went back to eating.

Lily crouched and stared at the fire. She wore a leather dress adorned with vines around the waist. Barefooted, he could see the mesh of mud and crushed leaves between her toes.

"Why are you here?" Tungsten asked. "Shapeshifters don't particularly travel far from their hunting grounds."

She lowered her gaze. "When necessary, I wouldn't dare invite trouble, even if some deserve it."

"Then what *are* you doing here?"

Lily looked at him. "To see if it was true that you would kill me like the others."

"You want to know?".

Lily pressed her lips tightly even as he went to one knee. He laid his hand on her head, and she jumped, shutting both eyes.

"Children are children," he said. "Even shapeshifters like yourself."

Her tiny hands squeezed his finger. She smiled and removed his heavy hand. "I'm glad."

"Now that we understand each other, why did you usurp that old man's daughter?"

"Because I ate his daughter."

Tungsten nodded. "To survive?"

"Yes." She pressed her knees together and stared at the fire. "But in consuming, we shapeshifters take in memories only." She crouched as if to see the fire more. "I didn't expect her memories to be filled with so much revulsion; she hated her life as much as I hated mine. Her mother didn't want her, and despite her father's sacrifices for the war, he slaved over the farm to make sure she lived comfortably. She suffered things she couldn't tell him, but she always came home, knowing he would die without her."

"So, you went back?" He grabbed a piece of uncooked bear meat and offered it to her.

She took it, and sharp teeth grew out of her gums. She chomped briefly before gulping the meat without chewing. Blood oozed down her lips as she gazed at the fire. "I saw an opportunity to survive, and I took it. But after meeting you, I began to understand what was going on, and why these creatures were overstepping on my territory. They're following you."

Tungsten looked at her. The girl was scrawny from little nutrition and dirty from her travel. He saw the truth in her, the same worry on her face she had for her adopted father.

"I better go," she said. "Da will be looking for me."

"Then it's not just territory you fear?"

Lily frowned and looked at her bare feet. "That old fool. He can't tell his daughter apart from the monster that killed her."

Tungsten sighed. "Sometimes we do things we normally wouldn't do because we're lost. That's why it's good to know your home."

"Home?" Lily rested her hand on her chin. "I don't know what that is. My parents were slaughtered by those Olivewood folks. Even then I was too much of a coward to go anywhere else."

"Home can sometimes instill a painful memory we don't want to remember." Tungsten crossed his arms and straightened his back. "But it's not about the location of your birth or who hurt you when you tried to build it. Home is the place where your loved ones always welcome you. Your longing to see them again knows no bounds, and wherever they may be, that place becomes your home."

Lily pinched her inner cheeks by how her dimples formed.

"Sorry, I gott'a go. If I see your friend, I'll tell him you're here."

"Hold a minute child, don't get involved."

Lily scurried out of the forest. "It's too late."

"Wait!" Tungsten went after her. "It's dangerous out there."

Lily's green body started to change into a pink lighter tone. Her height grew to match the identity of the girl she long usurped. "I'm taking my stand," she answered. "I've chosen the humans."

Tungsten watched as her figure disappeared into the night.

A shuffling of feet surrounded him, crunching the fallen leaves and disturbing the bushes. The place was as damp as any other day, covered in ferns and tall pine trees, but there was no creature.

"Have you drapes not had enough?" He fetched his blade and stormed out. He didn't have enough time to put on the rest of his armor, and it would be unwise to stay in the cave and risk getting trapped.

The shifting branches overhead slowed, and rocks crumbled down the mountains. The drapes were out of sight, but he had a sense that something was amiss.

A gray fog rolled through, taking the form of the Dwelling Devil. The fog wrapped him and in a split second, the entire forest was enveloped by it. "Recluse King, what have you done?"

"Pardon me?"

The wind picked up and stirred from his anger. "You've

done something." His eyes glowed like a mist, red and bright.

Tungsten searched for the Dwelling Devil but he was nowhere near. "You're not here, are you?" It seemed he had been conversing with him without his presence. "Did something or someone occupy you?"

"You let me worry about where I go."

The wind had picked up behind him, rustling the trees. By this point, he hoped Lancelot had returned to free him. Drapes or anything vile would have already lunged for the attack.

"It's not possible." The Dwelling Devil roared. "How did you get inside?"

The shuffling of feet went silent.

As Tungsten diligently searched for the intruder, the hushed stillness in the air conveyed a distinct message. If it wasn't for the small reflection of metal, he wouldn't have been aware of the thin blade approaching him. Before it went through his visor, he raised Calibor's sword and blocked it.

When the blades met, a burst of flames erupted into the air. Tungsten shuffled back, surprised by the effect. Fire shouldn't be spurting out of his blade unless it was made with the same material.

"Tanium?"

IX

I'LL JOURNEY WITH YOU
UNTIL WE PART WAYS

Covered by the fog, a figure emerged, wielding two swords in each hand. The blades were thin, but it was no rapier, no longer than twenty inches. The hilt was pointed with an angled disc.

"Pardon me," Tungsten began. "But the blade you carry belongs to our people. Before I retrieve it from you, I wish to know how you found it."

The intruder flipped the two short swords and crouched, ready to leap into another attack.

"Very well." Tungsten parted his legs and gave the hilt of his sword a slight squeeze.

The intruder charged with a speed that could cut the wind. Tungsten sent Calibor's sword down, forcing his opponent to bounce away, taking a new angle.

Metal collided as sparks of fire spurted out, the light giving way to the intruder's mask. By the second swing, he saw feminine features, a soft bridge of her nose, and catlike eyes that faintly glowed an amber color.

Tungsten pushed his blade to throw off the stranger, forcing her to leap back. A mask indeed covered her mouth. The front of her hair was mid-length, brushed to the side, covering her right eye. The rest of her hair was tightly braided and parted into two tails that went past her calves, tied by a red lace.

"Who are you?" Tungsten asked.

She flipped her short swords and used the distance to shuffle back; blades raised to the face. When she walked to the right, Tungsten raised his sword again and slashed at her side. Thinking he cut through her robe, her figure blurred until she disappeared. A surge of pain penetrated his side, followed by the crack of the tree before he realized what had happened. The shock left him fighting for air as he crawled to his knees.

Above he saw her pair of boots balancing on the branch. Her blades went on fire as they came down; Tungsten raised his arms, blocking her swing. The cold air whistled with the fumes only Orendor's tanium could cast.

"Enough!" Dozens of web-like strings broke between them, forcing her to step back. A form manifested from the black mists, revealing his long claws and the large antlers he wore like a crown

102

on his head. "Astra Degora." He sluggishly lifted himself off the mud. "He is my pet; go find your own."

"Before we start again." Tungsten climbed back to his feet. "What is your aim aside to assassinate me?"

"Do not bother getting an answer from her." The Dwelling Devil's black web coiled around her. "This Dranyth is a resourceful killer."

A sharp and intense pang of pain surged through Tungsten's chest. He saw himself standing at the edge of the bridge, watching Orendor's temple erupt in flames. "Impossible," he said. "Dranyth's were wiped out."

The Dwelling Devil chuckled and glided toward the Dranyth. Though his webs spun around her, she did not retaliate. "So you underestimated me and the Dranyth's existence? Like yours truly, they live a life deep within the woods, and in darkness, we know more than any person wishes to hide."

"Except the war finished the Dranyths," Tungsten corrected. "Though our fortress had a terrible vantage point over your kind, my father came out victorious. Many searched these lands, leaving no stone unturned of survivors."

The Dwelling Devil hissed. "And tell us, recluse king, how many of your men came back alive?"

Tungsten turned to Astra Degora. "You."

Her blades ignited with flames, the tanium responding to her will like before. She struck the Dwelling Devil's webs, tearing them into pieces that when they fell looked like black hair.

An arrow hit the ground between her feet. Lily gripped her bow, shakingly looking at the assassin.

Astra Degora dove at her, but Tungsten pushed the girl out of the way, the tip of her blades grazed his back, cutting blood but not breaking through his muscles.

"Run," he told Lily's wide eyes. "Go!"

"Help is coming," she said before taking off.

Astra Degora turned her blade and sped after her.

The Dwelling Devil grabbed her ankle and sent her crashing into the dirt with a downward swipe of his claws. She quickly countered, blocking the second attack with her short swords. The cut of her blade forced the beast to flee back into his dark mist.

"Your Majesty!" Lancelot rode on Indra's back, racing to him.

Astra Degora, seeing his friend charged at them but the webs wrapped her once more.

Taking his arm, Tungsten boosted himself onto Indra's back. "Lancelot!" he laughed. "You're alive."

They ran to the cave where Tungsten retrieved his armor. Astra Degora was distracted, cutting the reaching webs of a crying Dwelling Devil.

"Hurry," Lancelot told Indra. "Pick up those paws!"

"Where are you going!" the Dwelling Devil thudded behind

them, bending trees and snapping them out of his way.

"Shall we take him down?" Lancelot asked. "We may not get away again!"

Branches turned black as they started to swing at them but Indra dodged scarcely dodged them. Lancelot cut as many as they could, giving them space to escape.

"What will become of me?" The Dwelling Devil cried. "Everyone detests me, and the trolls do not speak. Who will keep me company?"

"Your Majesty!" Lancelot exclaimed. "Your order?"

"We leave him," said Tungsten.

"But—"

"Recluse King." The devil let wept. "Come back!"

Tungsten patted Indra so he wouldn't stop. "Dwelling Devils don't make friends with other monsters. He's lonely, that's why he didn't kill me." He looked back and saw he had given up, back hunched as he covered his face with one hand and leaned on the tree with the other.

The end of the forest of ahead, but he still felt unsettled. Something remained unresolved, and he had but only to uncover it. He gripped his ride's fur. "Indra, stop!"

His cat tore through the ground, sending Lancelot flying off and slamming into the ground. Tungsten, who braced himself, dismounted his cat.

The forest lay in silence, with only the leaves crunching

under his feet. Indra stood at his side, ears pressed flat as he sniffed the air, unable to locate the threat.

"Show yourself," Tungsten commanded. "I know you're there."

The sway of her braids uncovered her location. She was on the highest branch, her boots neatly pressed together. While her posture hinted no interest for another fight, her stare pierced through his armor, unblinking, and unmoving.

"Your Majesty?" Lancelot asked.

Tungsten turned back and mounted his cat. He ran his fingers down his coat, pleased to see him safe. "Let's go."

• • •

The fire crackled well into the late hour, and their cloaks were set out to dry while they sought rest after the long escape. It was the first night they could enjoy stars of this magnitude, spread out like a canvas with no weather or monster on their backs.

Tungsten checked Lancelot's wound from the tavern. The bleeding had stopped, which relieved him immensely. His friend was bruised on the shoulder and arms from the trolls and having combated the Dwelling Devil. It turned out his friend had been keeping him busy, enough to find his location.

Without their armor, their escape could've ended differently, leaving him with his own share of wounds.

"Told you I was fine," Lancelot said.

"And I can't rest without seeing for myself." He got up and went back to cozy up with Indra's belly. The cat slept soundly, and after such a long run, he deserved it. The hills they rested on were dry and had little sport, but he hoped once they continued, he could treat him to a good feast.

The crackling fire caught Tungsten's attention, the swaying flames reminding him of those two short swords. He frowned and looked at the stars for their silent council.

"You're not still thinking about that Dranyth, are you?" Lancelot said he would sleep, but it looked like he noticed his troubled mind.

"Ten years of peace and one of those dragon worshipers has been walking around these lands, planning her vengeance."

"At least we finally have an answer as to why some of your knights didn't return. Out of the fifty you sent, fifteen didn't return."

"I expected some beasts had gotten to them, but what if it was that woman's doing? Wielding tanium blades that belong to Orendor and using them against them." Tungsten breathed the cold air and let it all out at once. "During my time with the Dwelling Devil, I started to think about our travel, barren and fruitless as it has been."

"And wet."

"Calibor's death may have clouded my judgment, perhaps I should've returned to Excalibur than hunt for a killer we have no trace of."

Lancelot pivoted from his seat. "What are you saying? Don't tell me encountering that Dranyth has changed your mind."

"You know I want to avenge my sister, but her passing should have reached my mother." His gaze shifted to his friend. "Unless you did not convey the message clearly?"

Lancelot crossed his legs and rested his elbows on his thighs. "Are you doubting me?"

"Tell me."

"*Yes*, I asked for aid. If we had gone down King's Road, we would know. There could be many already at Crystal Lake as we speak."

"And chasing shadows has produced nothing." Tungsten slapped his thigh. "It's time that I return home, and bring with me a team to find Calibor's killer."

"We agreed we would return home afterward."

"I won't invite myself into another monstrous encounter unless it's absolutely necessary."

Lancelot frowned, counting only his silence. "Well, you can go, but I'm staying. I'm going to search for that shadow responsible for her death, so don't try to use your kingship over me."

"Friend, do not allow the weight of Calibor's death to hinder your thoughts again."

Lancelot slammed his fist onto the ground. "Leave her out of this!"

Tungsten sat up and calmly placed his hands on his knees. "You haven't changed, have you? You're still troubled as the day we left Crystal Lake."

"You couldn't possibly understand."

"I lost *my* sister. Is that not enough for you?"

Lancelot cursed and walked a bit ways from him to for distance and to lean back on a boulder. Something was bothering him, eating at him from the inside, and he had grown too angry to look beyond his grief.

Tungsten rested back on Indra's belly and crossed his arms. Sleep was calling him again, but he rejected it. He didn't know why he questioned Lancelot about what the letter he sent entailed, why he felt a slight mistrust in him. He left those thoughts and looked up at the all-seeing stars. If they could speak, there would be less trouble in the world.

• • •

Lancelot never left the boulder. He sat on the ground and while he said he wasn't going to sleep, emitted a gentle snore before jolting himself awake. He got up without explaining where he was going. He left his weapons behind, so he was likely off to relieve himself.

When he returned, he sat back down in his spot, shoulders slumped from exhaustion with little sleep to remain vigilant of intruders. "You keep looking at me," Lancelot said, still not looking his way.

Tungsten didn't hide it. "Your father, may he rest in peace, once told me the name Lancelot was given to his great-great-grandfather by Orendor himself."

His friend grabbed a piece of wood and threw it into the fire. "He spoke the truth."

"And one day you shall pass the name to your child?"

Lancelot was about to throw another piece of wood but stopped. "No, I've decided that I'm not going to marry."

By that alone, Tungsten looked at Calibor's sword. "My sister would want you to be happy."

"Of course she would, because she's good to me, like a sister who loves her brother. Maybe if I had married before she met Prince Valte, if I had moved on before her death then maybe it wouldn't hurt much, maybe I'd be more useful to you!" He said it with a bite, teeth clenched from having to repeat what he never wanted to know.

Though it wasn't his business, Tungsten felt responsible for what Calibor left behind, or perhaps he had to untie the knots Lancelot got himself in. "Calibor knew you had feelings for her." Lancelot ceased all movement. "I didn't want to make her death heavier on you, but she confided her long-kept secret the day before her wedding day. Of course, I had my suspicions when I watched how she gazed at you privately."

Lancelot got up and withdrew from their campfire. He spun one time and returned. "But how...?"

"When she told you she would marry Prince Valte, she saw your heartbreak. She told me she would never forgive herself for being the one to tell you."

"You're saying this to prevent me from looking for her, aren't you?" What should have offered him closure left Lancelot pacing back and forth, muttering in his denial.

It was any man's dream to hear his confession after they carried an unrequited love but it was too late to reclaim the words.

Tungsten rose to his feet despite the ache. "Calibor considered marrying you."

Lancelot stopped; this time his breathing was quickening. "Enough, Tungsten. You're just adding salt to my wounds."

"I do not wish to worsen the blows to your heart, but I can't see you this way anymore."

"*You* said she saw *me* as a brother instead of a man."

"And *she* said you were the second strongest man she knew.

But Calibor was no fool. She told me you were invaluable and it would be selfish if she took you from me."

"How could she think that?"

"Because a queen would need a king at her side, not her brother." Tungsten chuckled. "Calibor had no hesitation in telling me that if she was unhappy, she would leave Prince Valte to court you."

Lancelot shuddered. He looked like a child as he recoiled from the campfire. "But why—why didn't you tell me?"

"She made me swear not to, but I hope in knowing the truth, you can move on. Don't give up on that big-breasted woman or the gal in Olivewood."

Lancelot shook his head. "No, there is only Calibor for me."

"Friend."

"When that fairy took her in those waters, I saw my heart sink with her."

"Very well. It is your life, after all." Standing tired him, so he returned to Indra's side.

A change in the wind shifted the cat's fur. He swore to never unveil Calibor's secret but perhaps the uncomfortable feeling in his chest was of something much deeper. They had taken a great risk plowing into the unknown and harvesting nothing.

His mother came to mind, parading the quiet palace halls, wearing a dark gown with gold embroidery at the hem of her dress and sleeves. How she loved her dresses, and pinning up her brown hair, dazzled with gray lines. Did the news of Calibor's death break her just as Ecarus's death broke Father?

He had to return.

Home was calling.

X

TAKE OFF YOUR HELMET

Indra lay with his paws crossed, gnawing on the leg of the third deal he caught in his hunt. They had reached the end of the cliff and miles below was Three Rivers, coursing wildly along the edge of the sea. Beyond the end of the Cardon Forest were the Northstead Highlands, a land of rich green hills, and mountain peaks that cascaded through the forest like a fortress. After the highlands came the Wind Woods and the Kingdom of Atlios, home of the princess and Tungsten's childhood friend, Lady Casana.

"Are you sure you don't want to continue searching?" Lancelot asked. "If you're alone again, that Dranyth may return."

"As swift as that so-called Astra Degora was, she caught me without my armor. Things won't be the same for our next encounter." He stretched and gave out a long yawn worthy of making Indra proud. "Well then, shall we continue?" When he turned, Lancelot was on one knee, head bowing. "What now?"

His friend took off his helmet and tucked it under his arm. "Forgive me but I will continue my search for Calibor's killer. I will gladly accept full punishment upon my return, be it whipping, branding, imprisonment even the forfeiture of my estate."

Tungsten snorted and placed his hands on his hips. "I would never do that to you or your mother."

"Don't go easy on me," Lancelot said. "I've behaved bitterly toward you on the road, I could not be the navigator you needed, least of all the friend you depended on, never considered your burden as king, as Calibor's brother. Since you were children, you two were inseparable. I often wondered why she treasured you over everyone in the world. When Ecarus died, I realized it was because you were each other's pillar. If I'm wrong, please correct me."

Tungsten swallowed hard. "You are correct."

Hearing this Lancelot shut his eyes and continued. "And in nurturing her heart, she became the Sun Princess our people adored, the one I fell in love with." His friend placed his hand over his chest. "I will find her killer and they will pay a handsome price." He raised his face so he could look at the sincerity in his eyes. "When it's over, I expect full punishment for not following you back to Excalibur."

Tungsten turned to Indra and patted his head. The cat growled, hating the disturbance during his meal. "Take Indra with you." Indra cackled as if a ball of fur had been lodged in his throat. "Atlios is two days away, but your journey may require a greater distance. I'd feel a lot safer if you two went without me."

Lancelot didn't answer. He got up and went to finish tying up the cooked venison from his hunt. "Look if that cat promises not to bite my head off, he can join me."

Indra peeled his black gums back and snarled at him. Tungsten laughed. "Don't mind him, Indra likes you, he just has trouble showing it."

"Don't lie on his stead!" Lancelot exclaimed. "I still bear the scars on my arm when he tried to gnaw it off!"

Indra yowled and leaped off the ground, surprising them. A silver snake slipped past him and quickly hid under the shrubs. The rustling led Indra to lean toward it before he pounced on it and went for the chase.

"Oi, get back here you!" Tungsten exclaimed. "Haven't you eaten enough?"

Lancelot unhooked his crossbow from his belt and secured a bolt with incredible speed and pointed it at him.

Tungsten froze, surprised.

"Move aside, Your Majesty."

Tungsten did, realizing the sound of hooves was behind him, masked by the greenery and shade.

Lancelot took a step closer. "I won't deny that since the war, running into monsters again like this is hard to get used to again."

"At least, there's nothing you and I haven't faced," Tungsten unsheathing his blade.

The bits of rocks beneath them trembled from the hooves, growing ever so closer. Lancelot fired at the noise, his bolt whistled through, but it produced nothing.

On their right, Indra returned startling them with a lifeless snake in his mouth. Seeing the trees rustling he dropped his catch and leaped on Tungsten's side, growling. The fur on his spine was up, along with something he hadn't ever seen.

"Stay back," Tungsten told Lancelot, who was preparing his next bolt. "Hurry! Indra never tucks his tail."

"Just a second; I'm almost done!"

"It's coming!"

Lancelot looked up and barked. "Shit!"

A creature with brown skin sprang out of hiding and snatched Lancelot up by the neck, holding him six feet off the ground. The assailant's torso was covered in black armor, transitioning into a horse body below the waist.

"Your Majesty," Lancelot groaned, pounding his fists on the gauntlet. "Has a centaur taken a hold of my throat?"

"Like a chicken going to the block," Tungsten said. The beast stood five feet taller than him. "What is a guardian from the Isles of Avalon doing here?"

The centaur turned to him, grimacing. Such ancient creatures were not natives to their lands, but they were here just the same.

As Tungsten moved forward, the ground trembled under the thundering steps of someone else who followed closely behind, their grip tight on a mighty spear. Now there were two centaurs, clad in armor from hoof to head.

Tungsten gave them a deep nod. "Eógan and Ingon, sons of Ixion, the betrayer, and the phantom cloud-nymph, Nephele."

"Metal king," Eógan raised Lancelot above his head and walked back into the forest.

"Not so fast!" Tungsten shouted. "Return my knight."

Indra leaped on the back of Ingon, drawing his focus back to the other brother. His spear was in the air, giving Tungsten time to knock it aside. Ingon parted his feet and thrust his spear again.

Tungsten's next strike was more forceful, sending it flying with greater speed and power. "My father was a great spearman. If you wish to engage in combat, know that he trained me to take down fighters like you."

"You are small," Ingon said.

Tungsten chortled. "Well, that's a first for me."

Ingon spun his spear and thrust it towards him, cutting only air. Tungsten never intended to fight him but mounted Indra instead. They raced after Eógan, chasing after the disturbed vegetation, knocked-down trees, and the deep-seated hooves that marked the terrain.

Uphill, they picked up the sound of running water. Though he never intended to find it, he recalled seeing one on the map.

Indra came to a full stop. An old ruin made of worn cobblestone had been marked with runes.

Tungsten got off and looked around. The place was half buried with vines and leaves. Half-cracked, a stone pillar remained erect. When he smudged the grime off, he stepped back. The marking was the symbol of a dragon. "These are Dranythian lands," he said. "Vacant too. Long abandoned."

Indra growled and ran ahead, forcing Tungsten to follow him. The path led him to Eógan waited, holding Lancelot over the cliff edge.

Tungsten unsheathed his sword and slowly approached them. Lancelot had clipped his crossbow back on his belt, but his sword, dagger, and bolts had been thrown on the floor.

"Behind you!" his friend shouted.

Tungsten turned and saw the silver tip inches from his visor. He clashed the tip of Ingon's spear with his arm, bending it.

Seeing it was useless, the centaur threw the spear aside. At that moment, Indra leaped for Ingon's back. The cat sank his fangs into his arm and pulled at his pauldron, bending it.

Ingon grabbed Indra's scruff like a mother cat. "Touch me again and you will go over too." He threw the feline across, sending him crashing into the stone pillars the ancient ones marked.

Tungsten rushed to his cat and patted his side. Instead of a growl, Indra climbed back to his feet, his gold eyes focusing on him. "They spared you because you're like them, but this is not your fight." His cat clawed into the soil, growling. "Leave us!"

Indra snarled; his ears were pressed flat as he backed into the forest until he was out of sight.

"There," said Tungsten, eyeing Ingon and his brother. "The tiger will no longer trouble you."

Lancelot raised his knees to his chest and kicked his heel against Eógan's temple, cutting him to the point of bleeding.

In return, Eógan shook him like a doll. "Sir Lancelot," he said. "That was most unkind."

"Enough!" commanded Tungsten. "What are guardians of the Isles of Avalon doing here?"

Eógan stopped shaking his friend and slowly turned to him, bearing his gritting teeth. "We do not answer to the one who has gone against his own God."

Tungsten's eyebrows arched upwards. "Is that what *he* believes?" He waited, but he couldn't contain anymore. "Answer me!" A gust of air blew out of his armor, as the anger he felt couldn't be contained within and had to be released.

Eógan, seeing this fell silent and his brother Ingon said no more.

"You dare doubt two of Avalon's best protectors?" The new voice came from the surrounding ruins.

"Who said that?" Tungsten exclaimed. "Show yourself!"

Excalibarian knights emerged from the forest. Tungsten spun to count the twelve that surrounded them. Without their helmets, their faces were pale gray with grim lifeless eyes.

Long ago they once stood with him, knights who served under him during The Affliction War and fell.

Two of the knights parted, giving room for a man in full armor to stand between them. His armor was a copper-like color with bright yellow paint that crossed the breastplate where the royal crest was engraved.

He took off his helmet, revealing a young man, with a scar that ran down the bottom of his lip. His dark hair was damp and his eyes glittered the same blue they once had.

"No—" Lancelot started to heave, as little air could come through his throat. "I buried... you!"

Tungsten gripped the hilt of his sword as a wave of discomfort flooded his stomach.

Prince Valte raised his chin proudly. "No Sir Lancelot, you buried a shapeshifter." He fixed the ends of his blond hair and turned to Tungsten where his crooked smile curved the corner of his lips.

Twelve Excalibarians and fifteen soldiers hid among the ruins and trees. With two centaurs it was a disadvantage, and the only way out led to a mortal fall.

"Tactful as ever," said Valte. "You're devising a strategy, aren't you? How helpless you must've felt to know you couldn't do the same for the Sun Princess."

"You don't get to utter her name!" Lancelot raised his feet to his chest and kicked the centaur's biceps. "Release me!"

Valte cocked his head to the side and smirked. "Come now, Sir Lancelot. It's time to stop playing the tough guy."

"You just wait until I'm free. I'm going to send a bolt into that skull of yours and hang you for the vultures to tear apart!"

"Take his crossbow away!" Prince Valte ordered.

"He's got no bolts," said Eógan. Seeing no point in taking it from his belt, he let his friend keep it. "And you do not have full command over me."

"Then take off his helmet so I may teach him a lesson."

Eógan wrapped his entire hand over Lancelot's head. He squirmed until his helmet was taken and thrown aside. Without warning, Eógan slammed him into the ground and pinned him there.

Lancelot gritted his teeth; sweat dripped from his face from being under his helmet, but his eyes scorched with defiance. He pushed up, resisting the centaur. "Don't underestimate an Excalibarian!"

Eógan grumbled, seeing his true strength.

"So this is what she saw in you." Chuckling, Prince Valte

turned his horse to face him. "Did you know your mere existence delayed my courting with the Sun Princess? Fearing I would lose to you, I sought those old rumors that long followed your family of a Lancelot who will serve his kind and betray him in every way forever casting guilt and turmoil upon his very own soul." He left Lancelot as his struggles were ineffective and mounted his horse.

"Reveal your aim?" Tungsten said. "Is it the power of the Round Table? Excalibur itself?"

Valte's lips squeezed tight. He put his helmet on and closed his visor. "You will know as soon as we drag you back to Excalibur. You will come without a helmet, for your face to show in shame to your people."

"If you think I will cooperate, you are foolhardy."

Valte laughed. "I'm not the enemy you think you discovered. The real one lives in the dark and moves like the shadows."

Shadows.

Valte snapped his fingers. One of the Excalibarian knights came to him, dragging a little girl with green skin and blond hair. In her struggle to be released, she resorted to kicking.

Tungsten didn't shout her name, knowing if he showed he cared, she would be in more trouble.

"This little shapeshifter failed to lead you to the trap, and so we collected her and taught her a lesson by raiding her little father's home." He pinched her cheeks together and forced her to look at him. "She knows his body hangs, and I brought her here to you so she could see with her own eyes who is responsible."

Lily was thrown on the ground. Shaking, she looked up, red tears streaming from her blue eyes. "You're the king of Excalibur!" She exclaimed. "If you hadn't come to snooping around my Pa would've been alive!"

"Finish her," said Prince Valte.

Lily gasped and threw her hands over her head as the soldier, who pinned her, raised his blade into the air.

Tungsten powered forward and leaped just in time for the blade to hit his back. Lily peeked between her fingers, gasping for air.

"Run, child."

Lily shook her head and covered her face. "It's over... my da is gone and it's all my fault. I made him live a lie!"

The old man's face came to mind, following his plea. *I appreciate you not harming her. She's young and the world is cruel.*

"Do you think a retired captain trained to fight monsters couldn't tell his real daughter apart from a shifter? He kept you alive because he grew to love you as his own."

"Shoot the girl already!" Valte shouted to one of his men.

The soldier drew his bow and pointed his arrow at them. When Tungsten shielded her, another archer did the same.

124

An arrow whistled before it was sliced in half, missing the girl. A gust of wind stirred the leaves as a figure leaped from the branches and slowly rose. "The girl made a mistake, but I will not pardon any harm to an orphan."

Valte leaned back. "Stay out of this Dranyth."

"You already harmed one of her kind by forcing him to take your spot at Crystal Lake. That is enough sacrifice."

With a sneer, Valte dismissed the Dranyth and gestured for his men to withdraw.

Tungsten got to his knees when Lily sprang to her feet and punched his side. "I shouldn't have chosen you humans!" She fled back into the forest.

Tungsten turned to Astra Degora. "Shadow," he said. She turned and her one eye that wasn't covered by her hair met his. Her one eye suddenly widened as she turned to Prince Valte. An arrow whistled through and missed his visor by an inch. The arrowhead broke through, denting the side and knocking him off his horse.

Valte screamed as a bolt struck him. Lancelot had a bolt hidden in his gauntlet. It was too big to slip through his visor, but it dug through his eye. "Release him so my men can beat him!" He cried.

Eógan stepped away to give room to the Excalibarian soldiers who wrestled Lancelot down. They unbuckled his padding and threw it in the river.

Their steel fists went to his face while the others kicked his abdomen.

Valte moaned as he rose from the ground, hand still on his visor. "You stupid fool!" He ran to Lancelot and hit his chin, knocking him onto his back. "I will fix the war that blasted Merlin the Old tricked us into joining. Varil, the Iron Spear God shall return from the Isles of Avalon and reclaim his former glory. We shall not be mere humans no more but stand as equals to Excalibarians."

"Varil will not return!" Tungsten took one step, just one inch to that fool was enough but Ingon took a step closer. "It's over Valte, many ancient Gods have left, all that remains is stubbornness and wishful thinking for the old ways."

Valte stared at him with a crooked frown. "So easy for someone to say when their strength remains amplified by the Blacksmith God. In marrying your sister, bedding her, and being the only survivor, I will have Excalibur!" His blade went to Tungsten's neck. "Now take off your helmet."

Tungsten moved, and the men reeled back. Their fear of him made more sense, they were not his dead comrades brought back from the dead. They were shapeshifters; maybe drapes were among them by the reek of death.

Amidst the tension, Astra Degora stood firmly in place, fearless as the Dranyths he remembered invading the borders of Excalibur.

"Careful there," Valte panted with one hand covering his eye. He turned to Lancelot, who groaned on the ground, covered in blood. "You know, when I married Calibor, I thought I would find a hideous being, disfigured and infectious, something royal families like to conceal." He pressed his heel into Lancelot's cheek. "I didn't love her, but Calibor was a beauty. A masterpiece of a painting, the touch of her skin, as delicate as a flower, and her little squirms, music to my ears when the poison started to take effect."

"Fuck you, son of a whore." Lancelot was gritting his teeth, blood oozing from his gums. "Your Majesty! You have my permission to cast my life aside and finish him!"

"Not even for vengeance, friend," Tungsten said. "Valte, what do you want?"

Valte smiled; he looked at his blade and back at him. "Hand over Excalibur."

"I do not have it with me. It was buried with Calibor."

Valte frowned. "You gave the maidens of the lake their most desired weapon." He brushed his hair back, pacing a bit away from them, hands on his hips. The news irked him, but he concealed it by chuckling. "Oh, of course! You suspected something was off, didn't you?"

Tungsten smiled behind his helmet. "I attested that her death was related to me, but I am not the only one to blame."

"Hmph." With one command from Valte, Eógan grabbed

his friend by the neck and lifted him off the ground. Valte turned to his friend. "Then what shall you decide? Relinquish your helmet or surrender your friends to the roaring Three Rivers?" Lancelot barely opened one eye. He lay gripping the soil, battered, and bruised.

"Sir Lancelot will be tossed into the Three Rivers, and these centaurs will crush you from the inside out." Prince Valte moved his hand and the Excalibarian knights got closer. "Since the blade of Excalibur is lost, the wind sword of the former king still rests in his tomb. I was told his blade held the power of knives and the wind. What kind of fool uses a spear and forgoes a powerful weapon like his?"

"One who knows power isn't everything." Tungsten watched Indra lurking in the shadows. The only one who appeared to be tracking his every step was Astra Degora. She knew he was there, but his tiger couldn't intervene. When his golden eyes locked on him Tungsten tilted his head slightly, and Indra looked at Lancelot, understanding his command.

"Toss him," yelled Prince Valte. "Toss him!"

Tungsten dashed in Lancelot's direction. Eógan saw and swung his spear, but Tungsten dodged it, rolling to the side and slamming into Ingon's leg. The centaur leaned down and picked him up by the helmet.

"You'll pay for this!" Lancelot shouted. "I swear it!"

"Lancelot!" Tungsten reached for his friend but in vain

seeing him grow further from him.

"Get out of here!" Lancelot's voice quieted, taken by distance from the cliff edge.

Tungsten flung his head back, and the feathers from his helmet dove into Ingon's chest. Valte shouted something and arrows rained down on him and the centaur. He roared and raised his arms to cover himself.

"Valte!" Eógan shouted, standing on his hind legs and charging him. "You backstabbing—"

The Excalibarian shapeshifters changed form, turning into their adult versions, green with long claws. When they leaped at him, Valte made his escape.

Even with the arrows flying, Tungsten maintained his grip on Ingon's back. Everything was a blur until his feet were facing the clouds and the wind whistled through his armor.

He collided with the rocks below as he watched Ingon effortlessly sprint down the cliffs, his hand vengefully outstretched toward him. Rather than escape from him a second time, he took his hand and mustered his might to pull him downward, toppling the centaur off the cliff.

Tungsten used Ingon as a cushion against the sharp rocks, shielding himself from the first blow and the second until the centaur ultimately broke his neck.

Eógan screamed in the distance until the rough current of Three Rivers swept both he and Ingon.

The waters grabbed Tungsten and pulled him under the surface where he collided with the sharp rocks.

He fought the bubbles surrounding him and swam toward the surface, but in his attempt, he realized his arm had been dislocated from the fall. Every time he sank, the river would get deeper, and the ground harder to find. The feeling brought him back to Crystal Lake when Ecarus tossed him into the lake in full armor and told him to swim up.

You can't call yourself a servant of Orendor if you don't know how to swim in full armor.

Despite his attempts, it was impossible with one arm. As he sank deeper, he suddenly realized he wasn't in the river but in the deep end of an ocean.

Below a giant woman coated in blue, with a serpent's body and gills on her neck swam upward to meet him. "King Murenten!" She sang as her slender arms wrapped around him, pressing him against her breasts. "You returned me, just like you promised!"

Tungsten patted his side. Calibor's sword was left on the cliff. He searched for his dagger until he remembered he had given it to the woman on King's Road.

Her blue hair encircled him. She was no true Giantess, but she was big enough to take him to his grave. His fists were his only option, and he jabbed one of his fingers through her cheeks. She wailed and tossed her head back, sending him out of the water. He gasped and watched the sun and sky before falling back down.

"Why did you hurt me, King Murenten? Did you think I did not mean it when I said I loved you?" The water witch covered her face. Her tears came out like ink from an octopus. "I did everything I could to prove my love for you. I carved these rivers for you and gave you my precious venom."

Seeing there was no escape, Tungsten swam toward her, and the water witch's mood changed. Even though she bled from where he had struck her, she opened her arms, naively ready to receive him a second time.

Tungsten swam back when she tried to snatch him. He twisted around her and gripped her hair, yanking and making her lean back until he rammed his foot into her serpent body.

"Release me." She swam on, groaning from his tight hold. "This is not what we planned."

"Swim up."

"King Mureten!"

"Up!" He pulled, and the first crack of her bones sent her moaning. Screaming, she shot out of the water.

Tungsten landed on his dislocated arm. Grunting, he crawled away from the shore and the water witch followed him.

"Come back!" Her claws were out, and the pale-faced woman turned red. "Don't leave me!"

Sparks of fire erupted from the water. A woman in white

garments emerged from the water and upon her grasp, Excalibur. The water witch seeing the threat charged at her but in one strike her body was cut in half. Her serpent body slithered away, and the other half made it to the shore, dead.

The wielder was a woman with golden hair. Every feature of her was recognizable, from the freckles over the bridge of her nose to the blond hair that would be full of light if it were dry.

"Leave at once." Her voice reverberated like the maidens of the lake while Excalibur vibrated in her hold. "The waters are not safe for you."

Tungsten used his working hand to lift himself off the ground. He held his dislocated arm and came closer, bringing the maiden to step back. "Calibor."

"I am the Lady of the Lake," she answered almost in a haze. Her eyes were not as bright as his sister once bore. Her skin lacked any warmth of life, as if dead but decorated by the sparkling gems around the corner of her cheeks. "I am what became after Morgên took me. This Calibor you speak of, her memories live within clawing and disturbing me. Even after death she reaches out to you, knows the danger you're in but has no name to call it."

A shrill sky echoed in the distance, leaving Tungsten to squeeze his arm. "Lancelot, he fell."

"Lancelot?"

"You bore feelings for him although he did not know it."

The Lady of the Lake turned to the running river, where the cry resonated. His real sister would aid him without question. This was an imposter.

"If you will not help them, then I will!"

The Lady of the Lake raised Excalibur and aimed the tip at him, her eyes held a threatening gaze. "You will steer from these tainted waters, nothing awaits you here but death." The waters under her bare feet rose and rolled over, taking her back to the deep end, until she descended into the water.

One step and Tungsten crashed to his knees. Something was wrong. He merely dislocated his arm, he shouldn't have any trouble moving his legs. Fire burned within him, freezing all control of his body and sending him to plop on his back.

Lying still, he felt where the heat originated and touched his upper chest, finding black slime oozing from his fingers.

Poison?

"Tungsten," a voice softly said. "Tungsten."

A hand swam up his arms and locked him in an embrace.

The face of a woman showed herself before his visor. Her eyes radiated like starlight and her lips pursed before she reached down and kissed his helmet. "We found you."

"Mermaids," he grunted,

More voices of the sea women crawled out of the water, using their fishtail to pull off the ground and reach him. In minutes ten hovered over him, hands swimming over his armor

133

as they relentlessly tried to lift him. Without legs to steady their balance on land and skinny arms they were unsuccessful.

One secured a tight hold on his heel and the others joined. Together dragged him inch by inch to the water.

"Unhand me," Tungsten groaned.

"King of the Mountains," the mermaids sang. "Bid these dry lands farewell and embrace your new home under the sea."

"Your armor will sustain you like a statue and though your skin will rot and bones will wither, we will never."

"Take off his armor," one said. "We will carry them back piece by piece."

Their hands swam up and down pulling and tugging at his mail and pauldron, but his armor wouldn't budge. Not even a skilled squire could help them. For as long as he stayed awake, his tanium armor would open for no one but his will.

Tungsten rolled onto his stomach not caring whose hand got caught underneath his weight. As he guessed one was stuck pounding her fists at him for being too heavy. He crawled without apology, inch by inch he grew closer to the woods.

The mermaids, seeing his escape grouped up again to pull him back, but he didn't stop. If he was to finally get some sleep, he would do it out of their reach.

XI

DEATH IS KNOCKING AT MY DOORSTEP

The howling of wolves stirred him awake. A chill seeped into his breath, unbearable as the night fell over him like it had by the river.

The cold, wet ground had numbed his back, and what few stars he could see were hidden by the swaying branches. Another howl and Tungsten knew better than to linger. Everything hurt but he crawled aimlessly in the dark. Not far he picked up the footsteps of armored people; the clanking of their metal always gave them away. If they had been following his trail of blood, they were on the right track.

The howl came back with increased intensity, causing him to hold his breath. By the sound, they were wolves of Aarlin, the animal god who gave creatures like Indra their enormous size and strength.

Tungsten dug his fingers into the soil and got to his feet. He breathed calmly, but no effort made the pain more bearable. With this limp, he wouldn't make it far and the thick fog grew denser with each shaky step. No matter how hard he blinked, the dark only got stronger. He didn't know what the water witch did, or how her venom entered his body but it was affecting him even now.

Brushing to the vegetation, his footing dipped, and stumbled on the uneven terrain. With little to see, he expected a fall but rolled down a steep hill until the wet muddy ground caught him.

Groaning, he rolled to the side and chuckled. "I suppose everyone has a first fall."

A lantern hovered over him, breaking through the fog. He watched the gingery glow as another one came closer to his face.

"Should we leave 'em?" one said.

"Lower your voice, those wolves are out there," the companion snapped. "They'll sniff us out if we don't get moving."

A blue orb broke through the two men holding their amber lanterns. "He must come with us," his voice was fresh, and calm to his ears.

The second voice smacked his lips. "Don't tell me you

brought us out here in the middle of the night to find him. If we bring this Excalibarian back with us someone will come looking for him."

"I'll take full responsibility if something arises."

After some silence, the two pair tried to lift him.

"Oh hell," one of them said. "This man weighs like a boulder, we can't bring him with us."

"It's alright," Tungsten winced. "I'll find a way out, I always do."

The man who got closer brought the lantern to his face, revealing a toothless smile. "Give death the finger and focus on your breathing, will ya?" He left briefly and returned with a rope.

"What are you doing?" the other said.

The same rowdy man answered. "What do you think? We'll have the team pull him."

"Think that's wise considering his condition?"

"Excalibarians are hard to kill. Flesh wounds are nothing to their kind."

Tungsten shut his eyes, and a soft chuckle escaped his lips. "He is right." Though he'd be more capable if that venom hadn't paralyzed him. The team of horses went into motion and he felt rope pull his body down the road.

In that brief space of awareness before succumbing to sleep, his thoughts briefly touched upon Lancelot and Indra, only to be replaced by dreams of his father and the enigmatic water witch.

He was a boy when he last heard of her.

XII

OH, YOU CRAFTY FOOL, HOW YOU'VE BEEN MISSED

King's Road

*T*hirteen-year-old Tungsten held three-year-old Calibor in his arms, watching the campfire. His brother Ecarus fed it more wood while Mother tended the horses as nightfall had come.

For the past hour, Tungsten looked at the hill he last saw his father take. He was distraught when he left but intended on going alone, swearing he would get back at the man who tried to drown Calibor.

"Mother," Ecarus who stood as their guard always kept one hand on his hilt. His armor was painted black with some silver tones around the edges. "We can't linger any longer. The safety of King's Road will not last during an active war."

Mother started to walk back. It was just them, no knight to escort *them for the long trip, and even so they wouldn't take their helmets off until they were in the privacy of their home. "Let us wait one more hour. If your father doesn't return, we will go to him."*

Ecarus looked at Tungsten. Calibor was fast asleep, holding Tungsten's hand. "The risk is too great if it puts my brother and sister in danger once more and over a simple water witch."

"She is no simple water witch." Mother calmly sat down by the campfire. "Her name is Helena, a half-siren, half Excalibarian who was once a kind and very beautiful girl."

Ecarus couldn't hold his gasp. "You mean one of our own bedded a siren?"

"Helena lived and served under Orendor when she was a child. She cleaned his temple and made the peaks of his mountains her home. Seven years ago, she ventured far from the kingdom and never returned. After some searching and asking, we discovered she was kidnapped by the king of the dark waters and forced to wed him. We tried to bring her back, but she was impossible to find."

Ecarus rolled his shoulders. "Are you saying she was trying to escape now after all these years?"

"I believe she sensed your Father and probably decided this was her chance."

"Aye, by luring her Godforsaken king to attack us."

"She may have had no choice." Mother's voice fell short before she looked up at Ecarus. "Though she never admitted it, she was particularly fond of your father, in the way a woman sees a man."

Tungsten turned for the hill and saw a silhouette walking back, spear in hand. "Look!" he called.

Father was covered in what looked like black ink. Mother and Ecarus surrounded him, asking if he was well. "I had to kill the king, he would not let Helena go."

Ecarus wanted to know what happened but Father only looked at him and said they would speak on it later.

When they reached Crystal Lake, Tungsten was sitting by the bank, fishing with Father who hummed to himself. His mood always brightened when he enjoyed the sunlight upon his skin and not his armor.

"Why did you save the water witch?" Tungsten dared himself to ask. "Ecarus said that siren lost her wings, that she's bounded to the water because of what the king did to her."

Father's humming stopped. He placed his wide hand over his head and patted him. "She may have siren and Excalibarian blood, but she will always be one of us, and we help our people do we not?"

"But she's a monster," he corrected. "Ecarus said so."

"And I will tell you son that even the most heartless of beings bear the same sufferings as you and I. Retain this knowledge in order to protect the innocent."

Tungsten awoke.

Replacing the dream, was a small, quaint room, furnished with paintings on the wall, a rocking chair, and an area rug. The bed opposite of him was impeccably made and showed no signs of being used.

On the side table, a bottle of wine caught his attention; drops of it had spilled onto the wooden floor and his tunic. It had likely been used to treat his wound. An aroma of honey made him look at the cloth wrapped around his arm. Then there were his legs. One had been wrapped twice. The simple act of wiggling his toes sent an intense jolt of pain straight to his temple.

Blazes, why did he try that?

Soft steps were coming, bringing Tungsten to grab the bottle of wine. He wasn't going to take any chances, even if he was cared for.

The door creaked open, and a woman stepped inside, carrying clean wraps. She saw the bottle in his hand and shook her head. "Ah, he lives." She paced to the table and left the wraps there. "Layon!" She had a darker complexion, and her hair was short with gold hoops around her ears. She was thin, with a white-sleeved green dress and an apron.

Tungsten tried to sit up, but he could barely lift himself and flopped back on the bed.

"Layon!" the woman called again, hands on her hips. "Oh, that man."

The sound of hurried footsteps grew louder as they grew close. A tall man entered, surprised to see him. He rubbed his jaw as he stepped inside. "Ah, he lives."

"I already said that, dear." The woman turned for the door but before she left the man grabbed her waist and kissed her cheek.

"We didn't think you were ever going to wake up after the blood loss." That man's voice resonated with the sound of that night when one of the three men spoke over him.

Tungsten sat up and touched his chest again, feeling the wraps under his tunic. A shudder coursed through him as he repeated the same motion. He reached for his head and touched his hair and his nose. His fingers ran down and he touched his beard. "Where is my helmet?" he seethed through his pain and tried to sit up. "Where is my armor?"

"Easy, giant." Layon took a seat across from him. His eyes were green, like Calibor's, and his smile bore no threat. "Yer in Kemri, a village nestled far from your kingdoms or any proper civilization." He pounded his chest. "I'm the village chief. This here is a fine inn I own, but not for weary strangers like you."

Tungsten touched his side, feeling the wrap and the dent upon his skin. They touched him.

Layon grabbed the cloth his woman left. "Let's check your wrappings, shall we?"

"No, I shouldn't overstay my welcome."

"You were poisoned," he replied. "We had to do some bloodletting. You owe it to the kid that we brought you here, or you'd be dead. I later withdrew my vote, seeing it was in our best interest not to bring attention, with you being Excalibarian."

"Did history play a role in your decision?"

"We have finally found a decade of peace and we wish for it to stay that way."

The woman returned and gave Layon a bowl of hearty potatoes with celery. "Eat up. The food is good here."

Tungsten stared at the bowl, glistening with fat and the aroma of chicken broth touching his senses. He raised the bowl to his mouth and ate, doing more swallowing than chewing.

"Easy," the woman said with a stern look. "Those carrots and potatoes should be chewed."

Tungsten stopped, but only because he had emptied the bowl. He noticed another stranger leaning on the doorframe, arms crossed.

When Layon noticed her, he cleared his throat. "Listen, Excalibarian," he said. "I will be forward and inform you that if you bring trouble, we will sell you out. For now, you're welcome to recover until you leave this place."

"I would not endanger anyone on my behalf."

"Good." Layon took it and blinked at it. "If you wish to stretch your legs, you may do it at night when the hour is late. By respecting our rules, we won't have any trouble."

"You got a name?" the woman asked. "It is rude not to provide it after being taken care of by us."

Tungsten nodded. "I am Rode."

Layon nodded. "This is my wife, Yumna. She was a traveler just like you, and I was lucky to have convinced her to marry this buffoon." Yumna touched Layon's cheek before she left, passing a woman who waited at the threshold. "And that over there is Rella."

Rella smiled at the sound of her name. She entered his room like that was her invitation and took the wine bottle from the side table. "I didn't believe an Excalibarian would ever be in these parts, but my look at those muscles." She popped the cork open and gave it a hearty drink.

Fighting the aching in his entire body, he managed to rise by relying on his injured foot.

"By the Gods you are something," Layon said. "They told me that broken leg of yours will be healed in a week."

It was being Excalibarian, of course. The strength of their mountains was their own.

Ingon's words returned, of Orendor being unhappy with them.

"Who is the man who wanted to take me in?" he asked, hoping not to think about it longer.

"Man?" Layon rubbed his chin. "You must be talking about—"

"I think what you need, muscles, is some more rest." Rella closed in and gripped his shoulder, causing Tungsten to pull away. She flinched, surprised by his quick reflexes. "Is something the matter? Your arms shouldn't be dislocated anymore."

"Never you mind, dear." Seeing he was just in his trousers,

he grabbed the blanket and covered himself.

"Dear?" She released a lighthearted laugh. "I think we're the same age."

"Then you're old enough to keep to yourself and refrain from touching others who don't wish it."

Rella gave him a souring look this time. "My, you think you're special don't you?"

"Alright, let the man rest, Rella," Layon said.

"My armor," said Tungsten.

"It's in that chest over there." Layon whistled. "Excalibarians."

Rella shook her head and took the bottle with her before calmly shutting the door.

Tungsten immediately plopped back on the bed. Without his armor, there was no longer the aroma of metal or blood. There was a soreness everywhere, and the cast on his leg hindered any plans to leave and reunite with Lancelot, his bosom friend, the dagger around his waist he couldn't part with.

Tungsten rested his hand on his forehead at the thought of losing him. His screams before they pushed him off the cliff returned to his mind. Did Indra reach him when he fell into the river? Did Helena get to them before she got him?

A maiden in the river flashed back, holding Excalibur and bearing Calibor's likeness. "Sister," he said as he shut his eyes. "Lady of the Lake."

• • •

Tungsten spent the first three days asleep until Layon woke him up, thinking he had fallen unconscious. Being bedridden and seeing he was in good hands, he thought only of catching up on the sleep he missed since he left Excalibur.

For the next two days, he spent his time polishing his armor, stretching, and studying the map Layon who proudly declared they were drawn by his wife. The design was unique, with small roads that were marked safe. The three kingdoms, Atlios, Felmid, and Excalibur were drawn, from Cerrig Forest to Bromton. Even expanding little communities like Olivewood he was unaware of now had a place on this map.

It was hard to believe after The Affliction War that humans would expand at the rate they had. It didn't seem possible then, the war seemed never-ending.

With a knock on the door, Yumna appeared, wearing her usual frown. What she carried gave a scent of cloves, revealing his tray of soup and bread.

"Thank you," he said. There was not much meat in his serving, but he appreciated what they gave him.

Normally, Yumna would ignore him, but this time, she stopped. Something always appeared to bother her, but she said very little for as long as he minded his eating manners. "Is it true your bones have healed?"

"Aye."

"Then when can you leave?"

Tungsten moved to the side of the bed. "I was thinking tomorrow. If you're worried about the pay—."

Yumna harrumphed. "You can pay by *never* coming back."

Tungsten set his bowl down. "What grudge do you have against me, Yumna dear?"

"Do *not* call me—" Her raised voice fell, and she crossed her arms. "I do not like your kind. It's because you participated in The Affliction War that many suffered for decades, claiming war against the dragons and their people only to lead to more suffering."

"With fewer monsters prowling around, I'm certain you live peacefully now."

"Peace?" She moved to the window and looked out. "Being a cartographer, I traveled as my mother before me. In my travels, I found there is no peace as long as there are people who want control over what they have no claim over. Monsters? Humans? There's no difference, only the desire to kill and, if not, the desire to kill for peace."

"You are a wise woman." He got up and picked up his gauntlet.

Yumna crossed her arms. "And what do you think you are doing?"

"I've been cooped up in this room for a week. If I want to make sure I'm healthy for the journey, I must walk."

"Just keep your head low," she stammered. "Strangers have been coming by the village."

"Is Kemri not accustomed to strangers?"

"These were Felmidian soldiers. Soldiers from kingdoms have no business in an independent community such as ours. Not unless they're looking for someone, perhaps an Excalibarian?"

"Am I to expect them outside?"

"If they had been a threat, Layon would have traded you in, but they only passed by, and didn't come to stay."

"Then I'll make my walk short. It has been too long since I tasted the air." He still walked with an unsteady gait, but he was exceptionally better.

Downstairs, the room was warmed by the active fireplace. The hour was dark, and there wasn't much to see except candlelight by the side table flickering against the wall.

Layon was behind the counter, writing in his journal. He looked up, observing his armor from head to toe before returning to his writing. "You're not permitted to leave yet."

"I'm going for a little stroll."

An old man sat in the corner of the room, carving some wood. He looked up at him and nodded. "Looks like ye gave death one hella'va finger."

"I recognize that voice."

The man revealed his toothless smile. "Aye, I was the driver."

"Your idea to haul me with rope was a splendid idea."

The man laughed. "I've grown wiser to better think twice next time, ya almost broke me' wagon!"

Tungsten laughed and stepped outside. The cold mercilessly enveloped him. He only took a few steps and looked at the village. Small cottages lined the far side of the road, their chimneys releasing trails of smoke. Torches burned in the distance, along roads that went uphill to the countryside. He stretched, raising his hands in the air, and yawned.

"At long last," a soft voice said. "I thought you'd never leave the inn."

The shadow sitting on the roof was a boy, kicking his feet back and forth with a grin on his face.

"I don't believe we have met," Tungsten said.

"Well, of course, you don't recognize me." He rubbed his pink nose. "This is our first meeting."

The staff in his hand brought back his memory of an old man he used to know whose very own powers surged within his iris.

The boy leaned over and leaped. He landed on his feet without a strain and calmly stood straight. His cape was blue, but underneath he wore a white tunic, pants, and high brown boots.

"It's great to finally meet you," he said, extending his hand. "I'm Merlin."

"Merlin?" Tungsten grabbed the boy and gave him a tight hug, leaving him kicking the air. "Oh, you crafty fool, how you've been missed!"

"Oi! Let me breathe a little, would ya?"

Tungsten released him and laughed. "Only Merlin the Old would say that."

With a grumble, the boy adjusted his coat, making sure there were no wrinkles in sight. "I don't know how the other Merlin greeted you, but *I'm* not affectionate, understand?"

"Well, pardon me." He patted his head though he didn't seem pleased. "Goodness, you are tiny. Your nose isn't as long as it used to and your eyebrows have thinned out."

Merlin furrowed his eyebrows but said nothing.

"Keep it down," one of the guards said. "You'll conjure the beasts in the forests."

"Pardon us," Merlin said with a bow. "Let's go for a walk." Without waiting for his answer he marched toward the farmland, up the hill where a windmill turned slowly in the distance.

"I can't believe my eyes," Tungsten said. "You're back."

"Before you continue," he said. "Even if I am back as you say, I'm not the Merlin you remembered. His memories are not my own."

"I'm fully aware of reincarnations," said Tungsten.

151

"Then why did you nearly break my bones with an embrace?"

"Why it was pure and utter joy of course. I didn't think Mother Nature would have enough power to create another wizard. Such a feat requires old forests that still sing the memories of the ancients." Merlin didn't answer, but he intended on being followed. The countryside couldn't be livelier. Men and women wore veils to cover their heads as they worked in the night. "Such a strange hour to be tending the land, don't you think?"

"It's as you said, Mother Nature. Here, the moon makes their crops grow strong." Merlin stopped to watch them work. "I spend most of my nights outside, listening to the same whispers of the forests you speak of. News tends to travel in the dark quicker than in the day."

"And what did they say?"

"They talked about how you embarked on a quest to find your sister's killer and the loss of a friend."

Tungsten balled his hands into a fist. "His name was Sir Lancelot."

Merlin bowed. "I am sorry."

Tungsten placed his hand on the boy's head and tousled his blond hair. He shared the same high cheekbones as Merlin the Old, the same blond hair and blue eyes, but this one had a vibrant look around his irises, a certain glow.

Merlin climbed a wooden fence and sat, facing him. "Say, got any stories of the other Merlin to share?"

"Which one?"

The boy grasped the gold trinket that hung on his cloak. "You met two Merlins in your lifetime?"

"Aye." Tungsten leaned on the fence, it creaked under his weight, so he moved off. "Merlin the Old was my father's trusted advisor and my mentor. Merlin the Unremarkable was born shortly after, but he died quite young. He was a paranoid fellow, all bones by how little he ate. He didn't like that people looked him in the eyes and preferred to stay indoors."

"Strange," Merlin said. "How did he die?"

Tungsten shrugged. "He said he made a mistake by coming back too early. He left the confines of his room one night and we never saw him again."

The boy looked conflicted, his nose flared, but his eyes appeared to have changed. "And... Merlin the Old? What happened to him?"

Tungsten pinched his inner cheeks. "I... don't know. Nobody knows. We always thought he was never going to die. He was a powerful wizard? The strongest I have ever seen. He could cast lightning from his staff, and summon the elements into his hands. Dwelling Devils would let him walk their forests, even dragons respected him. Then one day on a campaign he bid my father and me goodbye and never returned."

"I've been meaning to ask what you're doing here." Merlin bowed his head. "King of Excalibur."

Tungsten faked a cough and looked the other way, resting his hands on his hips. "I spoke too much, didn't I?"

Merlin nodded. "I was told Merlin the Old was a friend of the former king of Excalibur, and from the way you speak about him, that can only mean you are the son of that former king."

Tungsten said nothing, it was better to let him think it than confirm it.

Smiling, Merlin leaned back and looked at the cloudy sky. "Don't worry, I didn't see your face when they treated you, just Layon, Yumna, and Rella."

"Somehow, I'm not comforted by that, nobody is supposed to see my face." He turned towards the inn and saw from the window Yunma was watching them. "I should return, don't want to conjure her anger."

"Wait!" Merlin leaped off the fence. "I can cast a spell that can alter fresh memories. I'll ensure they forget how you or your armor look." It was hard to take his word for it, but by the way he composed and spoke, he appeared confident, strange but confident at least. "Lord Tungsten."

"Rode from here on."

"Right. Rode. I was meant to venture to Excalibur to offer to warn you. Rumors are just rumors and I do not trust the words of man. But it is no secret that the shifting of this world is inevitable. Gods are leaving, the continent is changing, and the magic that once flourished is fading."

"This has already been into motion," he said. "Such news has been on every Excalibarian mind for centuries."

"And who had the foresight to foretell this?"

Tungsten suddenly stopped, and Merlin bumped into his back. "Orendor."

The boy walked around him, pleased by his answer. "Why, I didn't know the Blacksmith God with such a title would know the stars."

"A new era will unfold and Excalibur will not take part of it, that is what he said."

Merlin unclipped the gold trinket from his cloak. "Then I shall consult the stars with this discovery, and search for how I can aid you."

"Strange. Never thought you would pick up astronomy."

The boy gasped, appearing half insulted by his comment. "The other Merlins weren't?"

Tungsten laughed harder now, holding his side. "Well then, I'd like to walk back alone."

"Hey, wait!"

"It's late, and we have enough time to talk some more."

Aside from the few guards roaming the place, a group of women were packing crates in the lit barns.

A crash resonated from within. The crates had fallen over

and wedged a woman underneath. He went in and the worried faces grew silent while the woman buried under the pile cried for help.

"I got you, my dear," Tungsten winced at his attempt to kneel. He grabbed the first crate with two hands and placed it on another crate, taking the pressure off one after another.

Before the guards got to them, the women pulled the young one out. She looked at him wide-eyed, and the others started to giggle and whisper to each other.

An older woman ushered the crowd out, him included. "Men are not allowed at this hour of the night," she said.

Tungsten apologized while the other women said he came in to help.

It mattered not when one took his arm and led him back to the road. "Go back, stranger."

"I can assure you I am harmless."

She looked back at the way to the town's inn. "'Tis' dangerous at night; were you not made aware?"

"Dangerous?"

"The shadows," she said, peering at him. "A figure in black garments who assaults innocent travelers lingers by. Kemri has fallen victim, and a new face such as yours is likely to invite their wrath."

Shadows? Fighters in black garments? It seemed this village had confronted that Dranyth.

XIII

I FOUND YOU, GIANT KING

The unraveling stone steps were cold against his bare feet. Torches that burned without oil illuminated Tungsten's path as he descended to the point of feeling faint. More staircases, more dizziness, until he walked into a silent cavern. The place could fit an entire village, but it was a crypt for the royal family.

Tungsten ran down the wide road, his steps light—too light. He looked down and saw himself in the body of a child again. He made it to the recent tombs and climbed up for a better look. On the top was the tomb of his father, his armor carved in stone, holding the wind sword. Beside him was Ecarus's tomb, absent of Father's sword, for he was never king. The tomb following his brother was Calibor's. Instead of stone, it was made of white marble where it was to encase her armor for tanium armor corroded after the death of its carrier.

"Do you remember when we used to sneak here after dinner?" Calibor asked. Tungsten spun and found a little girl, bright-eyed in a simple dress. She went up the steps and placed her hand on the tomb of his father. "Do you remember?"

"Yes..." he said. "It had been nearly six months of regular visits from the nobles of Bengom, Felmid, and Atlios. We were eager for a break from donning our armor and this was the only place we could find it. Looking back now, I don't think it was good to visit the dead."

"We had to make do with the scant privacy available to us." She went to Ecarus's tomb and brushed her hand against it. Her smile fell and all the color drained from her face. Calibor slowly approached her tomb, but she dared not touch it. "Why does she have my armor? Why is my name written on it?" She spun back, eyes frightened as tears slowly rolled down her cheeks. "Tell me!"

Tungsten ran to her side. He took her hand and patted her back. "I put you to rest in Crystal Lake. Don't you remember?"

Calibor pulled from him, shaking her head in disbelief. In the blink of an eye, the girl had become the woman he remembered, covered in armor, but without her helmet and holding her side where blood ran. She descended the steps, her footsteps echoing as she made her way toward the rushing river that meandered around the tomb and carved its way through the mountain. Her arms spread open, and she shut her eyes. "That's right. I'm dead."

"Calibor!"

With a sense of surrender, she leaned back, letting gravity take over as she descended into the waiting arms of the river.

"Calibor!" Tungsten reached for the ceiling. Rella was

standing by the door, eyes wide. She grinned and sat on the empty bed across from him. "That was some dream you were having."

Tungsten wiped the sweat from his forehead What in Orendor's great hammer was she doing in his room?

"Calibor," Rella said. "That's the name of Excalibur's Sun Princess, isn't it?"

Tungsten didn't answer. He watched her fingers smoothing the end of the bed. "Did Yumna give you permission to enter my room?"

"I don't need permission from someone indebted to us, and you haven't answered my question. Is Calibor a lover of yours?"

When he didn't answer, she got up and sighed. "I came because of Merlin. That boy cooped himself up in the windmill and hasn't come down. Layon and everyone are out there, but he casts a spell to push back anyone who would disturb him. I thought you might help convince him to stop."

"And why do you think I can do that?"

"Because Layon and I suspect you're the reason he's losing sleep."

Tungsten got up, but she didn't move out of his way, invading his space. He sidestepped around her and headed toward the exit.

Her chuckling followed him. "You don't like to be touched, do you?"

"Not if I can avoid it."

She laughed this time. "You Excalibarians are as bizarre as they say. Hard to tell if you're righteous or self-righteous."

"That's for you to judge."

Outside the inn, a colder bitter night befell the community. A faint glow was coming from the countryside where Merlin must be. During the walk, he felt Rella's stare lingering. When he looked down, she was eyeing him before she averted her gaze. "So, tell me, how did you Excalibarians get your strength? All I have ever heard was that your people were the first to mark the southern mountains."

"Why do you wish to know?"

"Orendor has been gone for a long time now and look at you, it's as if he hasn't left."

"Felmid wielded their strength from Varil, the Iron Spear God but it was borrowed. Orendor sanctified us by giving us a piece of his unmatched strength and stature. His hammer and anvil that helped shape the mountains we see today shaped us."

Rella smiled, amused by his answer. "You know what irks me about such talk? Orendor is a creature of nature, but you call him a God. Gods don't die or cowardly leave their reign for the Isles of Avalon."

"Any deity who has power over nature or humans is a God in our eyes."

She didn't seem convinced but left it at that. The faint glow was getting strong, and the field workers appeared to be heading in the same direction, attracted to the light in the windmill.

Rella nudged his arm. "You're not going to ask me anything? It's rude not to reciprocate a curious mind."

Tungsten stepped away from her. "I'm not in the mood to talk."

"I hail from Bengom," she answered. "Five years ago, I was on the road when I found a pair of bandits bullying a poor boy no older than eleven Winters." She unsheathed her sword and gave it a few swings. "So, I saved him, and when I found out he was the great Merlin, I swore to protect that boy for the rest of my life."

"Strange," said Tungsten. "At sixteen, a wizard should be strong enough to defend himself."

"I thought so too," she said sheathing her blade. "Merlin the Old saved me when our family was raided during The Affliction War. I always wanted to give him my thanks, but when I got old enough to venture the roads, news of his death reached me."

"It seems everywhere I go there's always The Affliction War," Tungsten said softly.

Rella pressed her lips together tightly. "And who isn't affected?"

Tungsten came to a full stop. He swore he felt something, but had he imagined it? He held out his hand and waited.

A snowflake floated down and melted on his glove. "This

isn't good."

"What?"

"Snow."

Rella scrunched her face. "Is this another weird Excalibarian thing?"

"As Mother Nature wills it, the changing of the seasons puts some gods and monsters to sleep, but it awakens undesirable ones." He turned for the road out of the village. "Give Merlin my pardon, I cannot delay any longer."

Rella took his arm, and he winced. "What about Merlin?"

"I have other matters that need me." He yanked himself free. "Please give Layon and Yumna my gratitude."

Rella ran in front of him, she walked backward seeing he wasn't going to stop. "Now wait just a second. You said you would help me with the boy and that's what you're going to do."

Flashes of light erupted, illuminating Rella's face and revealing her surprise. Together, they ran to the windmill.

By the time they reached the creaking building, a protective orb that covered the place dimmed. Merlin walked out, aided by Layon. The boy was drenched in sweat. His eyes glowed a sharp sky blue; his hands were marked with the ancient mark.

"Merlin," Rella said as she went to his other side.

"I'm... I'm okay." He looked at Tungsten and what little color he had washed out and he fainted.

Layon carried him to the back, concern growing in his eyes.

Tungsten joined him, noticing the boy's racing breaths. He looked delicate, like paper against water.

"It appears seeking the stars comes with a cost," he asked.

"He's talented, and knows more than you know," Layon said. "The boy can predict what your eyes can't foresee."

Merlin was returned to the room he had been staying in. There were drawings of a child on the table, a toy sword, and markings of a height were etched on the wall. It was nothing like the place a wizard would keep, much less one fascinated by astronomy. This belonged to a boy and, knowing that cautious woman, she probably hid him.

"Speak of the devil," Tungsten said.

Yumna came with a bowl of water and cloth. Merlin was stripped of his cloak and tunic so she could wipe the sweat clean.

"This little brat," Rella said. "I told him not to do this."

Yumna looked at Tungsten. Her eyes were growing glossy. "I knew your arrival would disturb the peace of this place. Get out, get out before you cause more harm."

"Enough Yumna," said Layon.

"Wait just a minute," Rella said. "Merlin wants to talk to you. Don't make his efforts for naught."

"No, she's right. I can't wait another hour." In the Northstead Highlands, the cold claimed the frosty hills and cliffs. It was the last push the weather was going to have with him before the warm climate returned. "Hopefully, the boy will wake up and our paths cross again."

Tungsten made it out of the room before Rella took his arm, which he yanked away a second time. "At least tell us where you're going. When Merlin awakes, he'll be searching for you."

"If the stars are his friend as he claims then he won't have trouble finding me."

• • •

Two feet of snow covered Northstead Heights. He drew the cold air and peered at the map Layon gave him. He was grateful for the map and the blade. It was no two-handed weapon, but anything would do. He wondered what Merlin would think when he woke up and found him gone. Maybe he could have stayed a bit longer to hear what he had to say, but that look on his face. Whatever it was, it wasn't good news.

In the cold, his armor could insulate freezing temperatures, traveling throughout the night and day, seeping through his gambeson and leggings.

A pair of footprints in the snow stopped him, and he crouched for a closer look. "It appears someone passed through here." Tungsten unsheathed his blade.

"Indra boy," he said. "I guess I'll have to use my own nose."

He leaned down, imitating his cat, and sniffed it. There was no scent, just a cold nose from all the breathing. The tracks continued, and he followed them until they stopped at the trunk of a tree.

"What the blazes?" Tungsten raised his sword, blocking the two blades that came down. The flames of her two short swords spurred weakening the sword Layon gifted him. Fearing it would break, he grabbed her arm and swung her back. "You sure like to make an appearance."

Astra Degora tumbled back down before catching herself. He charged at her and she leaped into the trees, jumping from one branch to the other like a passing wind that Indra could not match.

"I've been waiting for a rematch," Tungsten shouted. "This time I'm hunting you!"

A weight landed on him until he realized her thighs squeezed him. "What's what? Who's hunting who?" She twisted with force he couldn't measure, and spun in mid-air before crashing into the snow.

Just as he tried to get up, he realized red was dripping on the snow. Her blade, thing as it was had cut through his armor and gambeson and crossed the flesh below his ribcage. He didn't know if it was during her first strike or when she landed on him that she struck. "Well done." He reached for the sword but stopped when he saw it was shattered into three pieces. "Who trained you to go against an Excalibarian so well?"

Astra Degora landed delicately on the snow. Her blades stopped at the end of his helmet. "It's true that Excalibarian armor is fortified and impossible to penetrate with magic alone. Even with tanium blades, it would take great effort." Her blade then went to his neck. He winced when he felt a sharp pain run through. "But as resistant your armor may be, there are air pockets one with a sword like mine can cut through."

Tungsten reached for her, in hopes of wrestling her down. He managed to grab her leg and trip her to the ground. It was solely because of her dropping that he noticed a greater threat coming at an accelerated pace, and she appeared to have taken no notice.

"You are strong." He covered his neck and rose to his knees. "Now step aside." Still unaware, she got up to confront him but he tossed her aside and slammed into Eógan's shoulder. They both pushed one another, holding little grip on the snow under their feet.

Using his mighty legs, the centaur slammed him against a giant spruce tree and roared. "At long last I found you!"

Tungsten gripped his wrist; being large was incomparable to a centaur. Eógan was filled with joyous anticipation, hoping for another encounter with him.

The centaur broke the tree using Tungsten's body alone and charged up the hill, passing and breaking through more trees until he stopped over a cliff. It was no bigger than the one down to the Three Rivers, but it was enough to break his bones if the one landing on him was Eógan himself.

"You will suffer the same fate you placed on my brother!"

As the centaur leaped over the cliff. Tungsten caught a glimpse of Astra Degora among the trees. She threw a blade at him, and he caught it surprised by what he held. Calibor's blade?

Without a second thought, Tungsten cut Eógan's neck, severing his head. The beast's grip on him loosened leaving Tungsten to climb over him and leap for the ledge.

A hand reached down and took his wrist, and he slammed against the cliff, sending powders of snow to fall. He looked up, surprised to see Astra Degora. Mermaids and man alike have tried to lift him, and yet this small woman was able to sustain the weight of a grown Excalibarian in full armor.

At that very moment, his heart skipped a beat.

Astra Degora pulled him up until he was back on solid ground. He rolled onto his side, hand grasping where the blood leaked. His clash with the centaur opened it.

As his vision blurred, Astra Degora stood over him. Her lashes and irises were a matching shade of red but her eyes carried a void of the light he never saw in the living.

Chatter was coming their way, and she slowly faded back into the forest. When he opened his eyes again, the chatter had turned into a group of men and women. There was an odor coming from them, a combination of alcohol and cannabis.

A man with a long mustache chuckled as he leaned toward him, eyes glossy. He was gray-haired with soot on his face and his belt had trouble keeping his bulging stomach in. "This armor looks mighty expensive." His red beret loosely fell over the side of his head. "Don't think it's yours now, seeing I'm saving your life."

XIV

MUST HACK THE DYING TIDE!

A tree, old and weathered, fell with a crash. Birds took flight and critters that made it its home scattered unto the cold and unforgivable snow. Tungsten cleared the branches first, tied them in a rope, and wrapped them around his abdomen. He then grabbed the leftovers, logs that weighed more than four men could carry. He flung them onto his shoulders and trudged through the forest.

Sweat fell onto the snow, and the weight tore through his tattered tunic. His stomach growled for the third time. When he left to collect wood the aroma of grilled meat followed him out, but food was earned here. He would not get a bite until his job was done.

A campsite with twelve tents lay ahead. Because a storm was

coming, these vagabonds had to stop their journey for shelter. Gilan was playing his guitar against his will. He was once part of a minstrel troupe that served his lord that is, until an unpleasant encounter with monsters led to the death of his lord and eventually to Gilan's capture and debt to Victor.

"Louder!" Victor, the troupe leader shouted. He yanked a boiled chicken leg from the woman who had presented it to him and moved her out of the way. "I want my feet burning to dance."

Gilan grinned awkwardly and started to sing.

Victor, Victor!
A man with no compare.
He'll knock you to the ground;
Steal your woman for the plow—

"And sister!" Victor interrupted.

And sister!

Gilan muttered, strumming his guitar a bit more, muttering something under his breath.

Victor, Victor!
His deeds are so great.

His mercy is valiant.

Like the old Gods' way.

Tungsten untied the rope from the logs. His presence always brought Victor satisfaction that an Excalibarian was under his thumb, knowing he couldn't leave without his armor.

"Giant." Victor got up and trudged toward him, shaking his belt so the pieces of chicken meat would fall into the snow and not another mouth. "Got us some fine burning wood for the storm, have ya?"

Tungsten said nothing and stacked the logs to the side.

"You've been a good boy since I saved your life." He grinned and scratched his beard. "But I'm no fool. You can spy on my men all you want. The armor you came in will be sold in Atlios, and it will turn me into a rich lord."

"Hmm." Tungsten crossed his arms. "And are you sure you would get a fair price?"

"Your armor's metal is like Damascus steel, with darker edges where the fire scorched through." He scratched his beard again and gazed at his fingers, finding them glossy from the chicken fat. "My guess is it's tanium."

He guessed that would happen. Taking down his group of men and searching for his armor himself was no trouble at all, but since they were heading to Atlios, he would get his armor one way or another.

"Alright men, start cutting the wood!" Victor shouted. "And you, Excalibarian, I trust you'll find a wonderful surprise when you return to your tent." Victor went back to eating, demanding more music from the bard.

Most of Victor's men let him be, some tried to tell him where Victor hid his armor but he didn't pay them any mind. They detested him and knew if anyone could harm him it would be him. No, he would not be used as bait just so one of his goons could take over.

To prepare for the storm, a wall of logs and a tarp was set up to shield the tents from the stirring wind. His own stood between the others, just big enough for his size. It was primarily used to dry fish and to store unused pots and pans, ropes, and hunting gear. On the corner was his sleeping area, made up of a thin blanket and one made of wool.

Tungsten curled himself into a ball and shut his eyes. His thoughts wandered back to his encounter with Prince Valte. He crafted a plot to kill Calibor and take his sword so he could rule. Everything Lancelot said about him was true, he was weak, a foreigner who lost his powers and envied theirs. His marriage to Calibor was arranged after The Affliction War ended, and while his sister had the choice to reject the arrangement she didn't see anything wrong with his intentions, and neither did he.

Tungsten groaned and rolled to his side. Lancelot was right, and now he could be dead, and Indra, where had he gone?

Outside his tent, Victor's men were getting louder for another drunken night.

• • •

The glowing light from the campfire stirred before his eyes. He felt warm, awfully warm. His wool blanket was tossed aside and yet he felt the soft texture brush up against his skin chest.

Suddenly something swam into his trousers.

"Wakey wakey," she whispered. Tungsten turned from the blanket and found a pair of hard nipples hovering over him.

Tungsten raised his hips and tossed the woman over. He realized how poorly he had underestimated his strength when she soared over him and crashed into a pile of pots and pans.

A peel of laughter broke from outside.

Picking herself up, was Zaria, everyone's favorite company, tugging at her robe. "How dare you!"

"Do not make another step in my tent," he said.

She rolled to her knees and stood up. "What are you, a eunuch?"

Tungsten took hold of her arm to escort her out himself. He must have been rough because she scratched his arm to free herself.

173

"Victor will hear of this!" Before another word shot out, he threw her single cloak over her face.

The men who sat by the campfire laughed and whistled.

"Looks like ye' gonna have an awful night Zaria!" one of the men said. "Come sit on my lap, I'll keep you warm."

"Fuck off," Zaria spat before she stormed off.

Tungsten returned to his tent. He barely sat before he saw a head peek through. The bard, Gilan, entered without permission, carrying two tankards in hand. He sat near the corner as if to give him space, taking his guitar from his back first so he wouldn't damage it.

"Saw what you did." He offered one drink to Tungsten. "You'd be the first man to deny Zaria's offer. Well, aside from me."

Tungsten took the tankard. "I made an oath of chastity."

"What a pain that must be. Denying urges for the flesh."

"There is no temptation of the flesh for an Excalibarian who is just before his god."

"You know, I almost fell for an Excalibarian man myself, I say almost because I'm not an attainable man." He crossed his legs and gently plucked at his guitar strings, producing a relaxing melody. "The thing is, he never made the move. Any reason why?"

"Hmmm." Tungsten crossed his arms. "If you had won his heart, then I don't think he would hesitate with any urges of the flesh, as you like to put it."

Gilan snorted and strummed harder before he laughed. "So, the bastard didn't like me as I thought. What a cruel fate to find that out like this."

A powerful gust of wind made the tent shudder as if it was being tugged at by unseen hands. Gilan stopped his strumming and scrunched his face, knowing something didn't feel quite right.

A sudden impact reverberated through the earth, followed by the summons to prepare for battle.

Tungsten barely made it out with Gilan following him but before the bard could run with the others he grabbed his shoulder. "Don't move."

A giant made of blue ice stood before the campsite. Shards of ice protruded from his back, and his legs and arms were skinny compared to his long torso. His head stood above the pine trees and his icy beard ran past his knees.

"What is that?" Gilan whispered.

Tungsten breathed the robust wind he conjured. As he feared, the arrival of winter has disturbed the slumber of more powerful monsters. "That is Huliar, a spirit of winter and servant of the God of Snow."

The stirring flames grew stronger and bewitched, for the ice would not blow out.

Gilan used his arm to shield himself from the biting wind.

"You don't suppose he's peeved with us, is he?"

"If we leave calmly, there's a chance he will leave us alone."

"Oi!" Victor ran to him with one leg in his pants. "Wadd'ya waiting for? Go and kill him."

Tungsten crossed his arms. A slow chuckle bubbled inside his chest. "For such services, I request my armor in return."

"I saved your life!" Victor raised his blade to Tungsten's neck. "Kill him or I drop you."

Tungsten pressed his hands on his hips and laughed. He looked at the other weary men, sword and bow ready. "It appears you made your campsite on the property of another dying God, and their protectors are the most violent."

"We don't need him." Victor stammered. "Fire!"

"Wait!" Gilan said.

The sound of arrows whistling through the air was quickly followed by the sensation of them penetrating Huliar's chest. The giant stumbled back. He released a powerful roar summoning an even greater storm. The tents took off into the air with some people still holding on.

The men who drank outside of his tent hung from the spikes of ice that grew from his arms.

Victor, gritting his teeth, called for his right-handed man. "Unbury his armor at once!"

"But Victor, the coins!"

"There are no coins in death, now fetch it!" He unsheathed

Calibor's sword and gave it to him.

Huliar went on his fours and charged once more. Tungsten leaped for the ground and covered his head as the wind towered over him. Looking up, Victor's men were by a campfire, digging.

Desperate to reclaim his armor, he dug with his bare hands, biting his lower lip as the flames burned his arm. Somehow the wind would not blow campfires out.

Just as his nails grazed cloth a force pushed him, sending him across the campfire.

Huliar's screamed as more arrows rained on him. He flinched, crawling on all fours, and quickly scaled the trees to prepare for another assault.

Tungsten pulled the bag out of the ground. The metal clanking and the weight promised it was his armor. The wind blazed through; icicles scraped his skin as he raised his helmet.

"Orendor," he called. "God of metal and hammer, if I am still in your favor, aid me."

Tungsten put on his helmet first and with little effort the rest of his armor floated to him and snapped together, binding to him. The feathery layers on his gauntlet snapped up and down securing his shape. The weight, warmth, and metallic scent became an integral part of his soul. True discomfort was being without.

Huliar let out an icy cry and charged through the campfire for a third time. Before the Snow God's servant touched him,

Tungsten leaped into his legs and started to climb. The thud of the ground shook him but he didn't let go until he broke through the spikes and made it to the back.

"Huliar," Tungsten said. "Heed my words. The God of Snow has gone to the Isles of Avalon. There is no one to protect anymore!"

Huliar's spikes retracted. Tungsten raised his arms to his face as pounds of ice struck him. The frigid cold seeped through him, adhering it to his armor.

"Heed," he pleaded. "Go in peace!"

Huliar's arms soared over him, claws swiping down. Tungsten dove to the front, squeezing the hilt of his sword as more and more spikes piled over one another.

Victor's people hooted amidst the chaos. "Kill him, kill him!"

Between two rods of ice, a shadow broke through. He turned his blade flat, blocking the two short blades at the same time. Her eyes fell on him once more.

Tungsten chuckled. "I knew you were nearby!" He swung his blade at her, forcing her to leap back.

She raised her blades toward him. "You will not kill him."

He charged forward and swung his blade down. Astra Degora skidded to the side of Huliar to evade his swing and started to climb back up. She kicked the spikes to spear him but he hit every single one with his gauntlet.

Amidst the fight, Huliar turned for the others but Victor's people sought shelter among the trees, some even cheered his fight with Astra Degora.

Gilan who was among them played his guitar and shouted against the wind.

The nameless Excalibarian;
A mighty giant lord.
He lay in wait for his armor,
And fooled that smelly Victor!

He fought a God's Servant,
And gave him mercy's time.
But even great Excalibarians,
Must hack the dying tide!

Tungsten cut the space between them and kicked Astra Degora down Huliar's lower spine. One of her short swords fell, wedged between the spikes of ice.

Tungsten glided down to claim her weapon, but she was quick on her feet and managed to hold on to the hilt. He pulled hard, but she held on tighter, yanking the blade from his grip and sending him on his back.

When directed the tip toward him, he broke the ice underneath and lodged it upwards missing her head but splitting some strands of hair. He kicked her and tossed her back to the lower back of Huliar's spine.

With no time to waste, he sped to the shoulder blades until he reached Huliar's neck.

Tungsten raised his blade and penetrated the neck. At that moment he saw Orendor in the grand temple, his hammer coming down the anvil, birthing sparks.

The centaur's words whirled back in his mind. *We do not answer to the one who has gone against his own God.*

He did it again and again, his arm muscles burned until his head dropped. Huliar's lower body ran toward the trees, forcing him to land back on the ground, the body crashed down with a loud thud.

Tungsten fought for air. Even when the storm momentarily subsided, his breathing remained feeble. Was Orendor really displeased with him? Had he committed an offense by becoming king when he was only meant to serve?

Victor was among the last to climb down the spruce tree, he pushed the others away and went to see the head of Huliar.

Astra Degora was the first one who stood before it, watching the guardian slowly close his eyes.

Like ice that had been let out in the summer, the head started melting rapidly into a pool of water. Twinkling were shards of diamonds.

"I'm rich!" Victor shouted and scooped two handfuls of

diamonds.

Astra Degora pointed her tanium blade to his neck, leading him to cry. "Your disturbance cost a life, one I will not forgive so easily."

A pair of weapons rattled as his men pointed their crossbows at them. Seeing their support, Victor smiled. "Let's see who gets out of this one."

"Drop those diamonds," Tungsten said.

Victor coughed up phlegm and spat before his feet. "Our deal is over, you go on your merry way and I'll go on mine."

Tungsten pointed his blade next. "I didn't have to kill that guardian, but you had to send your men after him."

"You don't scare me." He scooped more of the diamonds and laughed. "I am Victor, thief and cheat of these parts and nobody tells me what to do!"

Astra Degora lowered her blade and sheathed it. "Then you leave me no choice." Her hand went under her cloak. She brought out a round iron ball shape like the head of a dragon with a fuse at the top.

"A bomb!" one of the men shouted. "She's a Dranyth!"

Victor dropped the jewels and stumbled out of her reach. He rounded up the survivors and demanded that they leave now.

Zaria who survived the ordeal was among them, her wavy hair tossing and turning from the stirring wind. She sneered at Tungsten and left.

"Until our next meeting," Gilan sang, strumming his guitar. "If you ever need a bard to sing in your lands, I'll be in Atlios."

Tungsten nodded and watched Gilan sing the same song about him and when Victor told him to stop, he continued.

Tungsten endured the cold and stalled his journey until all the diamonds receded into the ground. Now and then he would look at the weapon in Astra Degora's grasp.

That bomb she presented. He hadn't seen one in years.

The Dranythian attacks on Excalibur returned. The siphon they pumped out of their posts, spitting fire upon his people. Shooting from the hip, they fired what they called rockets, burning liquid that stuck to their armor. "I thought those things were destroyed."

"It's a fake," she said putting it back under her cloak. "Those fools didn't see it had a missing rudimentary fuse much less any powder."

The wind whipped around them, knocking them a step to the side. Astra Degora raised her arms as the frigid winds spiraled through the forest, coating everything with snow. "Staying here will kill us both." Her two braids were the last thing he saw as she sliced through the running fog. He had no reason to follow her, but the brewing storm had blinded his sense of direction, and alone, he could be lost to other awoken beasts.

His enemy surely valued herself, and in her company, he only had to worry about her.

Tungsten followed her footprints, sword still in hand should this be another trick. The wind howled, and with each step, he cracked the ice chips on his armor.

Astra Degora was not far, but she seemed to know where to go.

"Could this be supernatural?" he asked, choosing to walk behind. "A last cry from the Huliar or perhaps his God mourning for him?"

"Maybe both?"

"No, Huliar had no master to serve, there was only malice left in his heart."

She stopped and turned to him. "Truly? I saw a creature in pain and the Excalibarian before me trying to silence him." That was the first he heard a Dranyth care about another person's pain. Her breath formed delicate wisps of clouds, smaller than his, but it reassured him that she was warm-blooded.

There were no signs of Victor and his group, and there were not any villages or cabins to seek shelter from the storm. The creaking of the trees stirred his senses, and his armor was starting to case itself with more ice.

"Hurry," Astra Degora continued. "The storm doesn't appear willing to rest."

Tungsten steadily gripped the hilt of his sword. "If this is a trap, you'll be sorely disappointed."

"Are you sure Excalibarian King? In this weather, the

elements are in my favor."

"Confident, are we?" Tungsten laughed, sheathing his blade. "Very well, I'll let you surprise me."

Through the dense forest, the wind began to intensify. Astra Degora used her arm to guard herself from incoming icicles. "There's a troll not far from here. It's dead, but will make a fine shelter."

More icicles came, to his armor was just an annoying pecking. Astra Degora had no helmet but her arms to shield herself. Tungsten went to her side and blocked the ice, allowing the crystals to encase his armor. She looked up at him, and he looked back, hand steady on the hilt of his sword.

Amidst the turbulent storm, he managed to pick up the smell of smoke. Ashes were spiraled with the current of the wind. A troll lay sideways, with its legs partially tucked to his chest.

Astra Degora leaped to the top of the troll's shoulder. The wind pulled and lifted her cloak revealing the two sheaths she kept her swords on each hip. There was nothing she wore that wasn't black. Her black leather pants were tight fitting, with black high-knee boots and armor on her upper chest and arms.

His gaze fell on her buttocks, and the cut on her inner thigh before he looked away. He unsheathed his sword just in case and slowly crept around the troll.

• • •

As the night fell, Tungsten kept watch on top of the troll's shoulder. The wind was dying, but the cold persisted. Sharing a campfire was a sacred space. It was a time of not just rest but where he could be among his comrades and friends. When he was a prince he spent many nights sleeping outside the kingdom walls, sharing in company with his people, preparing for the next battle, and trying to make jokes to ease the wounds and spirit.

Those same thoughts brought him back to his two closest companions.

Tungsten leaped off the troll. Upon landing, a bone in his hip popped. Astra Degora raised an eyebrow, and he cleared his throat. His age of thirty-five and carrying weighted metal all his life hot gotten to him.

He scraped what he could off his armor, particularly where the melted snow had seeped through his mail. Craving warmth, he raised his trembling hands toward the fire, hoping to thaw the icicles clinging to his knuckles.

Astra Degora used a travel bag and rested her back against it. By the pieces of wood she collected this had been her shelter for some time, but did that mean she knew where he was heading?

She reached behind her, and Tungsten immediately went for his blade. She stopped, noticing his alertness but revealed a bottle of wine. Sliding down her mask, she gave it a few gulps. She then offered it to him. "To stay warm," she said.

Tungsten didn't take it.

"Suit yourself." The wind lifted her hair a few times, and he saw she wore an eyepatch under where most of it fell.

Her one eye fixated on the fire. There was an absence, a hollow space he saw it in the Dwelling Devil's bleeding eyes.

XV

YOU LET YOUR GUARD DOWN

The tumultuous storm of the night had waned, granting way for the sun to ascend in a tranquil, orange sky. As the fire crackled, he found solace in what little warmth it gave him, and while he didn't sleep a wink, he was ready for the new day.

Astra Degora hadn't moved since she crossed her arms and closed her eyes. It was hard to believe she was asleep. Tungsten got up and stared at her, but she didn't budge. He left the troll's corpse and picked up some twigs and branches that had fallen from the storm.

Without being discreet, he snapped the longer pieces upon his knee and threw them to feed the fire.

"Did you sleep?" Astra asked, waking to the noise.

Tungsten didn't answer.

She rubbed one eye and yawned. Her nose crinkled, and she looked, for a second, like an ordinary woman. "Sleep is important, even for Excalibarians."

"What do you know of our people?"

"Enough to know they're difficult to kill." Her stare fell on his armor briefly before looking at him. She knew where to look through the visor to catch his gaze and lock them. "Tanium is a complicated steel, not any fire can melt it, and the kind of metal your knights wear is but a downgrade from it. Better than plated steel but just enough to break open with my tanium blades."

"They're not yours." Tungsten placed his hand on his sword and got up. "The storm is gone."

Astra Degora leaned back, but her gaze didn't leave his grip on the hilt. Despite a clump of snow falling between them, neither of them showed any reaction.

"Since you have been working with Prince Valte, you must know how Crystal Lake was raided," Tungsten said. "Did you kill Calibor?"

She uncrossed her arms and gave her two sheaths a tap. "If you desire my answer so much, then you're going to have to get it by force."

"I'd be happy to."

A chuckle left her. "First you have to find me, big guy."

"No need!" Tungsten parted his legs and swung his sword,

cutting the troll's stomach in her place.

Astra Degora was gone, and clumps of snow drifted into the wind before they fell. He'd been underestimating her reflexes, that or he'd become slower. He swung his blade, cleaning it from the troll's blood, and leaped over the troll's arm.

A set of fresh tracks led him downhill where the lake he meant to cross waited. He climbed down with the tip of his sword marking a line on the snow. If he was going to face this woman again, then it shouldn't be to prove who was better. He had a mission to complete, and this Dranyth had the answers.

At the lake, Astra Degora stood at the center, looking up at the sky. Her arms were apart with her palms facing north.

Tungsten stepped on the ice and nearly lost his poise. The lower ends of his solleret unlocked the tiny needles on the sole giving him balance. Orendor. He thought about everything an armored man and the predicaments he may face.

He walked toward the assassin, giving his sword a few turns. "If this is your way of having the advantage, I'm afraid you're mistaken."

Astra Degora lowered her head and her one eye opened. "Oh, you're here."

He grumbled. "Did you not heed my words?"

"I was merely worshipping the north since you took your time finding me."

Tungsten looked over the peeking mountains. Nothing

waited to the north except for the Isles of Avalon. Worship of such things was unheard of, though it brought back that unsettling feeling.

Astra Degora brought her short swords from her sheaths and spun them, casting fire to spurt out. Her stance was low, her feet steady.

Tungsten gripped his sword firmly, his feet planted securely on the ice.

Her weight leaned on her right foot before she bounced off her left heel and sped toward him. As her blades descended, he raised his own, resulting in a collision that caused him to slide backward.

He charged this time and Astra Degora did the same, back lowered as Indra would before a pounce. He pivoted and swung his sword sideways. She skidded on her knees, swept under, and kicked his left foot.

He slipped but caught himself with his hands, one foot firmly on the ice until he heard a crack underneath.

"Is something the matter?" She mused, skating around him, her two braids swaying.

Tungsten got back on his feet. "I'm impressed; I'll give you that. You have fought opponents larger than you, haven't you?"

"More than I can count."

Tungsten laughed. "But not someone such as I!"

Her eyes squinted like she was smiling. "Let's find out."

The noise of the colliding blades gave a deafening sound to the silent lake. Each collision produced a harmonious disturbance, disrupting the birds' melodic tunes.

He stopped her on her next pass and brought his blade down. She twisted from him and circled to his backside.

Oh no.

Fearing her tanium blades would cut through his backplate, flames spurted out of his armor, sending her across.

Tungsten turned back, as those same flames swam up his body. "You seem willing to take any chance you can get me."

"I'm just waiting for you to let your guard down." Astra Degora climbed to her knees, studying the flames slowly dissipating from his armor. "You're not going to win this."

Tungsten laughed. His voice echoed into the wide-ranging mountains. "I admire your confidence."

The fissures on the lake started to enlarge, creating deep grooves that extended like roots.

There was a rumbling from below but Tungsten neither minded it, Astra Degora was slowly walking to him and she needed to be dealt with first. If he carelessly exposed his back like that again, those keen eyes might notice the fake tanium encased on his lower back.

Tungsten rolled his neck. He would not let that happen again.

Astra Degora spun her blades. "Well then, shall we waltz?"

"Dear, haven't we been waltzing since we met?"

"We have." One blink and she was unseen, leaving a gust of wind to whistle past him. Realizing she was once more going for his back. He raised his blade over his shoulder and blocked the strike against his back. "What are you hiding?" she said as he turned and stepped back. "You *are* hiding something, aren't you?"

Tungsten drew the cold air. "I don't know what you're talking about."

The fissures of the lake deepened, causing an uneven surface to hold a steady stance. The flaying wind passed him once more, and she was gone. Anchor ice emerged between them, stopping Astra Degora who used the crackling ice to strike at his back.

With each ascent, the anchor ice grew, bringing more to build over. There was a glimmer at the very top where a sword presented itself, blade lodged into the ice and hilt upward.

This was not possible. His sword had sunk at the bottom of Crystal Lake.

Astra Degora's unmatched speed led her to the top. She sheathed her short swords and brushed her hands at the pommel. "So this is the king's sword." She gave the hilt a good grip and looked at him. "You better start running."

Tungsten didn't run, instead, he watched her pull the grip, but the sword budged. Blinking, she tried again, but the blade remained encased in ice.

Tungsten charged up the mountain of ice. His nails penetrated the surface as he jumped higher and higher. When he reached the top, Astra Degora leaped back. He grabbed the hilt and pulled. With little effort, the blade unsheathed from the ice. Tungsten raised Excalibur toward the sun and laughed.

Below, Astra Degora waited for both swords in hand. Tungsten glided down, the scraping forming smoke of ice to build behind him.

In one leap he charged and swung his blade, forcing Astra Degora to block his strike. Excalibur came alive; gold marked the fuller until flames shot out.

Astra Degora skidded away. She tried to pull the same trick again, turning her focus to his back once more, but he turned and met her directly with his helmet touching her nose but not colliding. They quickly returned to dueling, without any hesitation.

"Did you think I would let you continue?" he asked.

Astra Degora didn't answer. Their breaths mingled in the air before they both carefully stepped back. The embers born from the conflict transformed into a blazing fire, sustained not by wood or sorcery, but solely by Orendor's might.

With Tungsten gaining the advantage, she was forced into a defensive stance, leaving little opportunity to escape or counterattack. He intensified his efforts while she poorly kept up with him.

This was indeed a dance. They were now surrounded by a sea of flames, waltzing on melting ice. Pieces broke and moved apart, some shifted and started to overlap one another.

Tungsten swiftly jumped onto a thicker platform and Astra Degora took the one across from him. The ice blocks ebbed and flowed as more and more started to break around them.

Tungsten smirked. "I do like your persistence."

Astra Degora looked down. The ice beneath her feet started to quake. A woman shot out of the water and slammed her to the ground, the impact caused the short swords to glide down the ice and sink into the lake.

The assailant was no mermaid, and certainly no water witch. She wore a gown that sparkled like a diamond under the sun. Her golden hair swayed as she and Astra Degora wrestled on the ice before she kicked her abdomen and sent her back to the water.

"Calibor!" Tungsten exclaimed.

Astra Degora looked at her hands, free from her blades. She took off her cloak and flung it behind her. With a grunt, she leaped into the water.

Tungsten cut Excalibur on the ice so it wouldn't sink again. He rolled his shoulders and dove into the cold abyss.

The lake was pitch black below but he could make out some light from the gown belonging to the maiden of the lake.

Bubbles surrounded Astra Degora and Calibor as they fiercely wrestled one another. Astra Degora seemed to be swimming upward but Calibor would pull her leg and bring her back down.

Tungsten kicked his legs with all his might, sinking deeper and deeper.

Calibor watched as Astra Degora stopped fighting, her body lingered there, unmoving. When she noticed Tungsten approaching, she told him to stop. "You're making a mistake."

Tungsten grabbed Astra Degora and started to kick upwards where the sun and warmth awaited. Each kick produced nothing, he was still far and would soon run out of air.

The Lady of the Lake grabbed his arm and with a power he didn't have, took to the edge of the lake.

Tungsten climbed the rest of the way back land, shivering and soaked with an unconscious Dranyth dangling under one arm. He fell to his knees, and freed her, allowing her to drop on the snowy ground. She managed to reclaim her short swords but remained still.

"Come on," Tungsten said, nudging Astra Degora's boot with his. "Wake up." He turned back to Calibor, or at least to the woman who took the form of his sister—it was hard to tell her apart. She didn't say anything but appeared upset at what he had done. "What did you do to her?"

"Only what she deserved," she said.

"That can wait until later." Tungsten uncurled her fingers with ease and moved the blades aside. Her bodysuit was binding her upper torso, possibly leaving little room for the lungs to expand. Her damp black hair was black as a moonless night sticking to her face. He brushed them aside, seeing her tanned skin had taken a bluish tone.

"She's not breathing." He took his helmet off, the weight carving into the ice lake.

"Why are you aiding her?" The Lady of the Lake asked.

"This Dranyth can disclose Prince Valte's plans." He gripped the fabric at the end of her chest and tore it in half, exposing her chest.

"She killed your sister," she said. "Is that not why you made the journey in search for?"

"Father once told me even the most heartless of beings bear the same sufferings as you and I. There is something in her eyes that I have yet to unveil."

"Metal king!" The waters that broke through the ice seeped out as if influenced by her emotions.

"I regret to inform you that you have made it abundantly clear that we are not siblings." He pinched Astra Degora's nose and blew air between her lips. He fed her steadily, watching her chest slowly rise.

After parting away, he observed her, lips parted, glistening from his own, but still unconscious. His mouth went back to hers, filling her with the warmth from his lungs again. Her skin gave a slight aroma, some kind of perfume the water couldn't wash away.

"Enough!" The Lady of the Lake called. "She's a Dranyth!"

"And she will die, but not now," he announced, tapping her cheeks. He went for another try and blew at a more even, and steadier pace. Something pained his side, but before he could make out the blade, a warm tongue swam inside his mouth.

Tungsten jerked back, touching the pommel of the blade at the same time. His body froze altogether, and he rolled to his side groaning in pain.

Astra Degora was awake. A gush of water dripped from his lips as she climbed back to her knees. She slyly licked her upper lip before flashing him a smile.

"You..." He crawled to her, gripping the snow and spitting the remaining water she put in his mouth.

Astra Degora reclaimed her other short sword and placed it back in the sheath.

Tungsten clenched his hands against the snow. Calibor was drawn back to the lake, disappointed.

Astra Degora crouched beside him and pulled out the blade from his side. As blood dripped, she used the tip to raise his chin. "Let this be the day you swallow two cold truths. You let your guard down, and I shoved my tongue down your virgin throat."

XVI

YOU'RE NOT A TROLL

The distant sound of chatter gradually pulled him out of this slumber. An aroma of spices brushed over his nose stirring him to open his eyes. Immediately the feeling of cold brought him to exhale. He touched his chest, feeling his skin, and trousers. He jumped and looked down finding he was indeed bare apart from his trousers.

Blasted. That Dranyth knew to remove his armor in his slumber.

Upon touching his face, relief swept over him when he felt the cold touch of his helmet. He got up and found himself trapped inside a steel cart with steel bars.

A group of people huddled around many campfires, their backs facing them as they conversed. By the look of the tents, they were a traveling group, much like Victor's party but it appeared that they were packing up.

"Fish soup is ready," an older woman said. Salmon appeared

to be their supper. They spoke with strange accents and were not dressed as soldiers or anyone remotely similar to Prince Valte's men.

Tungsten grabbed the bars and shook them. To his surprise, he only disturbed the people and their meal. They simultaneously fell silent as they faced him with unfriendly eyes. The color of their skin changed to tawny green wood, and claws grew from their fingers.

"Shapeshifters," Tungsten muttered. But what were they doing here? Disguised as common men and women?

A younger girl stepped out of the group to see what had caused the commotion. Her dark eyes fell on him with the same rage she bore before.

"Lily," Tungsten said. "What are you doing so far from Olivewood?"

Coming out of one tent was she, Astra Degora, covered in a blanket. "It's alright," she told Lily, her voice soft. "Everyone, fill your bellies; we're leaving soon."

Lily turned her back and sat with the others around the campfire. Her silence spoke louder than any words.

"Lily," Tungsten said again. "Are you being held against your will?"

The girl gave him one look and followed the others back into the forest, leaving him alone with the Dranyth.

Tungsten gripped the bars again and gave it a pull, hoping

his strength could bend the metal.

Astra Degora, seeing his effort, didn't seem worried. She sat by the fire, holding a tankard. "Lily chose to stay with her kind. At least, with what's left."

"Where are you taking her?"

Astra Degora was about to take a drink before she stopped to look at him. "Even now you ask for her well-being instead of yours. You are admirable."

"Answer me."

"Prisoners shouldn't ask questions they're in no position to demand." She grabbed a piece of some kind of tart from the bowl one of the shapeshifters left and took a bite. Such a treat was likely made or perhaps purchased from a town or village nearby.

Tungsten gave the cage another shake.

"You better not test the mechanism of that cage," she said. "Or did you forget your people made these cages for The Affliction War?"

Tungsten examined the composition of the cage with a focused look. It was all silver, expensive to make but perfect for Merlin the Old's spell to take effect. After the war, they were melted to help their economy. "Where did you get your hands on one?" he asked.

"You're not listening, are you?"

"What happened at the lake—did you kill my sister?"

Astra Degora seemed to have lost her appetite because she

dropped the tart and set her tankard down. "Perhaps you can ask these questions when I'm in the cage and you are free. You won't get a word out of me and you want to know why? Your ploy to save me from drowning for questioning flipped on you. You're my dog now, and soon you will see your kingdom fall."

Tungsten forcefully rattled the cage, causing the wheels to rise and slam on the ground.

The shapeshifters returned weapons drawn out but Astra Degora raised her hands to keep the others from coming closer.

The silver cage brightened to a porcelain glow static started to fill the air followed by the rumbling of clouds overhead.

"What do you intend to do to Excalibur?" Tungsten cursed. "Tell me your plans!"

A flash ignited and before he could say another word the bars vibrated from the surge of electricity. It coursed through his body like a thousand knives, dropping him to one knee.

Tungsten fought for air, still squeezing one bar. It felt as though a fever scorched his bones. His muscles were stiff, pulsing without control.

Astra Degora approached the cage, amused or satisfied by the result. "Most men piss themselves from that."

• • •

Toaren Mountains

The sun had gone past midday. The line of cliffs they followed was sharp and narrow, forcing horses to go one by one. Rocks crumbled with the slightest pressure, leaving a snap upon landing.

Astra Degora was leading them. He swore his armor was the large bag tied to her saddle. "Watch it," she warned the others. "One wrong step and we go down."

"Why did we half'ta take this path?" a shapeshifter who led the horse that pulled his cage said to his companion.

"Because it's faster." The other nudged him. "Now shut'ap before she hears you."

Tungsten crossed his arms and stared at the forests and unwinding terrain below. It was a fair distance, the gray stone, green gable roofs, life—civilization. He peered closer, recognizing a familiar mountain peak from his many visits to Atlios. The realization hit them—they were in the Toaren Mountains, overlooking the kingdom's border, where the majestic forests lay.

Tungsten leaned toward the bars and looked down. The fall would be about thirty meters high. One slip and a bed of deadly sharp rocks waited before reaching the forest grounds.

"Hmm." He stroked the side of his helmet. Such a height could be fatal for an Excalibarian. Without his complete set of armor, he might not have the legs or flesh left in his bones.

Tungsten touched the bars again, gently so he wouldn't

activate the spell. Merlin was resourceful and crafty, he'd made sure the interior of his cages was unbreakable but was the exterior the same?

"When do get off this mountain?" one man asked. "My legs are killing me."

The wagon began its turn around the mountain. If he was really going to do this, he had to act quickly.

I suppose I should never turn back from a challenge, even if it's the mountain itself. He looked to his right and saw Lily staring at him, eyes widening as if realizing what he was about to do.

Tungsten calmed the reminder of fire in his bones and slammed into the cage. The dormant magic awakened and unleashed another surge of electrical pulses.

"Oi!" the man said, taking out his blade. "What are you doing?"

Tungsten bit through the pain, went to the back corner and slammed into the cage again. This time the horses pushed back, and the noise rattled the others.

"He's gone insane," a shapeshifter said, backing away.

Tungsten rammed into the cage again, lifting the wheel slightly and causing it to lean.

"Everyone move back!" Astra Degora was trying to get through, but she couldn't squeeze through a narrow passageway of startled men and horses.

As pain penetrated his bones, the cage would lean again, but it wouldn't turn. Tungsten slammed into it again, again, and again causing more electric shock to penetrate him.

The carriage tipped, and the horse moved forward, trying to regain control. When he thought his efforts were for naught, he saw Lily push the raised wheel with her shoulder and screamed in pain.

"Child!"

"Go home," she winced. "Go back to where you're loved!"

The rocks crumbled under an unsteady horse and the cage leaned to the side. There was a moment of silence before he felt the descent. The man who drove the horse screamed and leaped off.

Tungsten curled into a ball as the world spun in a million directions, pounding and shaking him like sand in a bottle.

Gravity gripped him and shook his bones from the first impact. The electric spell stopped, but he wasn't suffering any less. With each blow, he saw flashes of his life. He saw his mother waiting for him with hands clasped in prayer as she looked upon the Round Table, in another, he saw himself fishing with his brother, Ecarus in the sunshine. One more and he saw his father carrying him on his back after his first battle. Calibor was missing, and it pained him not to see her.

When the world stopped spinning, he vividly remembered crawling out.

Lily's voice returned, and it gave him the courage to move.

"Home," he uttered, dragging himself from the wreckage. "I must... go home."

The ringing in his ears persisted. Every piece of him begged him to stop, but he continued thinking only of those memories.

A rock crumbled, leading him to look up. He doubted the shapeshifters would take the risk to catch him, but the Dranyth would.

Tungsten climbed to his knees and crawled away, blood leaked through his visor as he fought for air.

Atlios.

He was so close and yet the distance in his condition was impossible to reach.

His hand sank into a wet coat of moss, or at least it felt like it. The moss grew claws and trapped him, raising him from the ground.

"Meat," it groaned. "Meat!"

The moss melted, leaving hard scales protruding, and then a tail wagged from behind.

"By the gods," Tungsten laughed in mid-pain. "A dragon!"

"Servant of Orendor!" The dragon opened his mouth and tossed him inside. Tungsten reached for one of the teeth and held on. The dragon started to shake him off until he was flung and crashed into a boulder, having the wind knocked out of him.

The dragon wasn't as tall as he thought; his torso was short and one eye was glossed over, most likely blind. His mouth opened and flames spewed out.

Tungsten dove to the ground and rolled out of the way. He patted his chest, the solid reminder that he was without armor or weapon.

"Meat!" the dragon hissed. "Where are you?"

"If you keep behaving like that, Atlios' famous dragon slayers will come for you." Tungsten limped to the opposite side, seeking the shelter of a nearby boulder.

"Meat!" The wind of the dragon's tail swooshed, missing him as the dragon turned with flared nostrils. He breathed in, and flames rolled from his mouth. Each spark illuminated his scales, his slit pupils narrowed as he locked on him.

"Do you mind?" He panted, arm leaning on the tree. "You haven't given me a chance to catch my breath!"

A gust of wind swept past him, summoning her presence, short swords in hand as she faced the beast.

Instead of fire, a plum of smoke escaped the dragon's nostrils, leaving the flames flaring around his teeth. The smoke brushed across her as the dragon leaned toward her. His mouth didn't open, but his voice was booming, uttering something in a dialect Tungsten didn't understand.

"What did he say?" he dared to ask.

Astra Degora quickly raised one of her blades, silencing him. She responded to the beast with a rough usage of the r's rolling up her tongue.

The dragon's growl fell silent, and the noise of the forest came back.

"Shit." Astra Degora suddenly turned to him, her only eye visible to his wide. "Run!"

Tungsten didn't sprint, his shaking legs rambled all while the dragon's growl rumbled behind. The forest grew bright again, flashing by his sparks of fire.

Astra Degora gripped his arm and urged him to move faster.

"Careful," he winced. "I'm delicate."

"Oh shut up."

The flashing stopped, and the forest fell into darkness again. The next it was as if the entire forest suddenly went aflame. Tungsten felt a hard shove before crashing onto the ground.

• • •

Tungsten opened his eyes to a red forest. Wood crackled from the burning flames. His body pulsated with pain, recalling the biting heat that rolled over his body. He remembered climbing back to his feet, the shortness of breath as fled from the fires that had now caught up to him.

The smoke stung his eyes and brought him to cough. Beside him, a woman lay on her back unconscious, her short sword was half covered in ashes from the blast that knocked them out. He crawled to his knees and grabbed it. Without a second thought, he hovered over her, blade aimed at where her veins coursed through.

He raised the point to her neck. "How the tables have turned," he said.

She didn't respond.

"There's no need to keep up the act." The blade touched her skin enough to draw blood. Her life was now in his hands, but she didn't block him. "You and Valte will pay for what you did at Crystal Lake, for what plans you intend to do in my kingdom and this time you will answer every question!"

His booming voice caused the earth to shake beneath their feet. Nearby, the dragon loomed, its presence palpable in the air.

Tungsten gazed at the woman again, eyes shut, lips partly parted. "Blast you." He kept her daggers and used his free hand to grab her arm. With her securely on his shoulder, he made his way to the unscathed areas, avoiding the path where the flames had already passed.

As he trudged up the rugged terrain, the weight of the additional body he carried began to take its toll on him. Astra Degora slipped, bringing him to grip her waist to steady her. Women of her size were supposed to be light, but she was heavy.

"Hmm." With so much smoke and fire left to die out, he couldn't figure out the way to Atlios. For now, he had only to create some distance and avoid the falling branches and unbearable heat that wore him to his core. "I take it you came down the mountain empty-handed." He told her. "Wherever you left my armor, I expect you to retrieve it soon."

After a grunt, he felt her body jerk on his shoulder. "Cease your demands," she whispered. "Just finish me."

He squeezed her waist. "Not yet. I have questions that need answering."

"Perhaps we can waltz?"

He chuckled. "You and I are in no position to draw swords."

By trudging against the current, and climbing from the fire, Tungsten made it to a cool place that overlooked the rest of the forest. The flames didn't consume the whole forest, and the cold replaced the once scorching heat.

A campfire was lit, and for once in many days, he got some rest. Astra Degora sat across from him, leaning on a tree with her hand on her side. Now and then, she would fall asleep and wake up gasping until she saw him and grew silent.

Lady luck had guided him. From afar, Atlios awaited, bearing an impossible route to take in the dark but at the very least closer to home than he imagined.

"Where did you get these blades?" Her short swords were still in his possession. The craftsmanship was rather odd; there was fire emanating from them. Nothing like tanium, but it was tanium nonetheless.

Astra Degora appeared bothered that he had her blades in his hand, but she did nothing about it. As he guessed she must be wounded.

"I lied," he said. "I didn't save you solely for reclaiming my armor, but because you saved me." Her focus shifted back to the fire. He squeezed the hilt, prompting her to look at him. "Since you won't talk, I will see to your wound."

Her one widened eye looked almost ridden with terror before they narrowed. "You will *not* lay a finger on me."

That was out of the question. He was sore and suffered burned marks on his shoulder and upper back, but her breath was labored and she appeared to be growing a fever.

"Step back," she said after he invaded her space.

"Quiet, you'll stir the monsters if you shout, and I only wish to meet one dragon per night."

"There are much worse to meet than dragons."

"Yes dear, you."

"Don't call me—"

Tungsten grabbed her right wrist. Her left fist came to strike his side, but he caught it and held it with one of his hands. He paused briefly, aware of how small she was, both wrists in one grasp. Blinking away, he looked at her leg, finding the outer layer of her leather pants torn. Her upper thigh had a gash, enough for blood to pour out freely.

Tungsten laughed. "And here I thought you were

immortal!"

She sank her teeth into his arm, bringing him to wince. He placed his palm on her forehead to free himself but she was like a rabid animal. "Release me!"

"Lower your voice." He pressed his hand on the gash to her upper thigh, and she hit her head on the trunk of the tree, this time withholding her scream. It seemed she too knew there were much worse things to encounter than dragons.

He grabbed her blade and laid it over the flame.

"You can let go of my wrists now."

"So you will cooperate?"

One eye stared back, the other obediently hidden behind her layered hair. Tungsten released her, and she relaxed, staring at her blade in the fire.

"You're mighty strong," he commented.

Her eyes never left the flames. "I wasn't then."

His interest piqued, but he doubted she would answer. This woman was rightfully intimidated by him, but so was any animal that was hungry or cornered to survive. "This will hurt," he warned. He moved the blade from the fire and raised it over her thigh.

Astra Degora straightened her back and leaned into the trunk of the tree. She managed to look vulnerable at that moment.

"Why are you stalling?" she asked unmindful of his

thoughts.

"Nothing." Tungsten pressed the hot metal against her skin, it sizzled like hot iron on water.

Astra Degora's scream pierced the air, prompting Tungsten to quickly cover her mouth with his hand. The action suddenly caused her to scream more. She bit him again, but he endured it until he moved the blade out of her reach.

She still screamed, and he didn't know when to release his hand. She wasn't looking at him, but looking into the dark corner of the forest. He grabbed her and laced his arms around her. Holding her, he breathed her in, noticing the faint perfume on her body.

"You're safe," he said. "I won't harm you, not now." Her heart was pounding hard against his chest, enough for him to realize women had beating hearts too.

Astra Degora calmed down, and when she looked up, he froze and stared back. "You can release me now."

"My apologies." He let go and gave her room to move back to her spot. She tore what remained of her pants and tied it around her wound. The fire revealed where the blood had run, and there he saw a mark he did not expect.

A red tattoo of a dragon scale.

He was a bit perplexed by the symbol, the reminder of who she was. Before Excalibarians, it was Dranyths who were first blessed by nature's Gods—the ancient dragons. This woman had unthinkable strength and speed that was unmatched by his kind, but then, just how many remained after the war?

"You're not the last Dranyth, are you?"

Her gaze fell on him. She said nothing at first before her focus shifted back to the flames that always seemed to claim her mind.

"The war is over," he added. "I won't hunt your kind."

"You act surprised, metal king, that I'm here, but you're lying." After securing her wrap, she leaned back on the trunk of the tree. "Was it not you who sent your knights to hunt any survivors?"

Tungsten chose to sit cross-legged instead of returning to his usual spot across the dying campfire. "My father's advisors requested we measure the threat level of any survivors, so the past wouldn't repeat itself, so your bombs wouldn't enter our kingdom like they had when Orendor was attacked." He placed his hands on his knees and leaned towards her. "I stopped the search nine years ago, but it was started again because my advisors could not take the risk. Certainly one of you had to have survived, and... here you are."

"Then you have your answer."

He leaned back and crossed his arms. "Do not jest."

"Fifteen knights, that's how many didn't return to report to your advisors."

Tungsten said nothing. Fifty were sent in the span of nine

and a half years. Fifteen were reported missing, their bodies were never found, and there were no witnesses for foul play to take a role. By the accurate number, Astra Degora must've taken care of them. He turned to look at the blades he tossed out of her reach, of the tanium metal.

"It happened long ago," she said. "I found the tanium metal by mistake and kept it with me for a long time. Making explosives is my expertise, but like anything new, I studied its properties."

Tungsten crossed her arms, unconvinced. "No man or woman can melt tanium, only the fires of my God can melt them."

She shook her head, unconvinced, and that made him more curious. "By mere chance, I met... no I was saved by an old dragon who tested your precious metal. It was through her aid that I stood a fighting chance against you giants, but even revenge cannot heal old wounds." Astra Degora looked up at the stars. She raised her palm toward the air and closed her eyes. "Do I believe there are more Dranyths out there? No, I don't have that answer. Perhaps some survived but chose to start over, forswearing their former life. We are servants, and anyone who doesn't serve the dragons, are Dranyth no more."

XVII

NOT ALL WHO ARE STRONG START THEIR JOURNEY WITH STRENGTH

An owl hooted now that dying embers burned in the distance. The fires never spread throughout the forest as the dragon that caused them had put them out. According to Astra Degora, the dragon spent many years hiding so close to a kingdom, that it wouldn't dare cast any more unnecessary attention than his hunger for food.

After some time, the Dranyth appeared to have fallen asleep again. Did she not care that her enemy watched her or was she confident he wouldn't hurt her?

"What are Prince Valte's plans with Excalibur?" She opened

her eyes, but her gaze fixated on him. "If you cooperate, I'll consider giving you a lighter sentence for your crime, however, that choice is up to my people."

Astra Degora hissed and spat at the ground. "To *hell* with your people."

Tungsten pressed on her thigh again, and she bit her bottom lip. Droplets of sweat formed on her forehead when she tried to readjust herself. "*Your* people pushed two decades of unnecessary bloodshed, took my brother to an early grave, and wounded Orendor into exile! Do not think you're in a position to deserve any accommodation."

"You sound proud of the shortcomings of your world Giant King. Was it not your father and Merlin the Old who deemed us as dangerous?"

"*You* sided with the dragons and monsters who ravaged innocent villages." Lily and her father came to mind, and he squeezed her thigh. "And those bombs you wield, the mortars blasting into the sky and tearing limbs—were their lives not valuable?"

"You complain about our bombs when you wield Orendor's strength and hide behind your precious tanium, making it impossible for an average man or monster to break."

"My armor's sole purpose is to keep me alive, and my strength is my own." He shut his eyes and breathed for patience, but it was dwindling. Every word she uttered stirred the flames of that night. Dranyths invading his borders with explosives, of the dragons soaring over the darkened clouds to infiltrate Orendor's temple. His mountains quaked from that attack. It was so sudden that when Tungsten awoke, he was no longer on the battlefield but recovering in his room. His mother said he passed out from exhaustion. They found him curled, hugging his sword, half buried by other Excalibarians who were older and dead.

Astra Degora grabbed his wrist to move him off her thigh but his hold didn't loosen. "You fool. The dragons were going into exile. In slaughtering the lower dragons as part of your campaign, you tell me who made it personal first?"

Her words sank into his mind like poison. He squeezed her thigh once more and leaned toward her. A loud clank penetrated the side of his helmet. Seeing a rock in her hand, he grabbed her arm and flung her back, sending her rolling to the ground. She charged at him, teeth clenched with no regard for her condition, and kicked him.

Tungsten went crashing onto his back. Just as she was about to reach for her blades, he rolled over and thwarted her attempt. While trying to rise, she struck his helmet.

"Dammit!" She bounced on one foot while holding the other.

Tungsten got up, her blades tightly in his hold. His shortness of breath grew. "Do not speak to me about dragons. When Excalibur was attacked, I spent the longest nights of his life listening to the flaps of their wings flying over Excalibur." He wanted to protect Orendor's temple, but that job was for his father and his brother. Even with the weight of the sacred and noble responsibility bestowed upon him, he couldn't shake off the turmoil running within. "Nothing has been the same since... Orendor left while I was in recovery, leaving no instruction."

Anger boiled inside Tungsten and with no escape he charged at her with her blades but she dodged his swings.

"Do not underestimate me, Recluse King. I'm the only woman capable of defeating you."

Tungsten grabbed her shoulders, and she grabbed his. He attempted to lift her, but he was unsuccessful. But in pushing her back, she crashed into the tree. Like a phantom, Astra Degora left an illusion of herself and disappeared with the night.

"On might alone, Excalibarians are strong," Astra Degora said in the night. "But you're all still slow."

He looked at his surroundings and listened for her footsteps, where she slipped close until she hit him with an uppercut, sending him crashing onto his back.

She cursed, blowing air on her knuckles.

Tungsten laughed. The past consumed him so completely that the punch acted as a reset button for his thoughts. The night bore an uncomfortable chill, and yet, the ground made it enticing to simply lie still and revel in the comfort.

Astra Degora circled him, searching for where he kept her

blades. Despite her size, she possessed a strength that was equal to his.

His heart skipped a beat once more, and he cursed himself inwardly. "You know," he began. "If there was a way where man and beast could live in peace, then there would be no need for war. They outnumbered us, kingdoms could barely protect their own, and resources were scarce. Life for humans could barely hang on."

"You didn't go through anything, Excalibarian. You lived behind your wall, blind to what the war has done to those you now pity. You could not stomach watching the slaughter of your kind and being helpless to do anything."

Tungsten sat up, his swift move forcing Astra Degora to leap back. "Why are you afraid? Did you not say you're capable of defeating me?"

"Not all who are strong start their journey with strength. Even now I struggle with that knowledge."

"Such are the matters of war."

A cold silence descended upon them, made even more biting by Astra Degora's stiff posture. He thought he had sealed their discussion, but then she hunched over and began to chuckle.

Tungsten climbed to his feet, confused by her amusement, at the mocking way she laughed. "Tell me, Giant King, are your people not bound to uphold a high moral principle before

Orendor?"

He didn't know where she was going with this, but he felt a discomfort stirring in his stomach. "Yes."

"Then *such* are the matters of war. Until the end of time, soldiers will kiss their mothers, wives, and children goodbye as they venture out like cattle following a butcher." She spun and turned to him. "What do such soldiers do in solitude I wonder? What more than living out their urges they otherwise can't do at home?"

"Excalibarians would never—"

"Oh, but I've seen it from a particular rank among your kind. How they tortured and abused someone else's mother, someone else's wives, and tore the limbs of innocent Dranythian children."

Her amusement faded, and she stared into the flames with a vacant expression. Tungsten saw in them how the light reflected an anger and the emptiness she wasn't afraid to carry. "What did you see?"

"What I saw was that I could not kill any Excalibarian then." Her stare moved to him, and in them he saw the fire caught in her eyes, swirling in a circular motion without a break. "Have you ever been at home one moment and the next listened to the cries of your people forever echoing in the distance?"

"What happened?" Tungsten asked, his heart drummed by the unsteady feeling in his chest. "Who did this?"

"Your own flesh and blood, the heir of Excalibur."

"No!"

"He and his unit surrounded our village when our best fighters had gone to fight. He saw the weak stayed back, sick girls like me, the old, and mothers-to-be. I should've bitten my tongue like the others who knew what awaited but I fled. My bombs steered them off for a while, but my escape was short-lived. The prince of Excalibur and his captains took from me what should've been mine to give, shattering me into unmendable pieces." Astra Degora leaned by the tree, her eyes never left the comfort she probably saw in the fire. "When the light came, the remnants of my home had all been ash. They bonded me with stone and threw my body into Three Rivers, the exact one you and your friend fell unto."

Tungsten clenched and unclenched his fists. He recalled the rune stones during his chase to catch up to Lancelot and the centaur. A community that once thrived had been erased by the hands of his own brother.

Tungsten got up, but he didn't know why he moved at all. Perhaps it was because his heart seemed to have frozen in his chest. Despite his efforts to balance on his feet, it did not ease the buildup of acid he felt trying to tear open.

Astra Degora blinked from the fire. "And so laughing King, we can both now agree that such are the matters of war."

Tungsten released the hold of his tongue, the taste of iron

seeping through his teeth as he ground them. He breathed deeply, hoping to gain some composure. "If you want these swords back, you shall return my armor in Toren."

• • •

Main Road to Atlios

It was near midday when he reached the public road to the proud and hospital city in the kingdom of Atlios. Everything hurt; his trousers were charred and torn at the calves. At least he managed to get through the night without being held against his will or sought by another beast that detested him.

Astra Degora's empty stare returned. The burning hate in her voice was genuine when she retold what his brother had done. Her strife with Excalibur was enough reason for her to work with Valte and kill his sister.

The walls of a noisy city were coming up. Having traveled on the road and seeing only towns and villages, the sound was a soothing presence for his troubled thoughts.

Coming up the road on horseback were two familiar faces he thought he'd never see, Rella and the young Merlin.

The boy smiled wide as he caught his breath. "We saw a great smoke from a distance and thought it had to be you."

"That it was."

"You look horrid, and your armor, what became of it?"

"I will know soon enough."

Rella, upon seeing him, looked perplexed. "So, *you* were the king of Excalibur this entire time?" She looked at Merlin. "I swear you were not wearing a helmet when we spoke."

Merlin grinned. "I promised him nobody would remember his face."

"Good to see you hold to your word," Tungsten said, heading for the city.

Merlin nudged his horse to catch up to him. "You left before I could tell you what the stars said."

"I don't need fortune telling."

"Wait just a second," he stammered.

"Merlin," Rella said. "The king sounds convinced and don't you see he appears to be in a dull mood?"

Without wanting, his brother came to mind, followed by Astra Degora's claims. Such rumors never crossed the ranks of his men, and as far as he knew, Ecarus was a gentleman. He never saw him mistreat or force himself on any woman, even in a drunken state when many women tried to bed him for his crown.

Blasted. He had been going at this in circles again.

Merlin dismounted his horse and walked alongside him. Tiny as he was, the boy wasn't the fearful wizard who was afraid of his own shadow, but he also wasn't the strong old wise man he looked up to. Seeking counsel was out of the question, not when the condition was a family problem.

"I'm not great at reaching you, am I?" Merlin grabbed his compass and rubbed his thumb over it. "I'm a stranger, after all, and I can't keep the memories of my old self to prove I'm trustworthy."

"That is the natural order."

"But I'm different."

"You're a scrawny young man." He placed his hand on the top of his head. "Are you sure you haven't filled yourself with visions of grandeur?"

Merlin groaned and moved away. He ruffled his blonde hair in the same way Merlin the Old used to do out of frustration. "My gifts are for good, you're wrong to think I'm doing this to inflate myself."

"Then heed my advice and put more focus on becoming a powerful wizard, star seeker." There was no point in seeking any wisdom, what he needed to do was return to Excalibur, even if he returned with a wizard the boy was inexperienced.

Merlin stared at his fingers, bony and without callouses. "But I've survived this long without depending on power. Strength is nothing compared to knowledge. That's why the previous Merlin the Unremarkable failed and why Merlin the Old died."

"How would you know if you have no memory of how they fell?"

"In seeking the stars, I have something to offer that they couldn't." Merlin pressed his compass to his chest, a grasp that told Tungsten he was holding it for dear life. "I was reborn for this encounter, to warn you so that you may meet your destiny. Your kinghood shall one day lead these lands to another king but it has yet to come for his existence relies on your choices."

Tungsten tilted his head. "A king you say?" He shook his head. "Knowledge would not have stopped my sister from being killed."

"Your foolish thinking is the cause of that." Tungsten stopped, and the horses stepped aside as if responding with fear. Merlin, seeing he upset him, shrank before him. "Forgive me, I misspoke."

The gates to the city were coming up, and he had much to do beforehand. For now, he had to entertain the boy. "Since you came this fair to aid me. Tell me what warning the stars have for me."

Merlin looked at Rella, who nodded approvingly. The boy shut his eyes and raised his hands in the air. Slowly, the stirring wind pulled at his robes and his hands started to glow with the blue swirling patterns. When he reopened his eyes, they were white. A deep, darker voice took over his youth, one he recognized when he was a child.

"Merlin the Old," Tungsten said. "It's you."

"It is and isn't him," said Rella. "Now listen before he fades."

"Tungsten," Merlin the Old said.

"Teacher," Tungsten said. "I never thought I'd hear your voice again. You left us too soon, without telling us why."

"I ventured far in search of the truth, of the mistakes I unknowingly committed. Now our wrongs seek revenge."

"Felmid," Tungsten answered. "Prince Valte wishes to claim Excalibur for his own."

"Shadow again?"

"Don't interrupt him!" Rella warned.

"I must!" He asked. "What has happened to Excalibur?"

"To save your kingdom, you must eliminate the shadow, of the past, and shadow that bites at your heels."

Astra Degora came to Tungsten's mind again. The clouds parted and the blue markings faded from the boy's skin. The color of his eyes returned, followed by a look of worry. "At last," he said, eyes watering. "I have finally released this weight on my chest, one I held for long all these years."

Tungsten rested his hands on his hips. He must return to Excalibur, now sooner than later. He marched on to enter the gate.

Merlin followed, asking him to slow down. "Hold steady,

mighty king. Your mercy, fears, and pain; all of it has been cast beyond the stars and is far from fate's grasp. The choices you make from here on will damn this place or save it."

"Merlin," Rella said. "I think he understands the weight. There is no need to press him even further."

They joined him and entered the city. Now there was one thing left to do.

• • •

Atlios

50 Miles to Excalibur

A crowd of Atlians surrounded Tungsten. Even without his armor, they knew from his helmet the king of Excalibur walked among them. Many made paths for him, some bowing, but most of them cheered and begged him to look their way.

It was too much for Merlin, and he broke from the crowd, saying he would meet them later. Rella stayed with Tungsten, enjoying the attention.

"Lord Tungsten!" a woman wailed. "Lord Tungsten!" Several more shouted from the rooftops, waving their handkerchiefs.

Tungsten bellowed a laugh and waved.

A flower girl ran to his side and offered him a fistful of

Snowdrops. He took them and her face reddened.

"You must forgive me for my behavior," Rella said. "If I had known you were the king."

"Water under the bridge."

"But you know." She smiled, and he saw that same mischievous look again. "If I did flirt a little, it must be because I liked what I saw."

Tungsten shrugged. "Or maybe Merlin made you think so."

She frowned and looked the other way. "He wouldn't mess with my mind like that."

The baking store they passed jingled from the door opening. Behind, a baker left his store and offered him a loaf of bread. "It's so good to see you, M'lord!"

Across the street, a store owner handed him cured ham, cheese, and nuts.

Rella commented on how generous the city was.

"Hmm." Tungsten took a hearty beat of the cured ham. "I spent a few months in this fine place and acquainted myself with the locals."

"Just because you're a king?"

"And I am a childhood friend of the princess, Lady Casana."

Rella crossed her arms. "Now I'm more upset that Merlin erased my memory of your face. Just so you know, I wouldn't have told anybody."

"Traditions must not be broken." Tungsten offered her the

loaf of bread and she took it. If Rella couldn't recognize him, then the boy must have done the same to the others in Kemri. Now there was one more person left who knew his face, and Merlin the Old marked her as one of his prime enemies.

The crowd brought the attention of the guards who separated the horde that followed him. "Give the king his peace," they commanded, dispersing them.

Merlin, who waited ahead at the corner, appeared impatient fidgeting with his coat, tapping his left foot.

"He's a strange one, is he?" Tungsten said.

Rella only smiled. "He's anxious around big crowds and doesn't do well with new faces. I think it has to do with his past lives."

"Merlin!" Tungsten called. "Come over!"

"Oi!" Rella took his arm. "Not so loud; everyone knows that name."

Tungsten looked at her hand and she released him with a chuckle.

Merlin joined them, hushing them. "Please lower your voice. I'm not too fond of people."

Tungsten smacked the young boy's back and laughed. "If I haven't met the strangest Merlin of them all, I surely have met him now!" Merlin groaned, growing red in the face. "There is something I wish to ask since you claim to have all knowledge."

His annoyance turned to a smile. "Go on."

"What do you know about fairies?"

He seemed surprised by his question as his face scrunched for a moment. "They're maidens who have given up our world for a world of fairykind."

Morgên and the ladies of the lake, standing on the surface of the water returned. "Can they take the memories of others?"

"There is not much known about what they can and cannot do. They're private creatures." He crossed his arms and placed his index finger on his chin. "But since you mention it, it's possible."

"Why do you ask?" Rella said. "Don't tell me you swooned for one of those seductresses."

"Curiosity is all," Tungsten called to the nearest guard. The man's shoulders tensed up before he ran to him. "Fine man, is there any news from Excalibur?"

The man cocked his head. "No, Your Majesty."

"Has Sir Lancelot come through here?"

"I'm afraid I don't know, but if there is news, perhaps Princess Casana knows. Would you like me to notify her of your arrival?"

Tungsten adjusted the short blades on his hip. "I will come to her very soon."

The guard saluted him and left.

Tungsten's stomach twisted into knots. If they were unaware of his supposed disappearance or Calibor's death, then it meant that the news was intentionally hidden. If Lancelot survived and sent word as he said, he would have at least come here as he planned.

"Is something the matter?" Merlin asked.

"I'm worried." He looked up at the sky. Excalibur was not far, and yet information had not been leaked? No matter. He wasn't far from home. "I must see Lady Casana, only I'm expected to meet someone very soon."

"Send me," said Merlin. "I am small and light as you said and swift on my horse."

"Do you think they sell any good medicine here?"

Tungsten spun toward the smooth voice and found Astra Degora covered from head to toe, looking at a vendor's herbs. She didn't look him in the eyes, but it was her indeed.

"Perhaps you can come with us," Rella said, pulling his attention. "Whoever you are to meet can wait."

"No, this I have to settle."

Merlin looked at Rella, who shrugged. He wasn't going to explain, but it was safer if they weren't near him while *she* was lurking about.

"Then we're off," Merlin said.

"Don't worry, he has me," Rella said, winking at him.

After they left, he turned back to the same stall and found her gone. "Very well Dranyth."

Whether she was going to follow him or not didn't matter.

She made her presence known to tell him she was going to meet her end of the bargain.

• • •

Inns were an important business in Atlios since there weren't neighbors or villages between civilization and the major forests. Tungsten's favorite was a three-story inn with spacious rooms and a grand room for baths.

Bard was his old friend and innkeeper. His smile fell as he measured the state of his torn tunic and trousers. "Great Goddess of Spring, what happened?"

"Nearly got taken by a dragon."

"A dragon?" he asked with wide eyes. "Leave it to me to replace them. We have many Excalibarian-sized tunics and trousers at my sister's store."

"That would be wonderful."

"And I will prepare your usual lovely room with a wonderful bath."

"That would be marvelous, only...." Tungsten patted his trousers. "I don't have any coin on me."

Bard laughed. "Your Majesty please."

A young woman came down the stairs. Her face grew red

before she ran to his side. "Tungsten!"

"Sendora, address the king appropriately. Now go prepare his bath," Bard said, giving her the key. "Stay as long as you need, Your Majesty. And please do not worry about any coins."

"Thank you. I shall not forget this." He stayed a bit longer, bringing Bard to a wide smile. "Have you heard any news from Excalibur?"

Bard wrinkled his nose as if surprised to be asked. "None, Your Majesty." He looked at the state he was in once more. "Should we be concerned?"

"I don't know," he said. "But I have a favor to ask."

• • •

The iron pipe above dripped the last few hot drops upon his wide tub built for him to fit in and deep enough to reach his lower waist. Steam had covered the room, allowing an aroma of spices to fill the room.

Tungsten cupped the clear water and looked at his reflection. With his helmet covering his face, he sometimes forgot what he looked like. Even in the palace, when he could walk freely without armor, he always kept his helmet. Perhaps there was something about his armor that he couldn't let go, and he wondered if it had to do with what Astra Degora said, about tanium and the many times he dodged death.

The power of her tale penetrated, leaving him with lingering questions he hesitated to confront out of fear of guilt. If crimes were committed by his people, someone had to know, and whoever did, kept it from him.

His father's advisor and his mother often oversaw foreign affairs, but if they knew, why conceal it from him?

"What a fine bath." An invasive voice brought his attention to the shadow lurking in the corner.

"You!" Tungsten got up, and Astra Degora's gaze fell between his legs. He dropped back into the water, causing a big splash. "I expected you would make this kind of entrance."

"Then why are you surprised?"

"Because." He felt his manly hood shrink in the water. An embarrassment swept over him. "Do not look at me."

"Why?" That sly smile. It was nothing like the anger he saw in the forest. "You think I'm predatory?"

"I'm trying to salvage whatever remains of my reputation." He turned his back to her to finish his wash. "One you are invading by looking at me and..."

"Kissing you?" she asked. "I only did it to distract you."

He said nothing.

"Oh...," she continued. "It *was* your first."

He heard something fall on the floor, but it wasn't heavy or metal. Soft steps walked around him until her buttocks were the first thing he saw.

Tungsten drew a heap of air. "What are you doing?"

"Do you think I had time to wash since we left that forest?" The two braids were unmade, leaving an even wave to fall on her backside. There were old scars across her back, along we keloid wounds crossing her arms and thighs.

When she turned to face him, Tungsten used his hands to cover his visor. He listened to her dip into the water before she completely submerged inside, splashing excess water onto the floor.

Tungsten slightly moved a finger, and he saw the tattoo of the dragon scale on her thigh alongside the fresh wound he seared with her blade.

"Relax and give me room." She leaned between his parted legs. "Or are you not accustomed to seeing a naked woman?"

His chest pounded from her daring, foolish question that bore an easy answer. He cleared his throat to regain control. Bathing with him was the shadow he was to defeat, and he was recoiling like a child.

Tungsten uncovered his eyes. Astra Degora wiped the soil and ash from her arms, and from his view, her breasts were in his line of sight, half dipped in water.

"We have to talk," he said sternly.

She leaned forward abruptly as if something disturbed her washing.

He looked down and saw his manly hood had come out of

hiding. Tungsten shifted his legs to his chest and turned so his back was to her. "What does the dragon scale on your leg represent?"

"You truly are the recluse king," she said. He jumped when she pressed her back against his. "It's permanent, much like you Excalibarians are born with strength and your impeccable physique."

"You're missing some details," he said. "Young Excalibarian boys suffer from flushed cheeks until we become men."

She didn't answer, so he turned slightly and found she was looking at him. This time he stared back, finding her gaze slightly wide.

"What is it?" he asked.

"Is this what you wanted to talk about?"

"No." He turned back. "Did you fight during the war?" He meant to bring up Ecarus and what happened to her but it was harder to repeat.

"I was born ill and weak but was gifted enough to create explosives that went beyond the usual mixture of saltpeter, sulfur, and charcoal. It was more than my duty, it was a craft for me, crafting an effective mixture that could ignite a blast so strong it would stop the war and put an end to all I feared I would lose."

"Back when you said you were tossed into the river…"

"So that's what you wanted to talk about?"

"I didn't want to—"

"I'm not afraid to recall what occurred."

"Then how did you…"

"Survive?" She finished. "You fell into it yourself. The river the water which reigns is dangerous. I suppose they didn't expect me to make it out alive, and neither did I. With a boulder wrapped around me, I was too weak to cling onto anything. Luckily, the sharp, jagged rocks loosened my bind to the boulder. Even so, I was pulled to my very death until I was rescued by a dragon, an ancient one who was on her way to the Isles of Avalon."

"I see…" Tungsten cleared his throat. "And who did the war take from you?"

"Aside from my village? Four brothers and my parents."

Tungsten grabbed his loofah and handed it over to her. "You said you were an ill child?"

Astra Degora reached for it and took it. "I come from a lineage of skilled fighters who have faithfully served the ancient dragons for generations. My training began at the age of five, only as I already stated, I was too sick to complete it. Aside from suffering many fevers, I would sometimes lose control of my body. I'd lose consciousness and convulse uncontrollably."

"Looking at you now, it doesn't appear so."

Astra Degora scoffed, and he felt her lean towards his back shoulder. "Is that a compliment?"

237

"No." His back stiffened when he felt her breathing brush against his skin.

"And you? You must've been raised well or were you sheltered?"

"There wasn't a day I didn't train. When I turned ten, I came before Orendor and vowed to serve as Excalibur's stronghold, to set aside desires common to man. Since then, that has always been my duty."

"How noble." A finger swam up his shoulder blade, and he shuddered. "You were never tempted?"

Tungsten jerked his shoulder from her. "Never." He got out not caring what she saw and went for his towel. "I trust you brought my armor?"

"That depends, do you have my swords?" She followed after, taking the robes that were left for him, and covered herself.

"Produce my armor."

"Relax, Recluse King, I just need you to cooperate with me just a while longer."

"You meant to tell me to Excalibur, weren't you? Why must you be the one to deliver me?"

Astra Degora calmly walked to him. She never tied her robe, but allowed it to part in the center. In trying not to look, his vision blurred. He stepped back as if the mere distance would give him control.

"What's this?" he mumbled, seeing a smile curl the corner

of her lips.

"What's what?" she asked with an innocent tone.

Feeling gravity pull him, he crashed into the table. His fingers were tingling, all the way down to his toes.

In a crouched position, she observed him closely, her breath held in anticipation. As his eyes met hers, he couldn't help but notice the allure of her exposed breasts.

"Did you hear me tell the vendor what kind of medicine I was looking for?" She grabbed both arms and dragged him to the next room. "With the right combinations, some herbs can turn lethal, at least enough can take down a big ogre like you."

It took some effort, but she managed to roll him onto the mattress. She quickly grabbed the chains she had prepared and locked his wrists to the post. On the table were her short swords—the ones he had hidden with the innkeeper.

"Did you kill him?" he grimaced.

"That would be a stupid call." Her breathing quickened and sweat glistened on her forehead.

Tungsten chuckled. "It appears the ingredient you put in my bath is starting to affect you."

"Self-sacrifice is a powerful weapon, capable of inflicting the greatest damage." Her limbs buckled, and she came down on him, landing on his chest.

He let out an exasperated sigh, annoyed by the woman's actions. She was dangerous, repulsive, and intoxicating. She'd do anything in her power to get the last laugh—his laugh.

"I am enjoying this waltz," he admitted.

A MUCH STRONGER KIND OF METAL

The doors leading to the balcony breezed through bringing a combination of coldness and heat from the crackling fireplace.

Astra Degora was awake, observing the streets, the sound of horses passing by, and the noise of the citizens. She wore the black body suit she had worn before, nothing new had changed.

Tungsten moved the chains, testing his strength when she started to walk back. Her daggers were neatly back in their holder, one to each side of her hips.

She climbed on the bed and went on her fours. When she inched closer, he pulled on the chains again. "Stop. I made an oath to remain chaste."

Her face scrunched. "I don't see any advantage in mounting

you." She moved on and sat on his upper thigh like he was a riding horse. "It amuses me how the opposite sex's presence unsettles you."

"You're not the first to tell me that." Tungsten looked at his bare body. The tower he had remained wedged between the bathing room, keeping the door from closing. "Why do I remain undressed?"

"I hate answering your questions, but this one isn't so bothersome." She unsheathed one of her swords and pressed it to his neck. "Being exposed in front of someone like me is truly degrading, isn't it?"

Tungsten relaxed and calmed his mind. "Enough, I'm fully aware of your plans."

"Oh?"

"This pursuit wasn't about killing but to ensure I return to Excalibur one way or another."

Astra Degora kept the sword pointed at him but she didn't respond. She never did when he guessed something right.

"Then why—why did Calibor have to pay—why did she have to die?"

"Save your outburst for someone who cares." She unmounted his thigh and sat on the side of the bed. "We leave tomorrow. If you test me one more time, you will never see your beloved armor."

Merlin the Old's warnings flashed back. Since he left Crystal

Lake, Astra Degora was that unkillable shadow haunting his every step. "If only you had prevented me from escaping that cage, things would be different now."

Astra Degora slightly turned but didn't look his way. "And why is that?"

"Because you didn't use strong enough poison." He broke through the chains and tackled her to the ground. Amid the power struggle, the room echoed with the clattering and tumbling of furniture.

"Your Majesty?" A knock came on his door. "Is everything alright?"

"Quite fine, Bard!" Tungsten sang. "There's nothing to worry about."

"As you say." His steps faded and Tungsten focused on the Dranyth.

She turned to knee him, he expelled some air but managed to lift her and slam her on the bed.

He had to sit on her to wrestle for her wrists, but she fought back, nails clawed at his skin in an attempt to free herself. When he took hold of both wrists in one hand he used his free hand to lace his fingers around her neck.

Without delay, Astra Degora's face started to turn red. He tightened his grip, and she gasped, fighting for air. She was smarter than this, wit enough to find some way out, and yet...

Astra Degora's eyes started to gloss over, she was coming in and out of consciousness.

The prince of Excalibur and his captains took it from me, shattering me into unmendable pieces.

Beware of the shadow.

They left me for dead.

Excalibur.

Tungsten screamed and released her, tossing her onto the floor. He looked at his hands, shaking as he plopped back on the bed.

Knowing right from wrong never burdened him. Given the circumstances, he knew when to take a life and when to step back. Now it was as if the truth and lies had switched sides. Were these poor execution and obstacles the consequence of Orendor's favor leaving him?

Astra Degora rolled to the end of the bed, hand clasping her neck. "Why... did you... stop?"

He couldn't answer. No, he didn't want to admit it but if he kept it within then it would poison, and he would find some way to justify it. "I've witnessed death, corruption, vile things man and monster can do to the weak. Even so, I was ignorant of what my own people could do. We serve righteously or we lose Orendor's favor. Perhaps because of what my brother did, he lost it and died." He looked at her, finding her sitting with her knees gently to the side, hand still on her neck, hair messy and over her face, eyes piercing his. "I believe I too have lost it or at

244

the very least and losing it." He got up and turned his back to avoid her gaze. "Recluse King, the name is befitting for one such as I. My destiny has never been to rule and while I didn't listen to what my father's general and captain said, deep down I knew this was a crime itself. I'm not befitting to rule—I never was. Perhaps the sins of my brother have rightfully made Excalibur your enemy, but what have I done to you?"

Astra Degora left the bed and went for the cloak on the side table. "You did nothing to me Tungsten." It was the first time she called him by his name, and it stirred something in his chest. "You and Calibor are innocent in this." Without looking, she went back to the balcony and looked up at the stars.

Against the moon, he could see her for what she was—a woman made of steel—no this was a much stronger kind of metal. The kind he wore, breathed, and fought in. But what hearth had been used to craft a killer like her?

"You'll return to Excalibur eventually," Astra Degora turned and her red eye started to glow. "So it doesn't matter if I bring you myself or not." With a cloak billowing in the wind, she climbed the rail of the balcony and gracefully leaped into the darkness of the night.

• • •

When morning came, Tungsten's thoughts circled deep in his mind and well into the day; thoughts of the choices he had made and of better ones he could've chosen.

No matter how hard he tried, his mind kept wandering back to Astra Degora. She stood as a reminder of everything he opposed—a bomb builder, an ally of monsters, and the catalyst for Orendor's departure. It was in that night and those long hours that he could finally admit to himself he felt something else, something that went against his oath.

The sound of the door banging shook Tungsten from his relaxed posture. He opened the door, but before he could say her name a fair maiden embraced him.

"Lady Casana."

"Tungsten!" she wept. "Whatever has happened to you?"

Tungsten relaxed and placed his hand on her blond head. "It's not proper for a lady like you to burst into a man's room."

She looked up and placed her hand on the side of his helmet. "You must be swift to Excalibur. Sir Lancelot awaits you in the tomb of the kings."

Tungsten's mouth fell open, but Lady Casana could not read his face. "Sir Lancelot is alive?"

Lady Casana blinked, confused. "Why yes of course?"

He laughed as he raised her and spun her, bringing her to laugh with him. "Thank the Gods!" He never thought he'd hear that name again. His bosom friend—alive!

Lady Casana wrapped her arms around him and silently wept.

Standing in the hallway were Merlin and Rella. Despite not hearing their footsteps, he deduced that they were purposefully maintaining silence to ensure that his meeting with the princes was undisturbed but he couldn't stay for chatter.

"I'm sorry but I cannot stay any longer." Tungsten gently let her down.

Casana gripped his arm, unwilling to let go. "I did as Lancelot asked and kept this news from my father. Please, allow me to speak to him so we can offer aid."

"I'd appreciate but we don't know the risks." He gently removed Casana's hand and walked back into his room. He stopped halfway when he looked at the table. His breastplate, lance rest, gauntlets, knee cops, and greaves were neatly laid out. Did she come back to return his armor as he slept?

"You cannot go alone," Casana said. "I saw a look of fear in Sir Lancelot's eyes. Something is wrong is it not?"

"If it's something like an invasion, that could never happen to Excalibur. My people could stand a one-hundred-year army without my rule. I fear this is something more and I must find out what."

"We'll get ready," said Merlin, surprising him.

Tungsten shook his head. "I wish to go alone."

"But Your Majesty."

"If Prince Valte has successfully infiltrated my kingdom, then it means he has my mother hostage." He placed his hand on the young wizard. "To you, it would be a death sentence. You have spent too much time studying the stars than test your might." He went behind the room divider and dressed in his armor. The weight and metal shifted until they fit him.

In the meantime, there was a discussion between Lady Casana and her knights, whom she made them swear to keep what they knew to themselves.

"Merlin," Tungsten called.

"Yes?"

The boy joined him behind the divider, and Tungsten placed his hand on his shoulder. "Are you certain of your prediction? Of the shadow becoming the force I must stop?"

His blue eyes shifted from one eye to the other. "Yes," he said. "The shadow is a threat to your destiny."

Tungsten nodded.

"And what if you run into Prince Valte and his people?" Rella asked. "You need us."

"She's right," Casana said. "If the alliance of the three kingdoms is broken, my father will aid you."

"Where I'm going is a secret passageway that only Lancelot and my family know. I will not risk any lives when I don't know the length of the threat Valte has in store."

Lady Casana gripped his shoulder. "Worry not, for you will not be entirely alone." Taking his hand, she led him to the balcony where he had to bow to get through.

Below, the busy streets of Casana's people went on as usual but across the street, something stood from the rest.

A giant cat with orange fur and dark stripes was neatly sitting growling at anyone who passed him.

"Indra!" Tungsten exclaimed.

His ears twitched when he looked up. Laughing, Tungsten leaped off the balcony and landed, breaking the sidewalk with his sheer weight. His cat roared startling the citizens to run as he crossed the street and tackled him to the ground.

"He came to us wounded!" Lady Casana shouted from the balcony. "He stayed, waiting as if he knew you would return."

Indra had his paws around Tungsten's helmet as he licked him and growled.

XIX

DO YOU WANT MY HELP OR NOT?

Whirling River

Indra sped like a racehorse past the borders of Atlios. His stealth was unseen from the lurking monsters, his powerful roars served as a threat to any who opposed him. They ventured through the climbing mountains and slopes of the unwinding lands.

The south was cool and warm, but the spices and the aroma of honey he missed were within his reach.

Whirling River broke from the heart of Excalibur's mountains and broke through to the lands beyond. After running into some obstacles, Tungsten and Indra made the riverbed their resting spot. The waters ran calmly, and the moon glistened, illuminating the night. From the distance picked up a woman's voice, singing, her tune calling out into the night, almost calling to him. Sirens often toured the rivers with their songs, but this one felt different.

Indra who slept on his right, rose to his feet. He growled at the incoming shadow, who shook the ground with every step. Tungsten readied himself, sword in his grasp.

A head popped up from the trees, and as it drew closer, the campfire revealed her grand stature.

"Giantess Florenda," he said. "It has been so long."

The fair maiden with red hair smiled. "Hello, Tungsten." Her voice was sensual and delicate despite her size. Her focus shifted to Indra, who stopped growling. "My boy, look how you've grown." Her hand smoothed over his coat and Indra licked her fingers.

"I thought you fled to the Isles of Avalon," said Tungsten.

"Heavens no," she scratched under Indra's chin. "After our fight, I decided to rest in the mountains."

"But now you've come to stop me."

She looked at him. "Yes, to squash you like the bug that you are, but I decided on this full moon to accept my fate." She looked out toward the river as if taken by the harmonious natural elements of the night. "The whispers of the night told me the Sun Princess has become a Lady of the Lake."

Tungsten, seeing Indra trust his former mistress, lowered his blade and went back to sit by the fire. "My sister is dead. I no longer care what happens to me as long as my people and mother are safe."

"So you're returning to your kingdom without a plan? How unbecoming of you."

Tungsten had no answer to that. He had been fighting Giantess Florenda since he was sixteen years old. She knew better than to know he was taking a great risk, unplanned, and poorly equipped.

In the silence, the giantess shifted back as if to leave but Tungsten stopped her. "Will you keep me company?"

She smiled and sat beside him. Indra cozied by her legs and fell asleep. The fire burned through the night, lighting only their still faces, with no thought to share but the comfort of company.

The murmuring river suddenly grew quiet, intensifying the sounds of the trees as they moved. Though the waters ran like it always had, a faint glow started to surface, then the face of a woman, peeking out of the river.

It was painful for him to see her eyes, knowing she wasn't the sister who danced in their ballroom.

"She waits," said Giantess Florenda. "Meet her."

Tungsten left the campfire and exchanged the tawny glow for the cool blue light the moon gave to the river. The woman who took his sister's form rose from the waters without any effort, her presence resisting the current. He examined her intently while she returned his gaze, devoid of Calibor's light, her warm smile. On her hip was Excalibur, the belt that held the scabbard was tied neatly around her waist.

"I need your help," he said. She didn't answer, so Tungsten pointed upstream. "The walls to Excalibur are guarded by Valte's men and two sand trolls on both the east and main gate. To enter undetected, I must enter through the secret passage, the gate hidden by this river, where the current is strong and the depths impossible to take."

"Pray thee tell me, why do you think I would help you?"

"I hoped you'd have that answer," he said. "You've been following me ever since we met. Near any body of water, I sensed you, saw the same floating crystals from the lake, and heard your voice but I waited, hoped you would remember what you told me at Crystal Lake."

The Lady of the Lake didn't seem to make the connections. His real sister would know that answer. Calibor said she would follow him and yet this woman didn't know.

Tungsten jumped into the river, and he reached for her, but she drifted back. "If want me to acknowledge you solely as a fairy, and not my beloved sister, then help me. If not for me, help our mother and people who once loved the Sun Princess."

The maiden of the lake pressed her hands to her temples. "Stop talking."

Tungsten swallowed the rest of his words. He went back to the shore feeling he lost the battle.

Giantess Florenda, who watched, appeared to have been

listening. Before Tungsten could retreat to his fire, she placed her pinky on his shoulder, stopping him. "Fairy, surely you have a reason for contesting this handsome king? At the very least, you owe him an explanation regarding the memories you hold."

The maiden of the lake looked at her. Her piercing blue eyes never gave off a faint glow. "My memories are but a fog in a maze without an exit. They are untrustworthy."

"Then tell us," Giantess Florenda said. "Let this king come to terms with what happened to you, even if you do not care about it."

The Lady of the Lake looked into her hands, dripping from water. "I remember seeing myself sink with a sword in my grasp. There was only the sound of singing to comfort me until I awoke by the shores, and all I could think of was this desire to find someone, to meet him, to protect him." Her shaky gaze shifted to him. "Yes, I have been following you, and I do want to help. But if I am your sister, why can't I call you my brother?"

Tungsten fell silent. He asked Merlin for answers and at the moment there was still nothing he could say in confidence. What comforts could he offer if he wasn't confident himself?

"Very well," she said. "I will aid you, but only so I can free myself from this longing to be near you."

XX

WHY AREN'T YOU IN ARMOR?

When Orendor left Excalibur, his presence made the mouths of the mountain glow like a summer sunset. His fire would pour down his abode, followed by his great laugh and the clashing of the hammer and anvil. There was so much metal to craft back then, with many tunnels and channels for fire and water. Now, most of the mountains were almost barren and hundreds of mines had been sealed. The minerals were gone and the ores of tanium became a dream.

It was then that his father knew the Orendor's reign was coming to an end. But there was a war to finish, and a dying God to protect until his departure to the Isles of Avalon.

"It's open." Calibor's voice echoed through the tunnels. Her presence illuminated the hidden passageway as she swam under the current and pulled the lever that lifted the gates, allowing for him and Indra to pass. The way was nothing like their halls. The place was musty, with walls dripping from the moisture.

Indra went first, knowing what lay ahead, while Calibor stayed close. Even in a place ridden in darkness, her silver gown sparkled, enduring the warping darkness and guiding them.

"How much longer?" Calibor asked. "We've been cutting through this tight space for two hours."

"It's because no one is meant to be here. Where we are going is a sacred place and my damaging of this place could alert the palace."

If she was his sister, she would've known. The realization didn't comfort him. He wanted the Lady of the Lake to be his sister, his Calibor.

"Say, remember when we were children, and we used to watch our father and brother come home from the war? They would always bring us something from their journey."

She said nothing.

"Sweets from whatever nearby city he could find them," Tungsten continued. "Dolls from Bengom for you."

Rather than respond, she swam ahead. "I see a faint light."

"We're close."

She swam under to pull the lever. The next she reappeared, giving the gates a strange look before swimming back down. By the third attempt, she told him the lever wasn't working.

"Hmm." Tungsten nudged the gates, sturdy and stubborn as they should be. "It looks like I'll have to go down there with you."

"The current is strong. You'll be swept away."

"I have no choice and Indra is a good swimmer."

She bit her bottom lip and swam back.

Tungsten patted his feline friend. "Ready?"

Indra gave the water a menacing look. They jumped and crashed into the water, but like a gust of wind, the current pushed him back. Tungsten held on to Indra, who kicked forward. He squinted into the dark until a light came near.

The lady of the lake took hold of his hand and guided him and Indra with ease. The passage under the gate was narrow; Indra went first, leaving the maiden to lead him, hand still holding his.

The Calibor he knew used to always hold his hand in the same manner.

The dark cavern echoed his gasp as he crawled back to the walkway. Indra licked his paw, confident of the outcome.

"Thank you," he said, taking heaps of air.

Calibor ignored him, facing the mouth of the cavern, dim but giving light from the white fire that burned forever in these parts.

Without a word, she went ahead, and he followed behind.

The water went around the sacred place from a river that emerged from under the mountain. The way out had many stairs to climb, bright as they were in his childhood, as they were when he last told Calibor goodbye.

"Indra," Tungsten said. "Go before me and seek my mother. I don't know what we'll encounter in the palace, but you know this palace better than anyone to go unseen."

Indra growled and went ahead without him. The maiden of the lake had gone near the shore where the tomb of Excalibur's kings lay. Her widened eyes fixated on Father's tomb, the lid slightly ajar. It had been shattered into pieces and his coffin lay tossed sideways. The sabaton that once covered his foot slipped off of his bony feet.

Tungsten swallowed his anger and focused on the shaken water maiden. "Do you... remember this place?"

She gasped and turned to him. Her eyes held a look of surprise, but she didn't confirm his thoughts.

"This is the tomb of our forefathers," Tungsten went to one knee. "Where we will one day call home."

She looked up at the high ceiling and the many passages that led to the other tombs.

"We used to play here in the summer, to get away from the heat." Tungsten reached out and took her hand, feeling relieved when she didn't resist. "When you married Prince Valte, we came here to escape the crowd. This is where we said our goodbyes before you left for Crystal Lake. You told me we would see each other again, right here, like you and I are standing now."

"Valte." The water from the river shot towards the ceiling and started to spin around her. Her hand squeezed his. "He... he killed me."

"Yes, I know."

"No, he *killed* me." Her eyes pleaded with him. "He poisoned me!"

"Yes, but..."

She gripped his shoulders, her breath quickening. "I should've been dead before you arrived. But then I felt pain in my lower back. I didn't see then what she was trying to do—not then!"

"Sister?"

The waters flooded in, rising into the tomb. She yanked away from him and went underwater. Tungsten jumped into the river, if the Lady of the Lake made any hasty moves, they would be discovered. Her light and the force of the current left with her. Out of the water, he hurried for the stairs.

The grand painting of his parents blocked the exit. It was partially opened by Indra, who had stepped on the stone that opened it. There was a crackle of a fireplace, and for a moment, he feared any movement of the painting would reveal him.

A woman in black stood idly by, facing the round table where, as a child, he pulled Excalibur from the center and became the kingdom's stronghold. The woman turned slightly and a sharp gasp left her. She wore a long black dress with gold threads that trailed along the edges of her sleeves and skirt.

"Mother?" His voice fell like that of a child.

A veil covered her face, so she raised it, revealing her sad eyes. "Tungsten." She lifted her dress and ran to him, nearly tumbling over her own two feet.

Tungsten gripped her in a tight embrace and felt her tremble.

"Indra leaped into my room from outside. There was only one place you could've done it." She looked up at him and held the side of his helmet as if trying to brush his cheek. "We don't have much time. Prince Valte has infiltrated your father's resting place and claimed his ceremonial sword. Felmidian guards have infiltrated the palace, and our people are within the walls of the mines." She squeezed his arm. "My son... your friend..."

Tungsten took her arms. He found comfort that she was no longer a dream that followed him. She was real.

Suddenly, something sank in his stomach. "Why aren't you in armor?"

Mother held her breath. "He wished it so. My boy... everything happened so fast. The palace was infiltrated by the explosions of Dranyth bombs. The same they used against us when they attacked Orendor. I thought they had returned, but to my surprise, Felmidian soldiers and Prince Valte came to our doorstep. He threatened to blast the city, and I couldn't risk the deaths of our people. Then I got your letter, but these monsters, the shapeshifters, dressed themselves as Excalibarians to hide any suspicions from our allies."

"Step back from the queen mother," a voice said.

Tungsten shielded his mother so she could put on her veil.

These soldiers had to have been following his mother since she left her room. Among the ranks of the Felmidians, he picked out a few Excalibarian knights, real ones.

"Out of my way." A knight cut through, bearing an appearance he found all too familiar. On his hip was his crossbow. The purple pauldron was polished, and taken care of since they left Excalibur. "Surround the King," Lancelot commanded.

The Excalibarian knights raised their blades and circled him.

Tungsten said nothing, he stared at his bosom friend as his Mother extended her arm protectively from the knights. "Sir Lancelot, and knights of Orendor, will you not acknowledge your king?"

Tungsten took her arm and lowered it, his sight never prying from his friend. "Sir Lancelot, what is this?"

Lancelot's eyes, usually filled with sourness and grumpiness, now glimmered with an unfamiliar look—a look of pure hatred. Nevertheless, the knights who surrounded them crept ever so closely.

261

"Hand over your sword," one of the knights said.

"But of course, if you pry it off me."

"Don't son." Mother took his arm. She was shaking. Mother never trembled. "These people have chosen to follow Valte but not all—do not let the outcome of the palace fog your mind— wait for the right time to fight."

"It began the moment I arrived at Crystal Lake," he told her. "Has Sir Lancelot explained what Prince Valte did at Crystal Lake?" Tungsten looked at the Excalibarian knights. "Are you aware of what he did to your Sun Princess? The girl who entertained you with songs when your morale was low?" The Excalibarian knights looked at one another. "And you, old friend, you claimed to have loved my sister, but it appears the rumors about you were true. One day, a Lancelot shall betray his king."

"Surround him," Lancelot answered. "And don't let me repeat myself."

"Forgive me," one of the knights said.

"Don't ask for forgiveness," Mother commanded. "Take arms and join us!"

"Enough Queen Lailon." The incoming voice was none other than Father's old friend, General Armin. "Valte wed Princess Calibor and now carries the king's ceremonial wind sword. Sir Lancelot told us you gave in to the seduction of the fairies and gave them your right to the throne, abandoning

262

Excalibur."

"Hmm." Tungsten placed his hands on his hips. "I did give up my sword, but I did not abandon Excalibur!"

"Then have you come now?"

The steps old man entered the room. He was short but heavy with muscle and armor. Without his helmet, Tungsten could see his pale eyes fixated on him. "What is this noise at such a late hour?"

"Grand Advisor Edmun," Tungsten said. "Friend of my father and loyal servant of Excalibur, have you also sided with a traitorous knight and foreign prince?"

The advisor bowed. "Forgive me second born, I may have never approved of you taking the throne, but our people shall not fall into doom by your crown. The sun is coming, now return to your chamber until you are summoned by King Valte."

Tungsten laughed. "Why, I don't think I've been sent to my room since I was a boy." He unsheathed Calibor's blade and raised it at them.

"Tungsten no!" His mother exclaimed.

More knights entered the room to surround them and the Round Table.

"There will be no bloodshed tonight. Even you are not stupid enough to defile the palace like some animal," Advisor Edmun said. "You will see Prince Valte tomorrow, but tonight is not the time."

The Felmidian guards closed in on his mother, and Tungsten pointed his sword in their direction. "Not an inch closer."

"Go, son," his mother said, taking his arm once more to lower his blade. "For as long as I know you're still alive, I will not break."

Tungsten looked at the Round Table, at the twelve blades marking every generation of prince and princesses wielded as the kingdom's stronghold. The burden was now his, and he was failing. He cursed and gave himself up, but not before Advisor Edmun stopped him.

"Your blade; you won't be needing that tonight."

Tungsten gave it to his mother. She stared at it, knowing it was Calibor's sword, and pressed the hilt near her heart.

The halls of the palace were empty. Free of his guards and the royal knights of the castle. The place had never been as dark as it was now occupied by foreigners. They led him to the private tower that belonged to him, where only he could enter.

"Don't try anything," one of the Felmidian knights said. "You will not find any aide here."

Tungsten entered his grand room in silence and listened to the double doors shut. He could crush them. Open holes in the brick wall with their bodies, but his mother, her very life could depend on his actions.

• • •

The morning and afternoon had long past. Walking endlessly for hours had done nothing for his racing mind. He walked around the oval table in the center for the hundredth time. There were scratch marks on the surface from carelessly laying his helmet down. He dared not take it off now.

With the room darkening, he looked toward his oriel window, where it protruded from the main wall of a building many miles off the ground. Seeing it shut, he opened it and tied the red curtains back, allowing what remained of the setting sun to come through the gray skies.

The view offered him various angles of the city and was among his preferred spots to spend his time. Far below lay a ghost land of empty streets. There was smoke emitting from the central part of the city. Those Dranyth's bombs came again, her bombs. Unwilling to look more, he retreated to his bed and sat, but no longer found any comfort in it. Though the birds lamented the end of the day, waiting for the promise of a new day. Tomorrow had been promised to these creatures but Excalibur had no guarantee.

Prince Valte and his mother. He used to believe that he held her in high regard, but something was disturbing about the way the Felmidian guards treated her. Even so, she walked the palace without her armor and in the presence of invaders.

"Bastard!" He pounded his fists into the pole of his bed and crushed it.

"Careful now, you'll make a mess," said the shadow he could not be rid of, crouching on his windowsill.

XXI

CLOSURE, THE END TO MY EXISTENCE

Astra Degora sat on the window, arms crossed, with her back against the pillar. She had been gazing at the scenery while he picked up the wooden pieces from the floor.

"How you like to break everything rule I've built," he grimaced.

"What did I do now?"

"Rooms are cherished havens where one could escape from the pressures of the outside world and you're invading mine."

Astra Degora ignored his disapproval and coolly walked inside. "Strange, and here I thought you were held against your will." She touched the drapes on his bed and went to one of the shelves. Her fingers went to graze a toy of a soldier in bronze.

"What do you want?" he asked. "We said everything that

needed to be said in Atlios."

"We never finished our waltz."

"You wish to spar with me now? Do you think I wouldn't kill you after your bombs have brought havoc upon my lands?"

"You'd have an easier time understanding the reality of your situation if you let me deliver you to Pince Valte." She raised her blade toward him and swung at him. "Now let us end this waltz!"

Tungsten broke the other pillar of his bed and used it to block her second strike. Calibor's lifeless body flashed in his mind, followed by the fearful look in his mother's eyes. All his anger came back, and he backhanded her, knocking her across the room and into the wall. "Why now?" he shouted. "Tell me!"

"When did I try not to go for your head?" She struck him and sent him crashing onto the bed. Before he could recover, she leaped on top of him, her short swords coming down before he caught her elbows. He saw a bruise on the apple of her cheek, cut from what had to be a strike at her face.

"Coward," he said, intent on not falling for anymore of her distractions. He rolled to the side to knock her off. Her blades bounced on the floor.

Tungsten grabbed her sword and raised it over her. The blade came down and bit into her shoulder. She jerked and the part of her hair that covered her left eye slid down her cheek. "I dove into a pit by trusting you and hating you and I have yet not realized why I cannot forgive nor spare you." Seeing the eye patch, he grabbed the tie and yanked it off her.

Astra Degora gasped. A woman with two eyes stared back. The side she concealed revealed an old scar that ran from her temple to the apple of her cheek.

Tungsten could not move. His mind had gone back to that place, back where he was once a boy. A forest of smoke enveloped the borders of Excalibur as Dranythians tried to break down his walls. The roaring of dragons overhead drummed in his chest, the Dwelling Devils and drapes that aided the invasion of his land.

Amidst the clash of fire and sword, he saw a young Dranyth set up an explosive, unseen by his people who stood like giants over her. Fearing he was out of time, Tungsten swung his blade at her, cutting her left eye. She fell on her back taken by surprise. The flesh wound smeared down her face, but he did not cut out her eye. She stared back wide-eyed, stricken by fear, and told tears that cleared the blotches of her dirty face.

"You," he breathed, finding himself back in his room. "I remember you."

"Why did you miss then?" Astra Degora gripped the blade he stabbed into her shoulder and dove deeper. "Finish me this time!"

"No!" He pulled the blade out and tossed it across, sending it sliding across the floor. He got up and shuffled back to his knees.

Astra Degora pressed her palm against her shoulder. "I gave you so many chances and you still..."

The memory of that night circled back, of finding a girl his age in the middle of Excalibarian and Dranythian conflict. He didn't kill her because she was afraid, but because she was a child of war, born to fight until death freed them.

His heart twisted at those thoughts. "This is what you wanted, isn't it? To be killed by me, because the only thing a Dranyth cares about is dying with their dignity."

"And what is wrong with that?" she mumbled. "Taking my own life is not an option. The only one who has the power to make things right is the boy who fought me in the past and showed mercy by sparing my life."

"No, it is not right! Not after what my brother..." His heart pounded like the hooves of a wild horse. "If my father knew, he would've stopped my brother's vicious acts. If I knew, I would have dragged him before you and let you deal with him and torn your enemies asunder." He reached to her and cupped her face, and he was surprised she didn't jump. "I *know* you didn't kill Calibor. You could not save her, but cut her to let the poison out, didn't you?"

Astra Degora didn't answer.

"Answer me," he pleaded. Did she not understand that he was opening his heart and she was throwing rocks? He went back to his bed and sat very still, hand against his chest.

She walked back to the window, hand still on her bleeding shoulder. The trail of blood dripping from her arm led Tungsten to open his drawer. He grabbed his best garments and tore them.

Upon his approach, she looked away from him. "Have a seat," he said.

Rather than take a chair by his table she went to the balcony instead and sat on the stone rail.

Tungsten sat behind her. He folded four layers of cloth over her wound and started to wrap a longer piece over her shoulder. At the least she let him tend to her wound this time.

"When the Dranyths attacked Excalibur, why were you there?" he asked.

"Why do you care?"

"I wish to know, a girl unprepared to battle suddenly joining Dranyths to combat the borders of Excalibur." He jumped when her back relaxed into his chest. He took one arm and placed it over her upper shoulder, awkwardly holding her. In return, she took his arm. "All those bombs they used against your kingdom were mine."

Tungsten didn't release her. If he was going to decide if she was an unfeeling monster he couldn't react by emotion alone.

She continued. "To ensure we successfully harmed Orendor I had to be present. Midway through the fight, I was separated from my brothers and that was when you found me where I was still that ill child." The cawing moved their attention to the sky.

Crows were soaring high, and the sun had turned a dark blue. "It's almost over." She looked north at the stars. "Almost."

Though she said it softly, he recognized a different side of her was speaking to him and it left a sense of discomfort in his stomach.

Tungsten grazed his thumb over the bruise on her cheek and she winced. "What happened?" he asked. "The bruise is too old to be caused by my hand."

"I didn't follow orders," she answered, her voice filled with defiance. "You were supposed to be subdued at the inn."

"Then it is my fault."

Astra Degora laughed. "What a *hero* you must be!"

"This hero might've developed a romantic attraction toward you." She didn't move, if anything she remained as still as the pillars surrounding them. "I understand that hearing this from me must be offensive. The weight of my brother's sins rests on my shoulders."

Astra Degora turned completely so they could face each other. She fell silent for a moment before she shook her head. "No, I pondered long enough to know you're not your brother."

"I can't help but wonder if you're saying that to lower my guard."

Her eyebrows furrowed. "I knew you were different the moment you saved the woman from the drapes on King's Road, showed mercy to an orphaned shapeshifter, risked your life for your friend, spared a lonely monster, and hesitated in killing Huliar. Even when I didn't want to believe it, you saved me at the ice lake. In my eyes? The past decides the future of those who are unwilling to set it free." Her hand rested on his chest plate. "I know you saw I was a weak, scared girl when you left that scar on my face, that's why you didn't raise your blade a second time."

Tungsten crossed his legs and planted his hands on his knees. "Why can I not recall our encounter? Why did seeing your scar only bring back those memories?"

Astra Degora pulled back the side of her hair that covered her scar, allowing him to see the cut through her eyebrow. "Before your blade crossed my eye I had ignited the bomb. Seeing I was within the blast zone I tried to reach for it but it was too late. You grabbed me and shielded me in your arms. Though you were young, your body was big enough to shield someone as small as me. The bomb's deafening explosion soared through the air and you took all the damage. You fell unconscious but seeing what you have done, I no longer saw my enemy. I dragged you among your dead knights to hide you. Before I made my escape I saw pieces of tanium had broken from your back cutlet where the most impact hit. I took them with me and fled."

"Your swords," Tungsten breathed.

Astra Degora nodded. "I've been carrying a part of you all these years."

"Astra—" She pressed her finger against his helmet where

his lips were. In return, he took her hand and held it. "Whatever you have to say, whatever you say you might feel, don't say it, for it will be wasted and carried with the wind."

There was a knock on the door, and a knight said, "Dranyth, are you done?"

His breath left him as her hand slipped from his. "Wait!"

"It was nice talking, for real this time." Astra Degora picked up the eye patch and covered the scar once more. "From here on, think of every danger I put you through because that's who you're going to see. Don't miss like you just did and stab my shoulder. Be firm and put your hands around my neck tightly."

Tungsten reached for her arm, stopping her. She looked up at him, eyes cautious but willing to listen to what he had to say. She asked him to leave his thoughts be, and he decided he'd never ponder it in Atlios but this was different. This felt different.

He pulled his helmet off and let it crash on his oval table like he had carelessly done before. He gently pulled her closer to him, eliciting a soft gasp from her. "You're not the first woman who tried to kill me but you're the first who stirred up emotions in me I'm not allowed to have, and for that—"

"For that?"

"Hmm." Women often kissed his helmet in attempting to reach his lips. He exposed his face to her for one reason but had doubts over what she would want. "Do you fear me?" He dared himself to ask.

She blinked a few times, and for a moment there was a look of realization. "I've known for a long time that there is only death for me. I was supposed to die when we attacked Excalibur when Ecarus tossed me at Three Rivers, but I lived. I survived somehow, and I accepted it is for this moment, for what's about to unfold." Astra Degora ran her fingers down his jaw. "Do not fall for a walking corpse. I exist only to fulfill my final act."

Tungsten held the frame of his face with his two hands. He leaned toward the direction of her desirable lips. "I wish to know your true name, so I will never forget you."

"It was always Astra Degora," she answered. "The meaning of that name, you must find out when I'm long gone." She gave him a soft smile. "Now will you kiss me or not?"

It started with an innocent press of two lips, but then it opened to a deep kiss, one they neither needed air for.

His intentions were good, and he felt his heart swell that she received him. When his mouth found her neck, she gasped and drew him nearer, pressing him against her chest. They held each other in silence, and for a moment it mattered not what tomorrow held.

Tungsten then exhaled and let her down. If this was what comfort felt like, then he understood his oath more, and why he had to be without.

Astra Degora slipped on her mask and went out the door.

Tomorrow they were back to being enemies.

XXII

BLACKSMITH GOD

The throne room remained the same as Tungsten remembered, grand pillars surrounded the space once ruled by many great kings. The paintings of his forefathers hung on the wall undisturbed, every precious vase and statue remained untouched.

The movement of everyone was reflected in the marble floors. To his relief, Mother was in her armor, but it made him sick to see her standing beside Valte who sat on the throne of the king. Though shackled, on her hip was Calibor's sword.

"Tungsten, I had hoped Astra Degora finished you." Valte got up and made his way down with his father's blade at his side. "I suppose that's why the war with the Dranyths was never ending with you Excalibarians." He stopped where his mother waited and firmly held her chin.

"Don't touch her."

Valte chuckled. "I can touch my future queen if I wish it."

Tungsten clenched his fists. "You're making a great mistake by saying that."

"Can you blame me? I was a pathetic little boy with a father who was nothing without the strength of our God. My whore of a mother ignored me and sought only her pleasures. It was when I came to Excalibur that my eyes were changed. King Murenten doted on you and your siblings, and your mother—" Valte turned and brushed the back of his hand on the side of her helmet. "I fell in love with her voice, the grace of every step from the only woman who had been nothing but kind and accepting of me."

"If you dare lay one more finger on her—"

"Don't worry. I'm reserving our special moment until after our wedding." He stepped down resting his hand on his sword. "I'm sure you're wondering by now why your people are following my orders. Your mother has asked me plenty of times, but it was not worth revealing until her little boy came home. Even so, I tried to bring you back, but you kept resisting." Valte clapped his hand. Ten Felmidian soldiers and five Excalibarian knights surrounded the Round Table his line had protected. Seeing now, the blades that no man could pull out of the table glowed brighter than usual, pulsing as if breathing, the gold marking running from the hilt to the fuller as his own.

"What's happening?" Tungsten asked. "What have you

disturbed?"

Prince Valte leaned against the round table and grinned at the light fading from the blades. "Your strength is no more. Soon your armor will be but a useless shell."

"How many times must I tell you people? My strength is my own!" Tungsten grabbed the man at his right and swung him before tossing him through the window. It shattered as he crashed through and fell, his cry fading.

Prince Valte unsheathed his sword and called his knights.

"Tungsten!" His mother ran to his side giving him the chance to unsheathe Calibor's sword.

As the knights came, he did not hesitate. They chose their path and his return did not sway them. The swing of his sword sent both Felmidian and Excalibarian knights in his path flying, denting their helmets. They never got up after the impact.

"Alright, you brute." Valte's retreated, pressing his back against his table. "Kill me, and your corpse will hang before your people. My armies will flood your stronghold on the morrow." His stare shifted to his mother before back to him. "I will make a greater nation and unite us all."

"Bring all the allies and monsters you can summon. It will give me the pleasure of smiting them." Tungsten raised his blade. "But nothing will give me more pleasure than cutting down my sister's killer."

Tungsten's stroke fell, his blade clashing with another.

Prince Valte panted with surprise, arms raised to his face. A robed man had come between him. His presence sent a wave of familiarity. Unease washed over him just the same, causing his chest to tighten.

The robed man's sword gave a faint light. The blade Merlin the Old crafted was his father's wind ceremonial sword.

Excalibarian knights promptly bent a knee, and that unsettled him.

The robed man pulled back his hood. The all too familiar branch designs he used to admire were engraved into the man's helmet. When he discarded his robe, all eyes were drawn to his chest plate, which had a conspicuous crack, allowing a glimpse of the weathered mail underneath.

In the depths of his mind, a lone word emerged, clear and undeniable—Ecarus.

XXIII

OR MAYBE SOME OF US ARE BORN THIS WAY

Mother ran toward Ecarus, wrists still shackled. In her haste, she stumbled forward, but her firstborn son caught and embraced her.

"Ecarus," she wept. "Ecarus!"

"Mother," he said softly.

"How is it possible? We found nobody."

"I'll answer soon." He turned to Tungsten and reached for Calibor's sword. It slipped through his fingers as Ecarus gripped it.

Coming to his brother's side was Lancelot. He did not flinch when he noticed him, but only stared at Prince Valte.

Ecarus released his mother, pivoted, and struck, cutting Prince Valte in half. Blood spilled onto the Round Table before the rest of the mess puddled on the floor.

The sound of Lancelot's voice echoed through the battlefield as he directed the Excalibarian knights to swiftly overwhelm the astonished Felmidian soldiers.

Prince Valte let out a cry, his head nodding up and down. "Why...?"

"For daring to think you could bed my mother." Ecarus kicked Valte's torso, sending it across the table. "Get rid of the rest of Valte's men that plague this kingdom. They have served their purpose."

Lancelot walked past Ecarus, his crossbow was in his hand prepared to answer his brother's order. Valte, dragging himself by the arms to Mother. "I told you I would get you." Lancelot released the trigger and sent a bolt into his head.

Ecarus swung Calibor's blade to remove the blood and returned it to Tungsten. He held it but not with the same strength he had.

"Ecarus," his mother said. "Were you working with that man?"

"Not now, Mother."

"Answer me!"

Ecarus turned to her, and seeing her shackles, he broke them in half. "For a long time, I had been aware that Felmid was our enemy, but the idea of going back and getting involved in another war was not something I wanted."

"But King Fernam."

"He is dead, or do you think Valte wasn't willing to kill his father to make you his queen?"

He placed his arm around Tungsten like he would when he was younger, but this time he stiffened. "Now excuse us, I wish to speak to my brother."

"Tungsten," his mother said. Her voice was full of worry, but she was safe, and that was enough for now.

Tungsten followed him to the main hall decorated with multiple grand statues of women depicting Mother Nature standing in their long gowns as if watching them, head down. Painted only with gold, they had no expression, but the way their hands appeared to hold the vaulted ceiling gave the impression that they could come alive and drop it all at once.

"Remember we used to climb them?" Ecarus asked. "I think the farthest we ever made it was the hips before we slid down. You could never catch up to me; I wonder if that has changed."

Tungsten said nothing. Behind, Lancelot and his knights followed, obedient to his brother alone.

Off the main hall led the way to the garden, it was still well kept despite their world being turned upside down. It was when Ecarus continued north that he realized they were going to the main rope bridge, the only passage to Orendor's temple.

The bridge was over two thousand feet in the air, crossing from one mountain ridge to another, and was supported by twenty main ropes and two hundred wind ropes.

Ecarus first stepped onto the bridge. Tungsten followed, looking below where the Whirl River passed through.

To enter the many mines in the surrounding mountains that encased the kingdom, bridges were made. In the city, many were corbal arch bridges made of stone, sturdy for bringing their ores to the blacksmiths. The one that led to Orendor's temple, however, could only be accessed from the palace, while the others connected from mountain to mountain.

Ecarus stopped halfway and stood at the edge of the bridge. "Do you hear that beautiful sound?" he said.

It was barely noticeable, but there was enough light to see something stirring in the city. "Excalibur has broken in half, those loyal to my return, and..." He looked at him. "Those who are loyal to you."

"What will you do to them?"

"What I have been doing to all who refuse me, they go into the mines to work." He placed his hand on the visible gap of his chest plate, one he never had when he last saw him. "Tanium was always hard to find without Orendor to guide us, and I will not waste another second."

"There is no more tanium," Tungsten said. "Orendor has gone to the Isles of Avalon; his flame and hammer have left these mountains barren."

Ecarus looked at him like he sounded absurd, and he patted

his back before he continued walking. "Did you believe everything Merlin the Old told you?"

"How are you alive?" Tungsten shouted. "Why have you come back from the dead now?" He watched him enter the temple alone before he looked back at the city. From this angle, he could barely see a glimpse of it, but there was smoke, evident of an active battle.

"Keep moving," Lancelot ordered.

Tungsten turned to him. "After everything we've been through. Father mourned you, he broke and died because of you!"

"I thought I was dead, I was supposed to be plenty of times but Mother Nature spared me so I can reclaim my crown."

"And my brother in arms? Was he also a farce—do you want me to believe you're doing this for the good of the kingdom?"

"If it means keeping Calibor from the Isles of Avalon, then yes."

Tungsten looked at the entrance to Orendor's temple. The opening appeared like any ordinary cave. Here Orendor would craft beautiful weapons and armor, but he was not vain. He was a humble God who didn't need ornate craftsmanship to celebrate him.

Ecarus stood before the altar, accompanied by the undying flames that lit the place.

"Ecarus!" Tungsten shouted. "End the bloodshed now!"

His older brother placed his hand on the black-marbled platform. "It was here where I received this armor, and as I grew, Orendor would melt it and rebuild it for my height and size. I remember being so proud of you when you were summoned to this place, readily taking the call as stronghold to Excalibur."

"If you will not heed me, then there is nothing for us to talk about." Tungsten turned from him but he stopped. Lancelot and his knights had been blocking him.

"I'm sorry Father died thinking I died. But I was not killed in battle as they made you believe, but I was nearly murdered," said Ecarus. He looked up at the great anvil. "I'm alive because that was the will of the Gods.

"It was during the cavalry war south of the Northstead Highlands. I made some plans that Merlin the Old discovered. He knew Orendor was dying, that we were killing him with these wars. Instead of stopping us, instead of preserving our way of life, he came to me with accusations about how I'd been running my army." Ecarus threw his cloak down, revealing a gap in the back of his armor. "He wizard was a sourpuss unwilling to see change or the possibility to deny the end of monsters and creation of man." The cracks revealed his mail beneath and even a dent on the side of his helmet. "This is what Merlin did to me. My impenetrable armor cracked, and I intend to mend it. I intend to make it whole, just as this kingdom will be whole when Orendor returns and denies the reforming lands."

"Orendor was never against The Affliction War," Tungsten said. "It was the monsters who in their refusal to leave that we were becoming a dying race."

"And you have done your part well, brother. Over the years, I've heard of your heroic deeds, of the admiration amongst the monsters who hate and despise you. You have stewarded my kingdom well, and I intend to return you to your rightful spot as the stronghold you were meant to be."

It was everything he wanted to hear but that dream had become a nightmare. "I've been asking myself why and now I see it. You did this because Calibor was to become queen!"

Ecarus frowned. "I admit I intended to delay Calibor's return. For if she had become the queen, I would have had reason to kill her, but that prince was sloppy in apprehending her, using the water witch's poison. You saw I dealt with that."

"And what role does Astra Degora play?"

"Astra Degora? What interest do you have in that woman?"

Tungsten didn't answer, and it made Ecarus chuckle. "Brother, it is against your oath to see any man and woman with lust or desire." He looked up at the anvil and raised his hands. "Was it not here before Orendor that father asked you, 'Do you Tungsten, swear to honor your birthright as Excalibur's servant and stronghold? Leaving behind all earthly desires and that of the flesh?' Did you not say 'I swear it?'"

Distant sounds of clashing swords and soldiers' footsteps

286

brought Tungsten to turn back. The battle was growing and to what degree he did not know.

"You know, after Excalibur was attacked by the Dranyths and you were recovering, I asked Orendor—no begged him not to forsake us, and you know what he said?" Ecarus remained calm and confident. "Nothing."

"You asked out of selfishness. You know the time of these monsters has expired and their refusal to go where they came from goes against the natural order."

"Why? Because our Gods chose to make way for one God to rule over our world? No brother, my armor, our provisions for metal, and the other deities are fading. That is the result of mankind's dominion, and we will fix that, reigniting the flames of the war, starting with Felmid. This time, it will be human and against human."

Tungsten placed his hands on his helmet and breathed. Any hopes of reasoning with him were fading. "Then you have lost Orendor's favor, and for much more, for your war crimes, and the assault you did to those Dranyth women and children."

Ecarus left the altar facing the anvil and came toward him. "I am a king. All threats must be cleansed from these lands and right now, has my blood chosen to become my enemy?"

"Your choice to turn the war against humans will not benefit us. If the monsters take over, humankind will not survive. That's why Orendor left, he chose *us*, and he left us his strength to overcome them, or have you forgotten our path?"

"And I disagree. Is that so hard to accept?"

The pounding feet of knights came into the temple. Upon seeing them, Ecarus passed Tungsten not once did he worry if he would attack but he gripped his father's ceremonial sword. The knights that surrounded him had gone through many to get to them, their bloodstained blades raised against him.

"Ecarus, the firstborn of King Murenten and Queen Lailon, quell this rebellion and bend to the rightful king."

"Fools." Ecarus nodded at Lancelot. "Take care of them."

Unsheathing his blade, Lancelot faced the five individuals his crossbow ready in hand. Just as he was about to fire his bolt he pivoted and turned to him. "You heard them bend to the rightful king—the true king, Tungsten."

Ecarus chuckled. "Sir Lancelot, loyal to the very end." He raised Father's ceremonial sword, and magical force pressed upon Lancelot's armor.

Lancelot backed away, and the others followed his lead. It seemed they were under his orders, and Lancelot was waiting for them to reach him.

Ecarus had played the patient game, even if he suspected Lancelot was leading him into an ambush. They retreated to the main bridge. Above them were many other bridges running from different parts of the mountain, where they met with ones that headed down to the city.

"Lancelot!" Tungsten intended on following him but Ecarus swept his blade, and the pressure returned, tossing him back.

Ecarus fought Lancelot, the clash of swords echoed through the air, filling the space with chaotic energy. Rella and the other knights went into combat with Ecarus's supporters.

When the ceremonial sword glowed again, Tungsten charged towards them. "Everyone stand behind me!"

Lancelot, Rella, and the other knights listened to his command. The pressure of Father's wind sword shot out. Tungsten resisted its push, drawing out his will through his armor. It lifted parts of his pauldron and chest plate, redirecting the force into the wind ropes of the bridge and snapping them.

The bridge quaked as a result, and Ecarus shook his head. "Brother, don't resist me. You may have thwarted my strike, but you won't a second time." As he raised his sword, he felt the familiar weight and power coursing through his arms.

A spark of electricity flashed before Tungsten, blinding him. Once he could see again, he watched as his brother pushed to one knee from where he had been thrown to the floor, static energy arcing along his armor.

"Tungsten!" A boy stood before him. The same electricity he cast swam around his hands.

Ecarus, seeing the young wizard grasped the gap in his armor. "Merlin!" he shouted. "So you're back!"

Merlin stepped back, hands open but ready. "I don't know

you!"

"Then let me remind you how I killed you the first time." Before he could touch them, Tungsten pushed his brother, sending him crashing to the end of the bridge.

"Brother," said Ecarus. "The side you stand on goes against your birthright. Will you save Excalibur? Or will you usurp the crown and become an enemy to us?"

Tungsten closed his eyes momentarily, taking a moment to steady his breath. "All kingdoms eventually fall, but Excalibur will not be undone by your hand!"

Astra Degora appeared at lightning speed, fiercer and swifter than he had ever seen. His heel smoothed back, shocked by the deadly look in her eyes.

Behind them, Mother unsheathed her sword and charged at Ecarus. With tears in her eyes, she whispered, "You took my daughter," the words filled with pain and sorrow. "You will not take my son."

"Mother lay your weapon down," Ecarus said. "Do not shed any tears for offspring born out of mere insurance. I am the one whom you should see as your priority."

"What has become of you?" she asked. "This isn't how we raised you. You've let the war change you."

"Perhaps," he said, swinging his blade at his mother, who deflected it. "Or maybe some of us are born this way."

His father's blade swiftly struck his mother's blade,

something his father would have never allowed. His mother flew five feet into the air and nearly slipped off the bridge before she gripped the edge.

"Mother!" Tungsten said, running to her. "Rella, take her. You'll need her strength to free the others!"

"As you command!" Rella shouted.

"Behind you!" Lancelot shouted.

A pain surged through Tungsten's shoulder, and he wailed! Tanium had finally cut through his body and it burned.

Astra Degora kicked him, unsheathing him from her blade.

"Wait..." he breathed.

"Take my brother back to the temple and lay him on the altar," Ecarus said. "Since he will not yield to me, then he will be properly executed for his tanium."

"Astra—" Her feet pressed against his back. She wrapped two chains around his neck and gripped the other ends with her fists as she dragged him back to the temple.

With her mask and eyepatch back on, her face was completely hidden, making it impossible to see if she felt any remorse for her actions.

"Astra Degora!" he panted as he reached for his neck. "This war, it was Felmid's doing. To grip Excalibur they pinned Dranyths' beyond our disagreements. Haven't you realized it?" He fought for air. "I've spent my entire life protecting this kingdom, but I never strayed from doing what is right. You may have no choice now, but let me fix this. Let me be the one who could've protected you."

"I don't know what relationship you two have, but the Dranyth will not listen to you." Ecarus followed from behind. "She is devoted to what's left of her dragons. They will die if I don't protect what's left of the weaker kind."

Tungsten grunted as he pulled the chain. Astra Degora, seeing this, took a slender chain that hung from her hip and added it to the others around his neck. The metal grew hot, surging from some spell that forced him to let go.

Servants of the temple loyal to his brother lifted him, placing him on the altar. The odor of smoke from the cave reached the temple, and the echoes of their steps invaded the dark corners where the light wouldn't linger.

Tungsten squeezed the chains which brought her to pull against it. "You would serve the man who destroyed your village and made you into a cold-blooded killer?"

The robed workers ignored him and stepped back so Ecarus could approach him.

The fighting resumed in the bridge, and he worried about the fate of his people, and Merlin and Rella, who were dragged into this.

Ecarus placed his hand on his chest plate. "To dismantle tanium, we need Orendor's fire and his mighty water." He raised his other hand to the other temple servants, who were near the upper mountains, where a seal held back the water for over a decade.

"Ecarus," Tungsten said. "If you do this, you will disturb Orendor's spirit. These are still his mountains. He will be aware of your plans and you may not like the outcome."

"Then let's hope he regrets his decision to abandon us." He raised his hand to the robed men standing by the two levers. "Release!"

A rumbling shook the ceiling, knocking dust and rocks loose to fall and plop into the slow-running lava. The metal's groan echoed through the mountain as it bent to the incoming force. Water roared into the temple, crashing like the sea against the rocks. Steam poured out, sizzling off the flowing lava that poured from the stalactites.

Tungsten started to shake as water flowed into the engravings on the platform. His vision blurred, and he was growing hot.

"Relinquish your armor," Ecarus said.

"No." He earned this armor, he lived in it, and his very soul belonged in it.

"Give it to me!" he commanded.

Tungsten fought for air as water and lava filled the engravings on the platform. His vision of his brother and Astra Degora washed away, along with the cave and the servants of the temple.

He could hear it now, as he could then. Orendor's mighty hammer, crafting for hours. His voice booming in the temple, stirring the mountains and bringing the fires to flare.

The temple disappeared, and darkness took him. He stood on a nameless black mountain. The ground looked like charcoal, cracking under his weight. Not far was Ecarus, staring up at the mountain with intent.

"Where are we?" Tungsten asked.

Ecarus didn't look his way. The mountain seemed angry from the quake underneath his feet. "He's coming."

Ash blew out of a crater, followed by a hammer held by a tight fist. Debris of lava and rocks fell around them, forcing both Tungsten and Ecarus to step back.

Rising from the depths of the crater, a hand emerged, firmly grasping the rim, and unveiled a magnificent gold helmet. It was intricately designed to resemble the blacksmith God, the deity they held in high regard.

XXIV

WHEREVER YOU GO, I'LL FIND YOU

When Orendor left, he gave one last command: never open the water that gave life to his mountains. Ecarus must've known such an act would stir his presence and now he was before them. A man of muscle, holding in a tight fist his hammer. He as he breathed slowly, watching them.

"Sons of Murenten." Orendor's voice towered like a rockslide, where even the mountain shook at his presence. "Who among you is the king?"

Tungsten took a knee but dared not utter a word.

"I am," Ecarus answered promptly. "Merlin the Old, who long served Excalibur, made an attempt on my life during The Affliction War. Drapes held me prisoner, but in time I swayed them to work with me. It was and has always been my goal to return to Excalibur." Even though Tungsten could sense Orendor's attention shifting towards him, he remained stubbornly fixed on the ground, avoiding any eye contact behind his visor. "Merlin the Old conjured a powerful lightning spell against me. Now my armor does not hold up as well as it used to," Ecarus continued. "I must find tanium, and right now, Excalibur is at war with Felmidian forces. Even so, my brother, second born and stronghold of Excalibur, refuses to serve me. He refused to step down and return the crown to me."

Tungsten deepened his bow. "What my brother said is true. I haven't stepped down because he intends to reignite the war. Our people have already suffered, and more will continue to suffer."

Orendor grumbled. "Tungsten, the children of the Round Table must protect the walls of Excalibur. Why do you care about the world?"

Tungsten searched in his heart for the answer. "My sister was a piece of the world I wished to protect, therefore I cannot..."

"Then you sought revenge and put the kingdom second."

Tungsten held his breath, feeling the tension in the air. "Yes, I sought justice. Calibor was going to be the new queen. She was capable and ready to lead—"

"And now she's dead," Ecarus cut in. "No secondborn has

ever bestowed the rights of the crown. That has always been our way—why should my absence keep me from my birthright?"

"Then I will lay my judgment upon thee." Orendor raised his hammer and brought it down as if he intended to hit them. Rather than being squashed into mush, an unbearable heat slammed unto him, breaking his and Ecarus's armor and burning their clothes, leaving them bare. "If you wish to claim the throne, then your strength will decide it. The loser will find their tanium armor brittle, and lackluster without my favor."

Where Orendor had hit, were two, still steaming, two-handed swords partially imbedded in the ground. In a swift motion, Ecarus stumbled forward and seized both swords from the ground, leaving Tungsten empty-handed.

"Where is your laugh now, brother?" In no time, Tungsten rolled away as Ecarus charged at him. "Were you not the favored?"

Tungsten kicked the rocks into Ecarus's face. He tackled him down. They wrestled unto the ground, their bare bodies covered with soot and ashes. Ecarus would not give up the swords and used the hilt of one sword to hit his brother in the temple.

Tungsten groaned as his brother quickly got to his feet.

Why have you been uncertain of your kinghood?

Shaken by the voice in his head, he looked at Orendor, who silently watched them. Did he speak to him? Seeing both swords in the air, mid-strike, Tungsten rolled, but it was not enough to keep one blade from grazing his shoulder as he barely made his escape.

"Enough, no more." Tungsten regained his footing, with blood slowly trickling down his arm. "I forfeit."

Ecarus grinned. "Then take a hit." He approached him with caution to avoid another grapple. Anything he could do with his bare hands against a blade of Orendor was impossible.

Tungsten, I did not give you that name by mistake. Such a metal is not as strong as steel, but it burns and bends under pressure in ways steel cannot.

Tungsten leaped back. His heart pounded wildly from the near miss to his abdomen. Ecarus cursed and swung again, forcing Tungsten to create more distance between them. This repeated on until he managed to read his footwork.

By the eighth swing, he grabbed his wrist and flipped him, sending Ecarus onto his back. With a powerful kick, Tungsten sent a jolt of pain through his abdomen, leaving him wheezing for air. The swords fell into his hands, giving him the advantage he needed.

Ecarus spat at the ground, panting. "Well come on then, give me your best shot."

Tungsten stared at Orendor's blades. They were his only chance to get out of this without losing the powers of his tanium. He tossed the swords on the ground.

Ecarus looked at him with both surprise and disgust.

"This is not my sword, and to be honest, I never wanted the position of king, nor did I think I could fill the space Father left." Tungsten turned to his brother. "If you wish to become king, then let our people decide. I didn't spend the last decade trying to put them back on their feet for you to ruin them." He walked back and started to climb the mountain. The hot wind brushed his face, his feet burned by the terrain. "Forgive me, Orendor, for I am not the man you believed in."

The Blacksmith God crossed his arms. The flames that crawled up his muscles did nothing to his might.

A growl stopped him in his tracks. He turned and caught a glimpse of Ecarus who thrusted his sword into his stomach. "I win," he panted. "I am victorious—" The forceful shot of water hit his back and flung him to the ground.

The waters took the form of Calibor, who steadily held Excalibur.

"You're late Sun Princess," Orendor said. "Have you embraced the understanding that your new physicality does not affect your standing as an Excalibarian?"

"My lord," she said, wheezing for air. The water surrounding her body began to sizzle and evaporate. "Do not heed any more of Ecarus's lies. Tungsten may have not wanted the crown, Tungsten may have done all he could to prepare, but *he* is the true king!"

Her feet burned from the escalating fires of the mountain, and she fell to her knees and screamed.

Tungsten picked her up and held her in his arms. For a moment he was back at Crystal Lake leading her to the waters. Her eyes half opened, and a smile grew. "Brother, I'm sorry I made you come to Crystal Lake."

Like a fading dream, the mountain and the heat faded. Tungsten was back in the cave. Ecarus was laughing, his armor glowing with the spirit of Orendor. "Now then," he said, spit hung from his bottom lip as he turned to him. "Let The Affliction War begin."

"Tungsten!" Calibor was coming down from the waterfall with Excalibur in her hand. "Don't let him win!" She swung Excalibur to him, commanding its fires to burst and penetrate the ground.

Tungsten fought to get to his feet, but his helmet and armor weighed him down. Was this true weakness? Had the tanium forsaken him as Orendor had?

"You should've stayed dead, dear sister." Using the ceremonial sword, Ecarus cut the air in Calibor's direction. The wind whistled and threw her against Orendor's anvil. Shaken, she clutched her side, bleeding while clinging to the edge of the anvil. Below the bubbling lava coursed ready to take her.

"Calibor." Tungsten inched off the platform and fell to the ground, rolling down the steps.

"Give Father my bed wishes," Ecarus said, raising his ceremonial blade once more.

Calibor lost her hold and fell but held on to the vine that wrapped Orendor's temple. Her blond hair fell over her face as she saw what her own brother was willing to do for power.

A bolt hit Ecarus's pauldron and bounced off. The fact it did no damage made him smile as he turned to face Lancelot, who had the second bolt ready.

"Hey bastard," Lancelot said. "Ease off the Sun Princess."

"Sir Lancelot," Ecarus said snapping his finger. "Charming as ever."

Lancelot ran to Tungsten's side. Astra Degora seeing this tried to intervene before Indra slammed into her, knocking her off.

"Friend!" Tungsten shouted. He managed to climb to his knees. "Take Calibor and flee!"

"Absolutely not!" Lancelot reached out a strong hand and helped him stand up. "I am committed to serving you faithfully and will continue to do so until the end of my life."

"How admirable." Ecarus raised his ceremonial sword against them. "Any last words?"

Calibor screamed.

Indra managed to snatch up Tungsten and Lancelot, narrowly escaping the wind's attack. Ecarus didn't stop, he swung the ceremonial blade, forcing Indra to leap and climb the

301

pillar with his nails.

"Lancelot, retrieve Calibor."

"Aye." Lancelot leaped from Indra and barely landed on the floating rocks.

Ecarus seeing his friend, smiled at the window of opportunity. Before he could react, a spear forced Ecarus to draw back. Mother had reached him, bringing with her several more knights.

Ecarus spoke to his mother, his voice heavy with hurt as he said, "Your rejection cuts deep."

"You are not my son."

His brother brought his sword around nearly splitting open her abdomen before he turned the blade and kicked her hard enough to send her to the temple's pillar.

"Mother!" Calibor cried.

Tungsten gripped the reigns, leading Indra to growl. "Indra!" His tiger leaped from the pillar and landed back on the altar. Tungsten barely held the hilt of his sword before he fell to one knee again. His mother lay sideways, unmoving from having lost consciousness.

Ecarus who had struck their mother was heaving, his arms shook at what Tungsten believed was regret. "I'm a monster, but even monsters can't harm their mother. Soon you will understand." The knights came at him, and he started to combat them, taking them down one by one.

Gritting his teeth, Tungsten peered at Orendor's anvil. Lancelot was easing into the bottom to get to Calibor.

"What are you doing?' Ecarus said as he pulled his sword out of the abdomen of his knight. "That sword is no longer yours."

With great effort, Tungsten managed to push himself up to his feet, his body protesting every movement. He patted his tiger's shoulder. "Take Lancelot and Calibor back to safety. I will be fine."

Indra growled, refusing to leave.

"If this is where we part, know that you have been a good and loyal friend to me."

Indra lowered his ears and fell silent. He passed him, tail brushed the side of his face.

Ecarus flicked the blade, and the wind careened at Tungsten, rattling and shaking his armor. "Why do you resist?" he said. "Did you not want Orendor's favor? Did you not admit you're not fit to be king?"

Tungsten planted his feet firmly, determined not to be thrown off balance. With or without tanium he had every right to confront any threat. He raised Excalibur from the ground and raised the blade against the wind. With his might alone he resisted with a newfound strength surging within.

Excalibur clashed with the ceremonial sword. The flames from his sword bellowed throwing Ecarus and casting the wind against him. His body rolled near the temple's exit, fumbling back to his feet, eyes widening. "Orendor" escaped his lips, his groan laced with disappointment and defeat. "What have you done?"

As Tungsten approached him, the flames dancing around Excalibur intensified.

"Get him!" Ecarus shouted to the others, retreating to the bridge. "Take down the wall!"

Excalibarian knights loyal to his brother raced to him. Tungsten tore through them, stampeding forward and breaking through. The ones who were far back dropped their swords and gave their obedience.

As Tungsten stepped out of the temple, the combat led the grand bridge to shift. On the other side were Merlin, Rella, and Indra, blocking Ecarus's loyal knights from entering, but some of the Excalibarian soldiers watched. Many who had escaped from the mines filled the bridge and watched him, the King of Excalibur, fight the true heir.

Ecarus, shaken by his approach, prepared another blast from Father's ceremonial sword. Tungsten raised his blade and ran it down, cutting through the wind.

The flames of the twin short blades broke through before he could reach his brother.

Tungsten didn't hesitate this time and made contact with her. There was no room for doubt anymore. The veil of lies has finally parted.

Flames danced just as they fought on the frozen lake. She was the cause of this. The shadow that had maimed his livelihood and brought back his brother from the dead.

Astra Degora's right swing lacked her usual strength, and this allowed him to counterattack, putting pressure and advancing on the offense.

He kicked her across the bridge, causing her to roll onto her side with her arm tucked under to protect her wounded shoulder.

"Tungsten!" Merlin's cry reached him as several bolts of lightning shot past him.

Heat pierced Tungsten like with any fire, but this came from a sharp cut. A shard of his tanium armor spun before him. The bigger part crumbled before his feet from the sword that wedged through his back.

Ecarus heaved. His helmet had been broken in half by Merlin's lightning. His skin suffered from scar burns; the brother he knew was buried under the scars. "It looks like you never mended the backplate."

Tungsten gripped the blade, barely capable of maintaining his balance from the swaying bridge.

"Brother," he squirmed with pain.

Ecarus's helmet clanked against his, his voice booming ever closer toward his ear. "Hush. It's almost over now." Ecarus laced one arm around his neck and stepped back, pushing him to the end of the bridge. "You are my brother and I love you, but if I'm not seeing this kingdom to its end, neither will you."

Amidst the chaos he only saw the blur of the mountain and the shifting of the bridge.

A woman crawled from the temple, her blond hair shifting from the stir of the wind. "Tungsten!" Calibor cried. "Tungsten!"

Her cry made Tungsten resist, and take his brother's arm. "Brother don't!"

Ecarus gave him a tight squeeze, his voice booming loudly in his ear. "Just as it is my birthright to be king, just as it's not yours to take. Such is tradition!" Ecarus's other arm came into view, where he presented before him a bomb. The slow match had been lit and was eating at the cord and twine.

Tungsten rammed the back of his head into his brother's face, but it didn't sway him. He was stuck to the ceremonial blade like a skewer. Astra Degora's bomb could kill everyone on the bridge and damage the mountains enough for them to cave in.

Ecarus resisted his attempts and shuffled back to throw them both off. "I told you it's over!"

The end of the slow match reached the neck, and Tungsten closed his eyes.

The stench from the fuse flared his nostrils, and he coughed whatever entered his lungs.

The swaying of the bridge brought him to open his eyes again. The wind was carrying a thin trail of smoke from the bomb.

Ecarus stared at it, his hand twitching in surprise. Tungsten gripped the blade and crouched, lifting his brother off the ground. He spun sharply until the weight of Ecarus and his sword released him.

Crashing to his knees he saw his brother stumbling back, unaware of the shadow that appeared behind him.

Astra Degora climbed onto Ecarus's back. She held something in her hand that sparked, a bomb that was flaring and flashing more intensely than the dud.

As the bridge swayed, a shot of adrenaline forced Tungsten to climb back to his feet. He ran to her, but despite his efforts, time seemed to slow.

Astra Degora shoved the bomb into the hole of her brother's shattered chest plate. She looked at Tungsten, who still raced toward her. She smiled at him and her lackluster eyes gleamed back to life as she leaned back, pulling Ecarus off the bridge with her.

Tungsten screamed her name, his cry breaching his brother's wails.

The stillness stifled his thoughts until a burst of sound shattered the darkness. Excalibarians from every bridge screamed as they clung to the bridges.

Light of every gold and blue shade imaginable swept over them in the form of a dragon, roaring and dancing towards the sky.

Amidst a cloud of fire and smoke, spikes shot out in every direction, burning everything as some carved the mountain and others whistled into the sky. The clouds grumbled as the smoke swept up to envelop them again.

The bridges stopped rocking, and the smoke dissipated. His sister, who watched from the temple, was carried by Lancelot, her expression saddened.

Indra sat at his side and listened to the fighting in the city. Something lodged in Tungsten's throat, a powerful emotion that couldn't be explained with words. He didn't feel again until his mother called for aid.

"Bring me a physician at once!"

More of his people came to the bridge, surrounding him. Among them was Merlin, he looked remorseful, but for once he had nothing to say.

"Tungsten." Lancelot carried Calibor in his arms. "More Felmidian troops have reached our borders. They're calling for war."

The threat itself invited a familiar welcome he had not encountered for ten years. He climbed back to his feet and looked up at the other bridges where his people watched.

"Giants," he called to them. "Mountain warriors of Orendor!" He reached for the blade his brother wouldn't touch and raised Excalibur in the air. "We will not give in to those who oppose us, nor will we be led by the predictions of others."

The sound of his people's cheers reverberated through the bridges. They chanted his name, fists in the air, while others crossed the bridge for battle.

"Laughing King!" his people shouted. "Long live the Laughing King!"

Tungsten held his side but managed to squeeze out a chuckle.

"Son, your wounds," his mother weakly said.

"I'm fine, for I'm favored by Orendor." The sight of Excalibur filled her with tranquility as it glowed with an intensity she had never witnessed before.

XXV

I HAIL FROM A TOWN IN THE NORTH

One Week Later.

Kingdom of Excalibur.

Tungsten watched from the balcony as more people were freed from the cave of their closed mountains. Ecarus had planned a great sacrifice and fed any monster who would fight for his cause. His victims were kidnapped from all over the continent, mostly women, children, and elderly men who were easy to enslave. By his brother's decree, the mountain that had long been the source of their rare metal was to be re-closed.

All this time, his brother had been within those abandoned mines, spying and preparing for his return. There were signs he searched for tanium for years, and upon finding none, he was forced to take extreme measures.

In the coming days, Tungsten's people respected him more than they already had, and their resilience fortified their desire to rebuild. But nobody saw the hurt or broken bones he suffered behind his armor nor the one he felt in his chest.

"There you are." His mother's dark gown was embellished with red jewels. Without her armor, she was a woman with radiant brown hair, high cheekbones, and soft brown eyes. "Lady Casana is here if you wish to see a kind face."

"I'm in no mood for company."

"Neither was I. Many are taken by your tales and they have bombarded me so much that I fled."

Tungsten chuckled but said nothing. He looked up at the window of his room. The shutters were still open since he last saw her sitting on the windowsill.

His mother took his hand, and he looked at her. "You know, back at the bridge, I have never heard you scream like that. The woman working the bomb, who was she?"

"She was like me, born into war. We met when I was shy of sixteen, on the night the Dranyths attacked Orendor."

"She was… Dranythian?"

"I can't say for certain why I allowed her to get so close. Perhaps what I confused for affection was her pain because I could hide what she couldn't or maybe I was envious that she could act on it."

Mother placed her hand against his arm. "In death, you believe it so?"

"There was no meaning for her to live again, but she hoped a day like this would happen, one where she wouldn't exist anymore. She must've wanted to kill Ecarus, but she couldn't get close to him. She wanted to die, but I couldn't kill her like she wanted. Only *he* could give her the redemption and the death she craved so much and I... I wanted something else."

His mother's skeptical expression revealed her lack of belief in his resolution. "If it was just revenge, why did she care who was caught in the crossfire?" Tungsten turned from his mother. "Son, if she jumped, it was so *you* wouldn't be hurt in the explosion."

Tungsten cleared his throat not wishing to let the thought simmer. "Now the weaker dragons will perish without her to safely lead them to the Isles of Avalon."

"Is that really what you want to say after I told you she spared you?" His mother looked over at the end of the hall, where some guards were speaking to Merlin.

Tungsten preferred not to torture himself with those thoughts and turned to the young wizard, seeing him quietly listening.

Merlin bowed before him. "I didn't mean to interrupt you two." He had bandages and was still using the staff the old Merlin left in the palace.

"He shouldn't be up," Rella said.

Merlin made one step but given he hadn't recovered from the battle with Felmid, he fell to his knees.

Rella helped him up, but he insisted on facing Tungsten with his strength.

"Have I pleased the stars as you so heartedly sang to me?" Tungsten said. "Did I defeat the shadow you and Merlin the Old warned me about?"

Merlin bit his bottom lip. He threw the staff and fell to his knees. "It was my arrogance that harmed you. I was selfish, wanting so badly to be better than the Merlins that I put you in an impossible spot. I failed to see who the enemy was, who could be the ally in the shadow I saw, and because of me, you lost someone." He planted his head on the ground. "I ask—no, I beg for your forgiveness!"

The young wizard covered his face as if that would help him hold his sniffles. Tungsten represented strength, and the boy didn't want to appear weak before him.

Tungsten reached down and lifted Merlin with his robe and put him back on his feet. "Stop all the groveling and waterworks. You're just a boy and you're learning."

"But."

"I saw you conjured lightning, a feat only Merlin the Old could do." He placed his hand over his blonde hair. "Now I'm no star seeker, but I believe you're going to be fine. No, the greatest Merlin that ever was. You wait and see."

Merlin's cheeks flushed, and while tears rolled down his cheeks, he worked a weak but guilty smile.

Tungsten looked at his mother, nodded, and started to leave.

"Where are you going?" Rella asked, following him.

"I'm tired," he said. "I wish to be alone." He returned to his private halls, empty and void of thought for once since his journey started.

In the courtyard that led to one of the bridges, he heard desperate voices. Lancelot, who was conversing with the attendants, appeared worried.

They had found more of Ecarus's victims. Tungsten sighed and cut through the long halls, his presence silencing the discussion. "How many more survivors have been found?" he asked.

Lancelot wanted to answer, but he had been doing the heavy lifting to not worry him.

"It's alright," he said. "I wish to know."

"Another thirty people have been successfully retrieved from deep within mines," replied Lancelot.

"Great. We don't want to seal them without making sure all have been freed."

The children, men, and women huddled together, their clothes tattered and covered with caked mud. The younger ones hid behind the taller ones. From the look of fear in their eyes, it appeared that they depended on each other for survival.

"You do not need to fear the king," his mother said, coming up behind him. "He may be strong, but he is kindhearted and compassionate."

The task of returning everyone home proved to be an arduous task. Scribes carried long lists that accounted for the sufferers and crimes his brother committed.

"We have written down everyone's name and location. I will send men to search for their people," a scribe said.

"I thought she would come for me," a girl said before another cry cut through.

"My husband said I only needed to wait, but he has not come," an older woman wept. "I have not seen him. He has not called for me. Where is he?"

Tungsten, seeing the matter being taken care of, decided to leave. The voices behind him became the aftermath of his brother and his search for more tanium.

"There is no other name," another freed prisoner said, like many who still hoped their loved one was alive.

"And what is the name again?" a scribe asked.

"Astra Degora."

Tungsten whipped around and looked at the crowd. "Who said that?" Several women and children who heard him looked at him, but nobody said a word. "I said who said that!"

His raised voice silenced the noise in the room.

"Whoever didn't speak, move aside now!"

The desolated victims parted. The only one left standing was a boy. Tungsten, shaken by the sound of her name approached the boy with commanding speed, leaving him to step back, visibly afraid. He had delicate brown eyes, big and full of wonder. His cheeks were freckled and flushed pink like all Excalibarian boys. And his hair was as dark as a raven's wing.

"Who are you?" Tungsten asked.

The boy bowed his head. "Naren. I hail from the north."

A sinking feeling settled into his stomach. "What is your age, boy?"

"Ten."

His mother, curious about the boy, got a closer look. Naren didn't move at his mother's touch even as she raised his chin. He looked up at her with wide eyes, his cheeks stained from working in the mine.

"Tungsten this boy... could he be half Excalibarian?"

Astra Degora never said she had a son, or any child at all.

"I am only half, Giant Lord," Naren said with a short nod. "But I know who I am. My real ma made sure I was aware."

"And you bear no hate to Excalibur?" Lancelot asked, joining the conversation.

The boy seeing his friend shook his head. "I can't let the past decide the future of those who are willing to set it free."

Tungsten heard those words in her voice and his wretched

heart beat with life again. "Your mother, she…"

The boy's eyes widened, and his expression softened. "You know her?"

At that moment, Tungsten saw it—all of Astra Degora's innocence poured into this meek and innocent boy. She had taken her pain and suffering away to let Naren look at the world in ways she never could.

Naren's eyes lowered as if knowing Tungsten's silence was the answer he sought.

"I'm sorry," Mother said.

The boy nodded with his lips pinched in. "She said it would come to this. That's why she gave me to good and loving parents. I didn't understand why it was dangerous to be with her until I was kidnapped." Naren rubbed his arm. "The Excalibarian with the broken armor came to us. My mother did what he asked, or he said he would kill me and my stepparents."

Tungsten bit his tongue. His brother had known she was alive. He found her after all those years and forced her hand because she was the only one who could build the bombs he needed.

"What can we do for you?" Mother's voice brought him back to the present. "Surely there's something we can do."

Naren smiled. "I wish to return to my birthplace; my Ma and Pa must be worried for me."

"Consider it done!" Tungsten's raised voice made the boy

inch back once more, as if suddenly aware of his stature. "But I will return you home personally."

XXVI

WE BETTER GET BACK IN ONE PIECE THIS TIME

Naren grew a habit of touching the Excalibarian cloth he wore, admiring the sheer gloss of the thread. Throughout the journey, he was a quiet boy. But in his silence, he was blessed with imagination. He kept a journal, worn from use, that he often tied with a piece of string.

On the road, he sketched endlessly, and to Tungsten's surprise, many drawings were of him. In one, he was standing by a nearby lake water where he had spoken to Calibor, and in another, he was talking with Lancelot.

Naren drew and drew, and it took one for Tungsten to mention her again. The drawing was old, depicting a woman sitting on the branch of a tree, looking up at the sky which he imagined was the way north.

"I'm sorry about your mother," he said.

The boy stopped drawing and looked up at him. "I bet she tried to kill you." Tungsten reeled back and laughed. Though it was a painful one, the boy smiled. "She did," he guessed.

"Aye, and there was never a dull moment with her."

"She protected our village," Naren said. "Kept everyone safe from robbers and raiders. When she wasn't home, she was protecting the dragons. She would come and visit at least once a year but otherwise kept her distance so the dragon's power wouldn't come to me. She wanted me to live a normal life, though she always worried about me just the same."

Tungsten had noticed it so. The boy looked Excalibarian, but he didn't have the height and build. Despite the strength of both Orendor and the dragons, Naren was only human.

The carriage went to a stop. "We must be here," Naren said, shutting his sketchbook. He left it on the seat and hurried off the carriage. Tungsten picked up the book and followed him out.

Merlin and Rella who joined them had dismounted their horses and went to talk to the locals. It took a moment for Tungsten to realize he'd been here before but only came out at night.

"Kemri," Tungsten said. "*This* is your home?"

Naren nodded. "This is where I was born. The owners of the inn are my parents. They found Mother when she was wounded, and helped her give birth to me."

The doors to the inn opened, and Layon was the first to come out. "Naren!"

Yumna swept past him; seeing the boy, she ran to him and embraced him. She wept silently, brushing his hair.

"I'm alright, Ma," he said softly. "I was saved by King Tungsten."

She wiped her tears and looked at him. For once that bitter woman smiled. "Thank you, Giant King."

Tungsten nodded silently, if she knew he was the man she despised she might think otherwise. Merlin's spell had taken effect, and no one in Kemri knew he was the wounded Rode they took in.

"Where is Astra?" Layon tried to whisper to the boy. "Have you seen her?"

Naren buried his face against Yumna. "Oh, my poor boy."

Layon saddened by the news scratched his back and looked at him. He bowed almost apologetically. "I can't thank you enough, Giant King."

"Can you stay?" the boy asked Tungsten. "At least for a while longer?"

Merlin and Rella shook their heads at him. "The kingdom needs him."

The boy looked saddened, but he didn't insist.

Tungsten returned Naren his sketchbook. "You'll see me again, I'll make sure of it."

"Here." The boy tore a page from his book and gave Tungsten a drawing of Astra Degora.

Tungsten took the paper and left. Everyone bowed to him as he mounted Indra. At once Excalibarian soldiers commanded their return home, and they headed away from the village.

With Lancelot joining him, they watched the farmlands expanding over the countryside.

Being back on the road, he no longer felt a shadow watching his back, nor the sense of threat at his heels, and he missed it.

"Say something," Tungsten said. It was worrisome that Lancelot, as worrying as he could be had been quiet. "Well?"

Lancelot whistled. "We better get back in one piece this time."

Tungsten laughed, and Lancelot joined him.

Indra growled appearing annoyed by their amusement until he leaped off the road, and Tungsten squeezed the reins. The cat charged at the fieldworkers, who started to scream and flee.

"Indra!" Tungsten shouted as they broke through the wheat fields and stopped near a group of women wearing linen caps to protect their faces from the sun. All had dispersed from the approaching feline, all except one. "Indra, what is wrong with you?" He looked at a woman who had turned her back to join the others. "I apologize."

The woman who barely faced him partially bowed.

A pang hit his chest, followed by a sense of disorder. "Halt," he said, dismounting Indra. The woman didn't stop. Fearing this was a trick, he pointed his blade at her. "Turn around."

The woman seeing his action screamed even though Lancelot told him to stop. "Your Majesty," he said. "What are you doing?"

In all honesty, he didn't know himself. But his heart was beating wildly, and he had to know why.

The woman accepted his command and turned to him. Her head was bowed, and the linen cap covered most of her face, except her frown.

"Heart be still." Tungsten's blade went under her skirt. "I spent my days of recovery reading about Dranyths with little hope, but hope nonetheless." The dress exposed her knees as the blade slowly went up. "Dranyths are gifted with immense strength, but that would detract from the meaning of the red scale. One you concealed from me. Dranyths are hardy against fire, maybe even an explosion."

The blade reached her thigh, where the point stopped on the scale on her right thigh.

The woman's frown turned to a smile.

XXVII

TUNGSTEN LAUGHED

One year later.
Winter.
Outside of Whirl River.

Tungsten and his mother sat at the nearest lake and breathed in the essence of the wind; its mild citrus aroma mingled with the fresh scent of pine. He hoped her long-awaited face would appear along the public road, but it was instead another traveler, apologizing profusely for even crossing before their presence.

Excalibur's knights let them pass, dismissing them without worry but among them, one carriage stopped.

"Your Majesty," a woman shouted. "Your Majesty!" A noblewoman, desperately waved at him from the road as his knights would not let her through.

Tungsten went to meet her, finding a familiar dagger in her hand. She was the woman he and Lancelot saved on King's Road.

"I came to return this," she said, head bowed, and dagger raised. "I made it back home, and to my son, as you said I would."

"Igraine, you have changed."

"You remembered my name," she said, surprised. "In my sorrow, I was given a second chance at life and remarried. That's why I came, to return this dagger and thank you."

Tungsten chuckled proudly. "You are most welcome. I wish you well on your travels to the new lands—I heard the weather is chilly."

An older boy peeked out of a carriage, leading the voice of the wet nurse called him back. "This is Ambrosius Aurelianus, the son of my late husband." Igraine turned to the newborn that the wet nurse shyly presented. "And this is Uther Pendragon."

The wet nurse curtsied, and Tungsten gave them an approving nod. "It is a great pleasure to see you once more, and to bear witness to your journey to the new world."

Smiling at his words, she bowed, offering his dagger.

"Keep it," he said. "May it provide continued safety to your journey."

Igraine smiled. She nodded and climbed into her carriage, taking her sons with her.

"Tungsten," his mother said. "Your sister has arrived."

Calibor had risen from deep waters, with the sword of Excalibur on her hip.

"Dear sister!" Tungsten leaped into the waters to embrace her but she pushed his shoulder, stopping him. "Careful you will squash him." In her arms, was a babe, eyes still gray from being two weeks old.

"What is this news I hear of you intending to court Lady Casana?"

Tungsten crossed his arms. "Oh, do not heed such things. It's purely a diplomatic arrangement."

"Casana has feelings for you, a notion you never reciprocated."

"A king needs a queen and my feelings have no weight on the matter."

Calibor shook her head with cold disapproval. Now and then, she would look at the mountains often without explaining why. She couldn't enjoy the food of their world anymore, but the ability to conceive a child equally surprised them. "This winter will be unkind," she said. "What an awful time to start a journey."

Orendor was calling them from the Isles of Avalon, and while men who crossed such waters never came back he owed the Blacksmith God his life, for allowing him to bear his armor in his favor.

The pair of new footsteps stopped his thoughts. Lancelot arrived, cautiously joining them as he knew who Calibor carried in her arms. Tungsten patted his back, but that didn't stop him from fidgeting with his fingers. "Can I see him?" he asked.

"Certainly." The river surrounding Calibor rolled under her feet moving her to Lancelot who met her halfway. The water reached his calves when he stopped, and her robes swayed as she leaned to show him.

Lancelot's fingertips gently brushed over the babe's forehead. "He is normal?" he asked.

"Normal," Calibor assured.

"Have you given the boy a name?" Tungsten asked, bringing the two to look at him.

"Lancelot," Calibor answered. "Our little Lancelot du Lac."

"Oh?" Tungsten said, turning to Lancelot. "I wasn't aware you two would extend the name to another generation."

Lancelot smiled, he took Calibor's shoulder and pulled her closer to him. "This one is a little different, it means Lancelot of the Lake."

"And yet my fears have not strayed," said Calibor. "Will such a name live in the hearts of many?"

"Merlin seemed worried when I asked," his friend said.

Calibor gently kissed the cheek of her babe. "Good or bad, I pray he will have atonement for whatever actions he takes."

Tungsten lost himself in watching the pair. Nothing could stop his friend from loving his sister. If only he dared to act on his feelings as boldly as them.

A hand went on his arms, leading him to look at his mother who smiled. "I don't like you venturing out after dark."

Tungsten whistled for Indra. The tiger slept under the shade of a tree. He yawned and stretched, taking his time to get to him like any other cat would.

"Promise me you'll return," his mother said.

Lancelot, hearing the concern in her voice, looked at Tungsten. After much debate, he convinced his friend not to join him on this journey.

Tungsten mounted his loyal tiger. Though he longed for company, he knew he had burdened his friend enough. Embarking alone to see Orendor was his duty and no one else's.

Lancelot stood among the knights who saluted his departure. Calibor and her child were no longer in the waters. He supposed his sister did not want to see him go and went on. Following the river was the swiftest course to reach the Oceans of Manar where the Isles of Avalon awaited.

A flash of light grabbed his attention. Calibor had been following him among the waters. Perhaps she wanted them to be alone.

"Have you come to bid me farewell?" Tungsten said, leading Indra back to the river.

Instead of answering, Calibor presented Excalibur. With both hands on the blade, she offered the weapon to him.

"We agreed you would be its protector," he said. "This weapon and my armor are the last pieces of Orendor's favor."

"When you don't need it, I will protect it but not today."

Tungsten took the sword and held it firmly.

A wide smile spread across Calibor's face. He inclined his upper body towards her, enough for his helmet to make contact with her forehead. "Until we meet again, Lady of the Lake."

She reached for him, allowing her pale hand to touch the side of his helmet. "If you ever need me, I'll be there. Wherever you go, I will follow you."

• • •

Tungsten savored the tranquil stroll along the serene road, reveling in the calmness of the surroundings. The way to the Isles of Avalon would unlikely harbor such a resemblance. Many isles needed to be crossed to get to the heart where rough seas, sirens, and those mermaids were sure to await him.

Without want, Tungsten turned back. Not a soul could be seen on the desolate road he took alone, not even a mythical beast lurking in the shadows.

Calibor's annoyance at him considering courting Lady Casana returned. "Perhaps I'm fooling myself," he told Indra and proceeded forward. "No oath is worth breaking unless it's with the person one truly desires, is it not?"

Indra growled.

"Well, of course, I couldn't tell her, that woman goes without letting her son know."

Tungsten sought Merlin for clues on Astra Degora's whereabouts. When he didn't know, he'd ask if his fate could be tied along with hers. Instead of answering, the boy gave him a cryptic answer, saying a star would smile at him. He'd been searching for one since, even now, there was none in sight.

"Perhaps that wizard needs more training than I thought." Tungsten petted his tiger. "Besides, I have you, and that's all a man needs."

"And you have me." Behind was Lancelot, riding his horse to meet him.

"Friend!" Tungsten said surprised by how much joy he felt to see him.

"I couldn't bear the thought of you embarking on another journey with no one to talk to but a big fat cat."

Indra growled, but it was not for Lancelot's comment. His shackles shot up and Tungsten twisted, raising his blade and splitting the body of a goblin that leaped at him.

Or so he thought.

It was already dead.

Lancelot pointed his crossbow among the branches before he relaxed.

Sitting on top of a branch was a woman in black. When she landed, Tungsten looked the other way. "Ah, Tungsten," she said. "Regrettably, I was unable to bid you farewell before your departure."

"Oh, you remembered?"

Lancelot chuckled but Astra Degora didn't seem to notice his tone of voice. She stared at the corpse of the drape she took down. "The migration of the last dragons has begun, and I'm to ensure a safe journey."

"All is forgiven," Tungsten murmured bitterly.

"Does that mean you're also heading to the Isles of Avalon?" Lancelot asked.

"I have been for a while." She crossed her arms and gave Tungsten a peculiar look, hooking him. "What did you think I've been up to?"

Tungsten cleared his throat. "Well, you came and saw me. Fare thee well." He encouraged Indra to go, but his tiger kept his paws rooted on the ground. "Indra!"

Astra Degora went to his right side, hand smoothing Indra's fur while the cat growled. She remained in her familiar leather garments, her hair still styled in the same way, as well as her preference to conceal her face. "I trust you three won't get lost trying to pay your respects to Orendor?"

"We'll be just fine," Tungsten stammered.

"No, we won't," Lancelot added. "I cannot navigate unknown lands without a map—not that one exists."

Astra Degora opened her mouth to say something, and

Tungsten held his breath for what would come. "Well then, I shouldn't keep you three."

Tungsten squeezed his reins. He dismounted Indra and went to her side. "I must ask you something."

The wind picked up and lifted her layered hair, and he saw both eyes looking at him, the scar still there. Her son told him in secret that she never wore an eye patch, and that told him she must've only worn it to conceal her identity from him. Now, seeing the scar over her eye so confidently gave him both warm and complex feelings.

Before he could utter a sound the galloping horses alerted them to the road ahead.

A team of horses were crossing through. The driver who led them was covered with blood as he passed them, warning them of a troll.

"Make it quick," Astra Degora said. "I hate fighting trolls."

Tungsten lowered his gaze, breathing the steel through his nostrils. "I'm contemplating the option of entering into matrimony with Lady Casana."

One eyebrow rose. "Do you want my blessing?"

"Hmm." Tungsten cleared his throat. By her expression, she barely moved a muscle. "You're not disappointed?"

"What do you expect me to say when it's decided?"

"You're right, it matters not."

"Oh, will you two just talk it out already," Lancelot

complained. "I'm getting second-handed humiliation over here."

"There is *nothing* else to say." Tungsten unsheathed Excalibur and stood in the center of the road, waiting for the troll to appear. "I saw you and you saw me."

"Truly?" Astra Degora said. "It beats waiting another year to see you again."

Tungsten's gaze locked onto her, eyes filled with curiosity. "*You* wanted to see *me*—"

Astra Degora tackled him to the ground. A gust of wind whooshed over them from the troll's fist. "Pay attention," she said. "Or is your poor form a result of you missing me?"

When a shadow cast over them, she leaped out of the way, leaving the troll to grab Tungsten and raise him in the air.

"Your Majesty!" Lancelot exclaimed.

"I am fine!" He assured, resisting the grip on his waist. "Astra Degora, you must know that our customs of living in full armor may be too much for you!" The troll waved him around using him as a club to hit the others but carving the ground instead. "The level of perspiration in the summer may be too great for you!"

Astra Degora leaped onto the troll and climbed his sandy back. "Yes, I'd imagine that'd be rather troublesome if I was Excalibarian but I'm not." She whispered something to the troll in the ancient dragon language. With her swords still concealed in her holder, she was likely giving the troll a way out before combating him.

"Moreover, you'd be expected to oversee the training of our soldiers." Tungsten's heart throbbed, but he remained unsure if it was his nerves or the troll squeezing his chest.

"And you'd have to deal with me." Astra Degora leaped back. "I'm not a morning person, and I like to sleep till noon."

Tungsten recalled the night they sought shelter from the blizzard. It's plausible she had been asleep then. "With the Gods and monsters leaving, we risk depriving our children of the same powers we currently possess." Sweat beaded under his armor wondering if she understood the conversation or at least what he was trying to ask.

Lancelot fired a bolt, leading the troll to roar. He dropped Tungsten and rolled back into the mountains, choosing peace.

Short of breath, Astra Degora turned to him. "*Our* children?"

Tungsten stood confidently with his hands on his hips. "You disagree?"

"Metal king, I fear your proposition is a hefty order."

"Is it?"

"A life of public service and a private one after, even raising children?"

His arms dropped, and he looked the other way. "Yes, I feared you would say that."

"When do we start?"

He turned back in disbelief. The wind softly touched her hair, moving it aside and allowing him to see her face in its entirety. She was smiling at him.

Tungsten took her hand, and she placed her other on his breastplate. They gazed at each other, lost in the moment, with no end in sight.

"Come on," Lancelot said, leading the way. "You two can make more plans on the way."

Tungsten patted Indra, who went ahead to catch up to his friend, leaving him to walk alongside Astra Degora. The challenges that lay ahead were uncertain, but he took comfort in the unwavering support of his faithful cat, his cherished friend, and a woman who shared his strength and determination.

A chuckle fizzed inside him that brought his companions to look at him strangely.

"I must be blind not to see the humor,"

"Alright, what is so funny laughing king?" Lancelot said, sounding half irritated.

Tungsten looked at the Astra Degora. Sensing the intensity of his stare, she felt compelled to meet his gaze. "That crafty Merlin," he said. "Maybe even craftier than Merlin the Old!"

The name Astra Degora meant Star Dragon. That's what the wizard meant when he said a star would be smiling at him.

Tungsten laughed.

EXCALIBUR'S KING

BY MRIAM YVETTE

About the Author

Miriam Yvette is the author of Dragon of Mirrors and Children of Rima. She writes about all things fantasy, from scenes that visit her in her dreams to nightmares she wishes she never had. She's a self-taught artist and has a passion for storytelling.

For more information of her upcoming works go to miriamyvette.com

KING CROW

Be a pal and support indie authors by leaving a review!

Until our next journey, safe travels.